Acclaim for Beth Wiseman

"You may think you are familiar with Beth's wonderful story-telling gift but this is something new! This is a story that will stay with you for a long, long time. It's a story of hope when life seems hopeless. It's a story of how God can redeem the seemingly unredeemable. It's a message the Church, the world needs to hear."

—SHEILA WALSH, AUTHOR OF *GOD LOVES BROKEN PEOPLE*

"Beth Wiseman tackles these difficult subjects with courage and grace. She remindsd us that true healing can only come by being vulnerable and honest before our God who loves us more than anything."

—DEBORAH BEDFORD, BEST-SELLING AUTHOR OF *HIS OTHER WIFE*, *A ROSE BY THE DOOR*, AND *THE PENNY* (CO-AUTHORED WITH JOYCE MEYER)

"Beth Wiseman writes with a masterful hand that reaches the recesses of the soul. Her capability for understanding the human condition exceeds traditional empathy and moves the reader to both introspection and exhilaration. Characters connect, transform, and redeem, making for a must 'one sit' read. Wiseman's comprehension of grace and redemption plays out in the subtle confines of the everyday and teaches the reality that new life is possible for all."

—KELLY LONG, BEST-SELLING AUTHOR OF *SARAH'S GARDEN*

"Wiseman's voice is consistently compassionate and her words flow smoothly."

—*PUBLISHERS WEEKLY* REVIEW OF *SEEK ME WITH ALL YOUR HEART*

"In *Seek Me With All Your Heart*, Beth Wiseman offers readers a heart-warming story filled with complex characters and deep emotion. I instantly loved Emily and eagerly turned each page, anxious to learn more about her past—and what future the Lord had in store for her."

—SHELLEY SHEPARD GRAY, BEST-SELLING AUTHOR OF THE SEASONS OF SUGARCREEK SERIES

Need You Now

Also by Beth Wiseman

The Daughters of the Promise series

Plain Perfect

Plain Pursuit

Plain Promise

Plain Paradise

Plain Proposal

The Land of Canaan series

Seek Me With All Your Heart

The Wonder of Your Love

Novellas found in

An Amish Christmas

An Amish Gathering

An Amish Love

An Amish Wedding

Need You Now

BETH WISEMAN

THOMAS NELSON

Since 1798

NASHVILLE DALLAS MEXICO CITY RIO DE JANEIRO

Published in Nashville, Tennessee, by Thomas Nelson. Thomas Nelson is a registered trademark of Thomas Nelson, Inc.

Thomas Nelson books may be purchased in bulk for educational, business, fund-raising, or sales promotional use. For information, please e-mail SpecialMarkets@ThomasNelson.com.

Scripture quotations are from the King James Version of the Bible.

Publisher's Note: This novel is a work of fiction. Names, characters, places, and incidents are either products of the author's imagination or used fictitiously. All characters are fictional, and any similarity to people living or dead is purely coincidental.

Library of Congress Cataloging-in-Publication Data

Wiseman, Beth, 1962–
Need you now / Beth Wiseman.
    p. cm.
ISBN 978-1-59554-887-0 (trade paper)
1. Domestic fiction. I. Title.
PS3623.I83N44 2012
813'.6—dc23

2011049553

Printed in the United States of America

12 13 14 15 16 17 QG 6 5 4 3

To Kelly Long (aka June)

Chapter One

Darlene's chest tightened, and for a few seconds she couldn't move. If ever there was a time to flee, it was now. She put a hand to her chest, held her breath, and eased backward, sliding one socked foot at a time across the wooden floor of her bedroom. She eyed the intruder, wondering why he wasn't moving. Maybe he was dead.

Nearing the door, she stretched her arm behind her, searching for the knob. She turned it quickly, and at the click of the latch, her trespasser rushed toward her. In one movement, she jumped backward, across the threshold and into the den, slamming the door so hard the picture of the kids fell off the wall. She looked down at Chad, Ansley, and Grace staring up through broken glass, then hurried through the den to the kitchen. Her hand trembled as she unplugged her cell phone and pressed the button to call Brad. *Please answer.*

It was tax time, so every CPA at her husband's office was working long hours, and for these last weeks before the April deadline, Brad was hard to reach. She knew she wouldn't hear from him until after eight o'clock tonight. And she couldn't go back in her bedroom. What would she have to live without until then? She looked down. For starters, a shirt. She was later than usual getting dressed this morning and had just pulled on her jeans when she'd noticed she wasn't alone.

She let out a heavy sigh and rubbed her forehead. Brad answered on the sixth ring.

"Bradley . . ." She only called him by his full name when she needed his full attention.

"What is it, babe?"

She took a deep breath. "There is a *snake* in our bedroom. A big black *snake*." She paused as she put a hand to her chest. "In our *bedroom*."

"How big?"

She'd expected a larger reaction. Maybe her husband didn't hear her. "Big! Very big. Huge, Brad."

He chuckled. "Honey, remember that little snake that got in your greenhouse when we lived on Charter Road in Houston? You said that snake was big too." He chuckled again, and Darlene wanted to smack him through the phone. "It was a tiny little grass snake."

"Brad, you're going to have to trust me. This snake is huge, like five or six feet long." A shiver ran down her spine. "Are you coming home or should I call 9-1-1?"

"What? You can't call 9-1-1 about a snake." His tone changed. "Darlene, don't do that. Round Top is a small town, and we'll be known as the city slickers who called in about a snake."

"Then you need to come home and take care of this." She lifted her chin and fought the tremble in her voice.

Deep breath on the other end of the line. "You know how crazy it is here. I can't leave right now. It's probably just a chicken snake, and they're not poisonous."

"Well, there are no *chickens* in our bedroom, so it doesn't have any business in there."

"Chad can probably get it out when he gets home from school. Maybe with a shovel or something, but tell him to be careful. Even though they're not venomous, it'd probably still hurt to get bit."

Darlene sighed. "Our girls are going to freak if they come home to find a snake in the house." She turned toward a sound in the entryway. "I'll call you back. There's someone at the door, and I'm standing here in my bra. I'll call you back. Love you." She clicked the phone off, then yelled toward the door, "Just a minute!"

After finding a T-shirt in Ansley's room, she pulled it over her head as she crossed back through the den toward the front door. This was the first visitor she'd had in the two months since they'd moved from Houston. She peeked around the curtain before she opened the door, realizing that her old city habit would probably linger for a while. Out here in the country, there probably wasn't much to worry about, but she was relieved to see it was a woman. A tall woman in a cowgirl hat. She pulled the door open.

"Your Longhorns are in my pasture." The woman twisted her mouth to one side and folded her arms across her chest. "This is the second time they've busted the fence and wandered onto my property."

Darlene thought this cowgirl could have walked straight off the set of any western movie. She was dressed in a long-sleeved denim shirt with her blue jeans tucked into brown boots. She was older than Darlene, possibly midforties, but she was gorgeous with huge brown eyes and blond hair that hung in a ponytail to her waist.

"I'm so sorry." Darlene shook her head. Brad should have never gotten those Longhorns. Neither she nor Brad knew a thing about cows, but Brad had said a move to the country should include some Longhorns. Although it didn't make a lick of sense to her. She pushed the door wide. "I'm Darlene."

The woman shifted her weight but didn't offer a greeting in return. Instead, she stared at Darlene's chest. Darlene waited for the woman to lock eyes with her, and when she didn't, Darlene finally looked down. Her cheeks warmed as she sighed.

"Oh, this is my daughter's shirt." *Don't Bug Me!* was scrolled across the white T-shirt in red, and beneath the writing was a hideous picture of a giant roach. Darlene couldn't stand the shirt, but twelve-year-old Ansley loved it. "Do you want to come in?" She stepped back.

"No. I just wanted to let you know that I'm going to round up your Longhorns and head them back to your pasture. I'll temporarily repair the fence." The woman turned to leave, and it was then that Darlene saw a horse tethered to the fence that divided their property. She stifled a smile. This woman really was a cowgirl.

"Know anything about snakes?" Darlene eased onto the front porch, sidestepping a board she knew was loose. The porch was on their list of things to repair on her grandparents' old homestead.

"What?" The woman turned around as she held a hand underneath the rim of her hat, blocking the afternoon sun.

"I have a snake in my bedroom." Darlene shrugged. "Just wondering if you had any . . . any experience with something like that?" She padded down two porch steps in her socks. "I'm not sure I got your name?"

"Layla." She gave a quick wave before she turned to leave again. Darlene sighed. Clearly the woman wasn't interested in being friends. Or helping with the snake. Darlene watched her walk to her horse and put a foot in the stirrup. Then she paused and twisted her body to face Darlene. "What kind of snake?"

Hopeful, Darlene edged down another step. "A big black one."

Layla put her foot back on the ground and walked across the grass toward the porch. Darlene couldn't believe how graceful the tall blonde was, how out of sync her beauty was in comparison to what she was wearing.

"Only thing you really have to worry about around here are copperheads." She tipped back the rim of her hat. "Was it a copperhead?"

At five foot two, Darlene felt instantly inferior to this tall, gorgeous, horse-riding, snake-slaying blonde. She wasn't about to say that she couldn't tell one snake from the other. "I don't think so."

"All I've got is a .22 with me." Layla pointed back to her horse, and Darlene saw a long gun in a holster. "But a .22 will blow a hole through your floor," Layla added. A surreal feeling washed over Darlene. She thought about their previous home in a Houston subdivision, and a woman with a gun on a horse wasn't a sight they would've seen.

"Do you have a pellet gun?" She stopped in front of Darlene on the steps. Darlene was pretty sure that was *all* they had— Chad's BB gun.

"Yeah, I think so."

Five minutes later, Darlene pushed open the door to her bedroom and watched Layla enter the scene of the invasion. The bed was piled with clean clothes, but at least it was made up. The vacuum was in the middle of the room instead of in the closet under the stairs. It wasn't the way she wanted a stranger to see her bedroom, but it could have been worse.

Layla got down on her knees and looked under the bed. From the threshold, Darlene did a mental scan of what was under there. Boxes of photos, a flowery hatbox that had belonged to her grandmother, an old red suitcase stuffed with baby keepsakes from when the kids were young—and a lot of dust.

"There he is." Layla leaned her chest to the floor and positioned Chad's BB gun. Darlene braced herself, then squeezed her eyes closed as two pops echoed underneath the bed. A minute later, Layla dragged the snake out with the tip of the gun. "Just a chicken snake."

Darlene stepped out of the room, giving Layla plenty of room to haul the snake out. Big, black, ugly. And now dead. Blood dripped all the way to the front door. Layla carried the snake to the fence and laid it across the timber, its yellow underside facing the sky.

"Belly up should bring rain." Layla was quickly up on her horse. "Tell your husband that I'm patching the fence up, but he really needs some new cross planks."

"I will. And thank you so much for killing that snake. Do you and your husband want to come for dinner tonight? I'd like to do something for you."

"I'm not married. And I can't come to dinner tonight. Thanks, though." She gave the horse a little kick in the flank, then eased through a gate that divided her acreage from Brad and Darlene's. She closed it behind her from atop her horse and headed toward the large house on top of the sloping hillside. Coming from town, the spacious estate was fully visible from the road, and Darlene's youngest daughter called it the "mansion on the hill." The rest of the family took to calling it that too.

In comparison to their run-down farmhouse, Darlene supposed it was a mansion. Both homes were probably built in the late 1800s, but Layla's was completely restored, at least on the outside, with fresh yellow paint and white trim. A split-rail, cedar fence surrounded the yard, and toward the back of the property, a bright-red barn lit up the hayfield not far from a good-sized pond. A massive iron gate—that stayed closed most of the time—welcomed visitors down a long, winding driveway. And there were lots of livestock—mostly Longhorns and horses. If the wind was blowing just right, sometimes Darlene could hear faint music coming from the house.

She was hoping maybe she could be friends with Layla, even though she wasn't sure she had anything in common with her. Just the same, Darlene was going to pay her a visit. Maybe take her a basket of baked goodies, a thank-you for killing that snake.

Brad adjusted the phone against his ear and listened to Darlene's details about her snake ordeal, then she ended the conversation the way she always did. "Who do you love?"

"You, baby."

It was their *thing*. Nearly twenty years ago, at a bistro in Houston, Brad wanted to tell Darlene that he loved her—for the first time—and he was a nervous wreck, wondering if she felt the same way. He'd kept fumbling around, and the words just wouldn't come. Maybe she'd seen it in his eyes, but she'd reached over, touched his hand, and smiled. Then in a soft whisper, she'd asked, "Who do you love?" His answer had rolled off his tongue with ease. "You, baby." Then she'd told him that she loved him too, and the who-do-you-love question stuck. Darlene asked him all the time. He knew it wasn't because she was insecure; it was just a fond recollection for both of them. That night at the bistro, Brad had known he was going to marry Darlene.

He flipped his phone shut and maneuvered through the Houston traffic toward home. He was glad that he wouldn't have to deal with a snake when he got there, but he was amused at Darlene's description of the tall, blond cowgirl who shot it with Chad's BB gun.

He had four tax returns to work on tonight after dinner. All these extra billable hours were bound to pay off. He needed the extra income if he was going to make all the renovations to the farm that he and Darlene had discussed. Brad wanted to give her the financial freedom to make their home everything she dreamed it could be. Cliff Hodges had been dangling the word *partner* in front of him for almost two years, and Brad was sure he was getting close to having his name on the door.

If they hadn't been in such a rush to move from Houston, Brad was sure they could have held out and gotten more for their house. As it turned out, they'd barely broken even, and just getting the farmhouse in semi-livable shape had taken a chunk of their savings. Buying out Darlene's brother for his share of the homestead had put a strain on their finances too, but it was worth it if Darlene was happy. She'd talked about restoring her grandparents' farm for years. The original plan had been to fix the place up over time so they could use it as a weekend getaway. But then they'd decided to make the move as soon as they could, even if the house wasn't in tip-top shape.

Forty-five minutes from his office, he'd cleared the bustle of the city, and the six-lane freeway narrowed to two lanes on either side of a median filled with bluebonnets and Indian paintbrushes. Nothing like spring in Texas to calm his mind after crunching numbers all day long, but leaving the office so late to head west put the setting sun directly in his face. He flipped his visor down, glad that the exit for Highway 36 was only a few miles away. Once he turned, he'd get a break from the blinding rays. Then he'd pass through the little towns of Sealy and Bellville before winding down one-lane roads to the peaceful countryside of Round Top. It was a long commute, almost an hour and a half each way, but it was worth it when he pulled into his driveway. Small-town living was better for all of them. Especially Chad.

Brad could still recall the night Chad came stumbling into the house—drunk. His seventeen-year-old son had been running around with a rebellious group of friends in Houston. And sometimes Chad's glassy eyes had suggested more than just alcohol abuse. Brad shook his head to clear the recollections, knowing he would continue to pray that his son would make better choices now that he had some distance from his old buddies.

Brad felt like a blessed man. He'd been married to his high school sweetheart for nearly twenty years, and he had three amazing children. He wanted to spend his life being the best husband and father he could be. There wasn't a day that went by that he didn't thank the Lord for the life he'd been given, and it was Brad's job to take care of his family.

⁂

Darlene finished setting the table. She regretted that her mother couldn't see her enjoying her grandmother's dining room set. Darlene had been surprised to find the oak table and chairs still in the house when they'd moved in. The antiques had been dusty and in dire need of cleaning, but they were just as sturdy as ever. She could remember many meals with her parents and grandparents in this house, at this table.

She still missed her grandparents—and her parents. Dad had been gone almost six years, and two years had passed since her mother's death. Her parents had started their family late in life, both of them in their late thirties when she was born, and

Dale was born two years after Darlene. She was glad her brother hadn't wanted the farm. It had been a struggle to buy him out, but no regrets. Someday, they too would have a "mansion on the hill," like Layla's. She cast her eyes downward, frowning at the worn-out wooden floors. She'd be glad when they could afford to cover the original planking with new hardwood.

Thinking of Layla brought a smile to her face as she mashed steaming potatoes in a pot on the stove. She couldn't help but wonder what the tall blonde was doing all alone on that estate. Darlene had never even been on a horse or owned a pair of cowgirl boots. Several of her friends back in Houston sported high-dollar, pointy-toed boots, but they didn't particularly appeal to Darlene. Her friend Gina had told her it was un-Texan not to own a pair of boots.

She missed Gina. They'd been friends since their daughters had started Girl Scouts together, but after Gina's divorce, they'd drifted apart. Gina's interests had changed from Girl Scout and PTO meetings to going out with new single friends.

She left the dining room and went back to the kitchen, glad that the aroma of dinner covered up the dingy old-house smell that lingered, despite her best efforts to conceal it with air fresheners.

"Mom! Mom!" Ansley burst into the kitchen with the kind of enthusiasm that could mean either celebration or disaster; with Ansley you never knew. At twelve, she was the youngest and the most dramatic in the family.

Darlene gave the potatoes a final stir before she turned to face her. "What is it, Ansley?"

"Guess what?" Ansley rocked back and forth from heel to toe, and Darlene could tell by the grin on her daughter's face that the news was good. "I did it. Straight Cs and above!"

Darlene brought her hands to her chest and held her breath

for a moment, smiling. When Ansley was in grade school, early testing indicated she was going to struggle, and Darlene and Brad knew she was a bit slower than other kids her age.

Not so thrilling was what Brad had promised Ansley if she received a report card without any failing grades. "Sweetie, that's great. I'm so proud of you." She hugged her daughter, knowing it was highly unlikely Ansley wouldn't remember her father's promise. Ansley eased out of the hug.

"I know they scare you, Mom, but having some chickens and roosters will be so much fun! We'll be like real farmers, and every day after school, I'll go get the eggs." Ansley's dark hair brushed against her straightened shoulders, and her big brown eyes twinkled. "Think how much money you'll save on eggs!"

Darlene bit her bottom lip as she recalled the chickens her grandparents used to keep on this very same farm. And one very mean rooster. Eight dollars in savings per month was hardly going to be worth it, but a promise was a promise. She'd told Brad before they'd left Houston not to offer such a reward, but Darlene had put it out of her mind. At the time, it seemed a stretch for Ansley to hit the goal and make all Cs.

"Maybe just have laying chickens. You don't need a rooster." Darlene walked to the refrigerator and pulled out a tub of butter.

"Mom . . ."

Darlene set the butter on the table and raised a brow in time to see Ansley rolling her eyes.

"Even I know we can't have baby chicks without a rooster." Ansley folded her arms across her chest.

Darlene grinned. "I know you know that, but how many chickens are you hoping to have?" She recalled that on some of her visits to her grandparents' house, if the wind blew just right, she could smell the chicken coop from the front yard, even though the pens were well over fifty yards away, back next to the barn. When they'd first moved in, Brad had fixed up the old coops as an incentive for Ansley to pull her grades up. Sitting on the porch swing with Brad late in the evenings had become a regular thing, and smelly chickens would be an unwelcome distraction.

"Not too many," Ansley said as she pulled a glass from the cabinet and filled it with water.

One was too many in Darlene's opinion, but it was a well-deserved reward. Darlene gave a lot of the credit to the school here. Much to her children's horror, there were only 240 students in grades kindergarten through twelve in the Round Top/ Carmine School District, but Darlene felt like they were getting a better education and more one-on-one attention. Darlene had been on the verge of homeschooling Ansley before they left Houston, but Ansley threw such a fit that Darlene had discarded the idea.

Ansley chugged the water, then put the glass in the sink. "I can't wait 'til Daddy gets home."

Darlene smiled. Her youngest was always a breath of fresh air, full of energy, and the tomboy in the family.

She thought about the snake and realized Ansley probably wouldn't have freaked out after all. She heard Brad's car rolling up the gravel driveway, and moments later, the front screen door slammed and Ansley yelled, "Daddy! Guess what!"

❧

An hour later, everyone was gathered at the dinner table except Chad. After about ten minutes, he finally sauntered into the room, slid into his chair, and folded his hands for prayer.

"It's your turn to offer the blessing, Chad." Darlene bowed her head.

"Thank You, Lord, for the many blessings You've given us, for this food, the roof over our head, and Your love. And, God . . ." Chad paused with a sigh. Darlene opened one eye and held her breath. More often than not, Chad's prayers included appeals for something outside the realm of what should be requested at the dinner table. Like the time he'd asked for God to help his parents see their way to buying him a better car. Darlene closed her eye, let out her breath, and listened.

"Could you heal Mr. Blackstone's cancer and bring him back to school? He's a good guy." Darlene's insides warmed, but then Chad continued, "Our substitute stinks. Amen."

"Chad!" Darlene sat taller, then cut her eyes at Brad, who shouldn't have been smiling.

"No, Mom. I mean, *really*. He stinks. He doesn't smell good." Chad scooped out a large spoonful of potatoes. "And he's like a hundred or something."

"Even more reason you shouldn't speak badly about him. Respect your elders, remember?" Darlene passed the meat loaf to Chad, who was shoveling potatoes like he hadn't eaten in a month of Sundays.

"Grace, how was your day?" Brad passed their older daughter a plate of rolls.

"It was okay."

Grace rarely complained, but Darlene knew she wasn't happy about the move from Houston. Mostly because of the boy she'd left behind.

Ansley turned her head to Darlene, grunted, then frowned. "Mom, why are you wearing my shirt?"

Darlene looked down at the big roach. "Oh, I had to borrow it earlier. I sort of couldn't go in my room for a while."

Darlene told the full-length version of the snake story that she'd shortened for Brad on the phone.

"I've seen that woman," Chad said. "And she's *hot*."

"She's old like Mom, Chad! That's gross." Ansley squeezed her eyes shut for a moment, then shook her head.

Darlene took a bite of roll. At thirty-eight, when had she become *old* in her children's eyes? "I believe Layla is several years older than I am, Chad."

Her son shrugged. "Whatever. She's still—"

"Chad, that's enough." Brad looked in Chad's direction, and Darlene was glad to see him step in since it seemed like she was the one who always disciplined the children. Brad, on the other hand—well, he promised chickens.

They were all quiet for a few moments before Chad spoke up again.

"Did you know Layla drives a tractor? I've seen her out in the pasture on the way to school." He shook his head. "Seems weird for a woman." He laughed as he looked to his left at Ansley. "Can you picture Mom out on a tractor plowing the fields?"

Ansley laughed. "No, I can't."

"Don't underestimate your mom. You never know what she might do." Brad reached for another roll as he winked at Darlene.

Darlene smiled. She found herself thinking, yet again, that this was a good move for them. They all needed this fresh start. None of the kids had been particularly happy at first, but they were coming around.

"Can I be excused?" Grace put her napkin in her lap and scooted her chair back.

Darlene knew meat loaf wasn't Grace's favorite. "Whose night is it to help with dishes?"

Grace and Ansley both pointed at Chad.

"Okay," Darlene said to Grace. "You can be excused."

Darlene watched Grace leave the table. Her middle child was tiny like Darlene, and she was the only one in the family who inherited Darlene's blond hair and blue eyes. And her features were as perfect as a porcelain doll's, complete with a flawless ivory complexion. She looked like a little princess. Chad and Ansley had their father's dark hair and eyes—and his height. Darlene loved her children equally, proud of them all, but sometimes it was hard not to favor Grace just a little bit, especially since they'd come so close to losing her as an infant. Grace had come into the world nine weeks premature, a surprise to everyone, including Darlene's doctor, since Darlene had delivered Chad at full term with no complications just two years earlier. Grace struggled those first few weeks with underdeveloped lungs and severe jaundice, and twice they were told to prepare themselves for the worst. But their Grace was a fighter, and as her sixteenth birthday approached, Darlene silently thanked God for the millionth time for His grace.

There'd been issues and struggles with both Chad and Ansley from time to time—mostly with Chad. But Grace had never given them one bit of trouble.

Chapter Two

As Darlene neared Layla's estate, she stopped to admire the view. Even Layla's entryway was something she could only dream about. A flight of sculpted blackbirds arched above the iron gate, and rosebushes bursting with red grew in front of white-rock columns. She thought about her family's metal pipe gate, which required you to push the button three or four times before it opened with shaky effort.

She was surprised to see Layla's gate already open. Darlene drove onto a beautiful cobblestone drive. She tried to speculate what such a project would cost, especially a driveway as long as Layla's. After only a few moments, she gave up, knowing it was completely out of reach for her and Brad. They were just hoping to get some gravel poured over the dirt driveway. As it was, someone got stuck every time it rained.

The closer she got to Layla's house, the more nervous she felt. Layla might not like unannounced visitors in the middle of the afternoon. Darlene thought back to the days when you looked up a person's number in the phone book. Now everyone had a cell phone. On the off chance Layla was listed, Darlene had checked for a landline but hadn't found one.

With a quick glance in the visor mirror, Darlene saw that

her makeup and gloss were in place. Then she fluffed her hair and stepped out of the car. Smoothing the seat-belt wrinkles from her sleeveless white blouse, she felt much more presentable today.

She looked around and gaped at Layla's amazing flower beds, a mix of begonias, lilies, and tulips. With her decorative tin of chocolate chip cookies in hand, she breathed in the aroma of freshly mowed pastures and walked toward the door, her heeled sandals clicking against the cobblestones. Her black sunglasses slid down her nose, so she gave them a push upward. It was only the beginning of April, but already the temperatures were in the 80s.

She knocked several times and waited. No answer. She shifted the cookies to her other hand and knocked again, but still no answer. She was heading back to her car when she heard movement to her left. Layla was closing the barn door and heading across the yard.

"Hello!" Darlene waved, feeling intrusive. She'd just give her the cookies and go.

Layla was dressed the same way as before—blue jeans tucked into pointy-toed boots, long-sleeved denim shirt, and the cowgirl hat. The woman had dirt on her face, yet Darlene was sure Layla still presented herself better than she did.

"Hi, Darlene." Layla stopped in front of her, expressionless. "What can I do for you? Another snake?" She grinned. Only briefly. But enough for Darlene to see that her teeth were as perfect as the rest of her.

"Oh no . . ." Darlene waved a hand and squeaked out a laugh. "No more snakes. I just wanted to bring you something, you know . . . a thank-you for slaying my intruder." She pushed the tin toward Layla.

Layla pulled off one of her work gloves, took the tin, and

wasted no time prying off the lid. After studying the cookies for a few moments, she chose one and took a big bite. "Thanks," she said after she swallowed. Then she proceeded to polish off the rest of the cookie.

"You're welcome." Darlene wondered if Layla would invite her inside, or if that was Darlene's cue to hit the road. She pushed a strand of hair behind her ear and once again gave her sunglasses a heave-ho up the bridge of her nose. "How many acres do you have?"

Layla pulled out another cookie, then shut the tin. "Thirty-five."

Darlene thought about their ten acres and the time Brad spent keeping it up. "Wow. That's a lot. Do you have help, or do you take care of it all by yourself?"

"No help. It keeps me young."

I'll say. Darlene watched her eat another cookie, feeling her own hips expand. She loved to bake, but seldom partook. She was short, and she had to work at not being short and fat. "My kids love chocolate chip cookies, so I make them a lot." She paused. "Do you have children?"

Layla swallowed. "No."

Hmm . . . No husband. No children. Lives in the mansion on the hill. And looks like a forty-plus supermodel dressed in cowgirl gear.

"Okay, well, I just wanted to bring you the cookies. Thanks again." Darlene gave a wave. Layla was taking off her other glove and didn't look up. Darlene had taken about four steps toward her car when Layla called her name. Darlene turned around.

"You don't know how to sew, do you? I mean, you kind of look like the sewing type."

The sewing type? "Um, yeah. I sew." Maybe the fact that she'd been a homemaker for almost twenty years showed.

Layla ran her sleeve across her forehead, which further smudged the dirt already there. "I have a formal event to attend." She sighed. "I've lost twelve pounds, and my dress is swallowing me. I'd pay you to alter it for me."

I should have such problems. "Uh, okay." Darlene pushed her glasses up on her head. "You don't have to pay me, though."

"Okay."

No argument? She stuck her hands in the back pockets of her Capri jeans and stood tall, but no amount of stretching would bring her any higher than Layla's shoulders.

"Can you come in and pin the dress now?"

Now? "Uh, yeah . . . sure." At least she'd get a chance to see the inside of Layla's house.

Layla started walking toward the house, so Darlene followed. Before Layla opened the door, she turned to Darlene. "Can you give me just a minute? I wasn't expecting company."

Darlene smiled. "No problem." She felt somewhat relieved that Layla's house might not be in top condition since Layla had seen Darlene's house on the back end of the cleaning schedule.

It still seemed odd that Layla would leave her standing on the porch. Usually folks just had to deal with an unexpected guest, clean house or not.

❧

Layla moved like a tornado through the living room and kitchen, clearing the areas of evidence. Last thing she needed was a nosy neighbor getting in her business, but at least she'd get her dress taken in. It was a great gown. Seemed a waste to go buy a new one for an event she didn't even want to attend. She reminded herself it was for a good cause and a way to unload some money for tax purposes.

She piled everything in her arms, dumped it on her bed to deal with later, then closed her bedroom door. Down the hall, she went into the extra bedroom and found her emerald-green gown. She draped it over her arm.

"Sorry about that," she said as she opened the door for Darlene.

"That's okay."

Darlene was a petite little thing with blond hair and a much-too-friendly smile, as if the world hadn't sucked the life out of her yet. *Give it time, Darlene.* Layla sighed, then motioned for Darlene to sit down on the couch. "Just give me a minute, and I'll go put the dress on and round up some pins." She went to her bedroom and closed the door.

A few minutes later, Layla stared at herself in the mirror. Wearing the gown reminded her of times past. She closed her eyes and pictured herself in Tom's arms, swirling beneath the twinkling lights in the Grand Ballroom of the Waldorf Astoria in Manhattan. Those days were gone, and agreeing to attend this gala alone was probably a mistake. But she'd already committed. The peppy woman who'd come calling a few weeks ago had promised that the plaza at Festival Hill would be transformed into an exquisite venue, and she'd said, "Your presence would make a huge impact on our event."

It better. Layla was just glad that Darlene hadn't figured out who she was yet, or so it seemed. Because then she'd want to be Layla's best friend, and Layla didn't have the energy for that.

⁂

Darlene took the opportunity to look around Layla's living room. Every antique was purposely placed and adorned with expensive-looking trinkets, the inside décor matching the early 1900s style of the outside. Shiny wooden floors were partly covered with

patterned rugs, and several glass hutches were filled with exquisite pottery and china. Darlene didn't know a lot about antiques,
but it seemed a hodgepodge of old collectibles and vintage pieces.
There was a certain warmth throughout Layla's home but also a
chill that Darlene couldn't quite put her finger on.

When Layla walked in wearing the gown, Darlene homed in
on the tiny lines feathering either side of Layla's eyes. The woman
had to have six or seven years on Darlene, but it hardly mattered.
Layla had gorgeous features. And Darlene was sure she could
never wear a dress like that. She just didn't have the figure for it.

"That's an amazing dress." Darlene stepped closer and
squinted as she leaned down and took a closer look at the tiny
crystals encircling the base of the gown. A light emerald-green,
the sleeveless, floor-length gown had a flattering V-neck, and
when Layla turned to the side, Darlene saw the open-draped
back. She stood straight, put a hand to her chest. "I'm not sure I
should even touch this dress."

"I thought you said you could sew." Layla frowned.

"Well, I can, but . . . this looks like a very expensive dress. I'd
hate to mess it up." She ran a hand through her hair. "Are you
sure you don't want to have a professional seamstress alter the
dress for you?" Darlene could see where it needed to be taken in
around the waist and in the bust.

Layla folded her arms across her chest. "Have you forgotten
where we live?"

"I know there isn't anyone in Round Top who can alter it, but
maybe go to Houston or to—"

"If you don't want to do it, just say so."

"I'm just worried. What if I mess it up?"

"Then just don't mess it up." Layla handed Darlene a box of
pins. "I don't want it too tight. If I have to attend this gala, I'm
going to enjoy the food."

Darlene took the pins and set to work. What a transition, from working cowgirl to glamour queen. "What's the event?"

Layla sighed. "Another one of the many fund-raisers I'm asked to attend." She paused. "But this one is for a very good cause."

"Why don't you just send a donation if you don't want to go?" Darlene carefully pinched the delicate fabric near Layla's waist and prepared to pin it.

Layla chuckled as she tossed her hair, causing Darlene to lose her grip on the fold. "They are expecting me there . . . in person." She shifted her weight, and Darlene wondered if she'd ever get the dress properly pinned.

After another few minutes, Darlene was finally done, and Layla walked to her bedroom. She returned with the pinned dress on a hanger. "The gala isn't for three weeks. Can you have it done by then?"

"Yes, I think so."

"You *think* so? Yes or no?"

Darlene wanted to tell Layla that she wasn't her servant, but instead she just smiled and said, "Yes, I can have it done."

∞

Later that evening, Darlene crawled into bed next to Brad. Her husband had his laptop in his lap and papers scattered all over the place. She'd be glad when tax season was over. She waited until he took a break before she told him about her time at Layla's.

"She's just . . . different. I can't figure her out." Darlene pumped lotion into her palm, then breathed in the aroma of lavender as she spread it up and down her arms.

"So why try so hard to be friends with her?" Brad took off his reading glasses and rubbed his eyes. He'd probably needed the glasses for much longer than he would admit, but when he turned forty last year, he'd finally stepped out of denial and purchased a pair.

"I'm not trying hard to be friends with her, she's just . . ." Darlene shrugged as she smoothed the last of the lotion on her neck. "Interesting, I guess."

Brad put his glasses back on and focused on the work in front of him. Darlene reached for a book on her nightstand and started to read, finding it difficult to stay in the story. Her mind kept drifting.

In Houston, she'd worn herself out by volunteering for too many things—Girl Scout leader, band booster sponsor, softball mom, room mother, T-ball coach, and the list went on. She'd been happy to do it, but her kids were older now and didn't need her as much. Even though she'd been enjoying a quieter life for the past two months, an idea had been rooting around in her mind.

"I was thinking about maybe getting a part-time job."

"What?" Brad turned to her and grimaced, a reaction she'd expected. "Why? I told you I think I'll make partner soon, and we'll have plenty of money to do everything you want with the house."

"It's not the money. I think if I was out and about, I'd meet more people in the community. The kids are older now, doing their own things, so I don't meet their friends' parents like before." Darlene knew Brad was a proud man, and she'd need to tread carefully around anything to do with money. Her husband was old-fashioned in that way, believed the man should take care of the family. She gave him a playful nudge before saying, "But you have to admit—any money I make would help."

He pulled off his glasses, leaned down, and kissed her on the mouth. "If you want to get a part-time job, you go for it. But *not* for the money. Do it for you. I'll take care of us financially."

"I know that. And it would be for me." She thought about having play money in her pocket, not a bad perk either. Then Layla's dress came to mind. She'd noticed earlier when she hung it in the closet that it was a Versace. Darlene couldn't imagine purchasing a designer dress for two or three thousand dollars, and she wished more than ever that she'd never agreed to alter the gown. She and Brad led a comfortable life and had never gone without, nor had their children. But her formal attire came from a local department store, and spending anything over three hundred dollars seemed extreme. She was worried about ruining Layla's expensive dress.

Brad closed his laptop, picked up two file folders, and gathered up some loose papers.

"Done for tonight?" She put her book on the nightstand, then edged closer to him.

Brad moved his laptop and files from the bed and took off his glasses. "Yep. I can't keep my eyes open."

Darlene was wide awake, but as Brad clicked his lamp off and rolled onto his side, she knew he was exhausted. She turned the knob on her light too and snuggled into the covers as she waited for his arm to drape across her.

She said her prayers the same way every night, checking off a list, never changing the order, and knowing that it was almost obsessive-compulsive. First she'd run through all the things she was thankful for, then she'd ask forgiveness for her sins—stating specifically the offenses she felt she'd carried with her the longest. That was followed by requests for her children's health and happiness, and she always asked God to continue to bless her marriage. At the end were all the extra prayers, for people she'd met, certain situations, or if one of the kids needed extra time dedicated to them. But all was well in her family this evening, so as she drew to a close, she felt a strong urge to pray for Layla. She kept it simple, unsure exactly what to pray for.

Lord, please bless my new friend, Layla. Darlene paused, wondering if she and Layla were really going to be friends. *I know that sometimes You put people in our lives for a reason, and I'm sensing a purpose. I pray that You'll guide my steps toward a friendship with Layla and all that I do in Your name. Amen.*

She pulled Brad's arm tighter around her, closed her eyes, and basked in the peacefulness she felt. Things had been rough in Houston. Chad hadn't been making good choices, Ansley had been failing her classes, and Grace had been all distraught over a boy. This move was exactly what they all needed.

"Who do you love?" she whispered in the darkness.

"You, baby."

Grace climbed into bed later than usual. She'd stayed up and watched a movie downstairs, despite her mother's constant push to go to bed. She'd been having a hard time getting to sleep since they'd moved.

The glow of her bedside lamp lightly illuminated her room in the old farmhouse. It was nothing like the bedroom she used to have before they moved to the middle of nowhere. Once she was tucked beneath her pink comforter, she reached into the drawer of her nightstand and pulled out her trinket box. She loved the lavender sachet she kept inside of it, right next to the necklace Tristan had given her for her fifteenth birthday. She didn't wear the heart-shaped pendant anymore. Except to bed.

She lifted the sachet to her nose and breathed in the floral scent, then fastened the tiny clasp of the pendant around her neck. She closed her eyes, anguish swimming through her veins. There was only one way she was going to get any relief. She stared at the shiny objects lying in the box.

She just wanted to feel better.

The next morning, she grimaced when she looked down at her sheets. She had to be more careful. She blotted the blood spots with cold water, stripped the sheets from her bed, then hurried to the laundry room downstairs. She stuffed the sheets into the washer, added detergent, and twisted the knob to On.

"I know why you keep washing your sheets."

Grace spun around at the sound of her mother's voice. Her heart raced. Mom walked closer and placed a hand on her shoulder.

"Honey, I don't mind washing your sheets. I know what's happening."

Grace was sure her mother could see her heart beating through her chest. "You do?" She stared at the floor, but Mom lifted her chin.

"Yes. It's happened to all women at some time. I promise. We've all had accidents during our time of the month. It's nothing to be embarrassed about. I don't want you feeling like you have to hide that from me."

Relief washed over her like water putting out a fire. "Thanks, Mom."

"Breakfast is ready. Go eat, and I'll get these in the dryer and back on your bed before you get home from school."

Grace nodded and walked to the kitchen for breakfast.

Her mom came in a minute or two later. "Your dad left earlier than usual this morning. He said to tell you all to have a good day and to have fun tonight at the youth group gathering."

Chad stood up as he shoved another biscuit in his mouth. "Hurry up, let's go," he said with a mouthful.

"Let your sisters eat, Chad. You've got plenty of time."

"I'll be in the truck." Chad left the room, and Grace knew in a few minutes, they'd all hear his music booming. Hopefully her parents would get her a car when she turned sixteen. She hated Chad's obnoxious rap songs. He was so juvenile. He thought it was cool to drive up to the school with that stupid music blaring, but it was embarrassing.

Grace was ready for school to end for the summer, but there was another six weeks left. She hadn't made any real friends since they'd moved. Acquaintances only—a group of girls she ate lunch with. Everyone was nice enough, but Grace just didn't fit in. That was fine by her anyhow. She didn't expect it would be any different at the "meet and greet" youth group party tonight.

She'd begged her parents not to drag the family here, but when Tristan broke up with her, she'd just given in. Chad and Ansley weren't for the move in the beginning, but they seemed to be adjusting better than Grace was. *Whatever.*

She put her napkin on her plate and waited for Ansley to finish her breakfast, which always consisted of two biscuits stuffed with peanut butter and pickles. Ansley's eating habits were as weird as Ansley was, but Grace didn't think anyone loved Ansley as much as Grace did. Not always the sharpest tool in the shed, her younger sister was the sweetest person on the planet. She'd never intentionally hurt anyone, and her bubbly spirit was the only thing that kept Grace going some days.

"Grace! Grace! Your arm is bleeding all through your shirt! Look, Mom!"

Grace grabbed her arm and jumped from the table as her mother drew near.

Mom grimaced as she held out her hand. "Grace, let me see your arm."

Chapter Three

"Are you sure you're all right?" Darlene yelled as Grace went upstairs to change her shirt.

"Yes, Mom!" Grace shouted back from the stairs. "I told you, I cut it on the fence yesterday. Quit making a big deal about it!"

Darlene waited until Grace came back down the stairs wearing another long-sleeved shirt. "It's so hot, Grace. Don't you want to wear something cooler?"

"Mom, please! Don't you hear Chad honking? We're gonna be late." She brushed by Darlene, gave her a quick kiss on the cheek, then turned to Ansley. "Come on. We have to go."

Darlene watched her children pile into Chad's truck faster than what seemed humanly possible. "Have a good day!" she yelled from the front porch.

Still sipping coffee, she moseyed back into the house, mentally planning out her day. She wanted to get Layla's expensive dress back to her as soon as possible, but first she wanted to reread that ad in the newspaper, the one she'd circled earlier that morning. She sat down at the kitchen table and spread out the classifieds.

Teacher's aide, special needs school. Experience working with children.

Darlene knew her two years of college, taking mostly core classes, didn't qualify her to work with children, but didn't life experience count? Ansley hardly qualified as a special needs child, but Darlene had spent years tutoring Ansley and searching for resources to help her. Maybe working at the school would give Darlene some insight into how to help Ansley better.

The Evans School was between Round Top and Fayetteville, less than ten miles from her house. She'd passed the small brick building plenty of times. There were always a few cars in the newly paved parking lot, and she wondered what areas the school served. Round Top had a population of only eighty-nine, but nearby towns, with populations from three hundred to three thousand, surely could benefit from the school too.

She decided to go by The Evans School in person. After showering and dressing, she cleaned the kitchen, put Grace's sheets in the dryer, and ran the sweeper across the floors. At ten o'clock, she arrived at the school.

The small waiting room was empty except for four chairs and a coffee table. She noticed a bell on her side of a fogged glass window. Gently, she gave it a tap. A few moments later, the window slid open.

"Can I help you?" A girl who didn't look much older than Grace peeked out.

"I'm here about the job in the newspaper for a teacher's aide."

"Oh, sure. Hang on." The window closed, and within a few minutes an elderly woman with gray hair and kind, hazel eyes stepped from behind the closed door.

"Hello, honey. Come on back." The woman motioned with her hand for Darlene to follow her. She turned and looked at Darlene over her shoulder. "Ever worked with special needs children before?"

"No, ma'am, I haven't, but—"

"No worries." The woman stopped in front of a closed door. "Really, don't *all* of our children have special needs?" She smiled, and Darlene instantly liked her.

∞

Brad walked in the door at eight o'clock. He could smell dinner, but it was unusually quiet. He set his briefcase on the couch and headed toward the kitchen. Empty. "Darlene?"

He loosened his tie and walked into the dining room. "Wow." His beautiful wife was sitting at the head of the table, dinner was laid out, and there were only two places set. "Dare I ask where our children are?"

"The youth group party, remember?" She smiled as her eyes twinkled in the candlelit room, then she winked. "So sit down, handsome."

Brad was so tired, he felt like he could crawl into bed and sleep for days, but he was going to muster up every bit of energy he had to enjoy this evening. He pulled out his chair at the other end of the table. "You look beautiful. What's the occasion?"

"I told you, the kids are at a youth group function." She smiled again. "The house to ourselves *is* the occasion."

"Good enough for me." But Brad could tell by his wife's giddy expression that there was more. He raised an eyebrow and waited.

"I got a job today."

Darlene was glowing, and if this was really what she wanted, then he was going to be happy about it too. "Baby, that's great. Doing what?"

"Let's pray so we can start eating, then I'll tell you all about it."

Brad said a quick blessing as his stomach growled, then asked what she'd cooked.

"Chicken spaghetti, the way you like it, loaded up."

"Aww, honey . . ." Darlene's chicken spaghetti was his favorite, but most of the time she left out the onions because Ansley wouldn't eat them, the celery because Chad insisted he was allergic to it, and some of the spices because none of the kids did spicy very well. It made for a decent dish, but nothing like this—with all the good stuff in it. "Have I mentioned how much I love you?" He scooped out a generous portion, then reached for a roll. "Tell me about your job."

"Brad, this is going to be so perfect for me. It's working with special needs children. It's a very small school, only seven students right now, and there is a lady named Myrna who runs it. Her granddaughter is a student there. She's autistic."

Brad nodded as he swallowed. "Are all the kids autistic?"

"No. But they are all challenged in some way. One of the girls is Grace's age, and . . ." Darlene paused as she took a deep breath. "She has the mind of a four-year-old. I met her today. Her name is Mindy. And I met another girl named Tina who is also emotionally challenged."

"So you'll be working with the kids?"

"Yes. I'll actually be working directly with a little girl named Cara. She's twelve and autistic. But she's high-functioning, meaning she can talk, just not a lot, and she's easily distracted." Darlene smiled. "I don't know much yet, but I met her briefly today, and she's a lovely girl."

"But you don't have a degree or experience." Brad looked up from his plate and wished right away that he hadn't made the remark. His wife bit her bottom lip and stared at her plate. "I'm sure you'll be great at it, babe. I'm just surprised that you don't need a degree."

"It's just an entry-level aide position," she said as she picked at her food. Brad could have kicked himself. Then she looked up, lifted her eyes to his. "I'm so excited about it, though."

"I'm excited too." He smiled broadly at her. "I think it's great. It's what you wanted, and you'll be able to meet more people in the community." Glad he hadn't hurt her feelings too badly, he reached for another roll. "So how often do you go in—one or two days a week?"

"Every day."

Brad stopped chewing. "For how many hours?"

"Eight to five."

"I thought you were looking for a part-time job, Dar. Eight to five?"

"I know I should have talked to you before I accepted the job." She squeezed her eyes closed for a moment, then looked up at him. "But I really want to do this. I know it's a lot to take on, but it's right down the road. I'll still have time to make dinner for everyone when I get home, and . . . maybe I'll learn . . . you know . . ." She shrugged, then started picking at her food again. "How to deal with Ansley better sometimes."

Brad stiffened. There wasn't anything wrong with Ansley. "I don't think you can compare Ansley to the kids at that school."

"I'm not comparing, just saying that sometimes I don't understand what's going on in Ansley's head is all."

Brad pushed his critical thoughts aside and refocused on his wife's new endeavor. He had plenty of friends whose wives worked full-time jobs and tended families, and he'd heard their mixed reviews. He put his fork down and looked up at Darlene, her beautiful eyes longing for his approval. "I think you will be the best teacher in the world. I think all the students will love you. And I think that school is blessed that you walked in their door."

Her face lit up instantly. "Thank you, Brad."

"When do you start?"

"A week from Monday. And I don't have to dress up or anything. Just jeans or Capri pants. Very casual."

"My wife, the working girl. Guess you've already been doing it for years. You just didn't get paid for it before." Brad smiled. Darlene had always been a homemaker, and although he found it challenging to be as excited as his wife, her happiness was the most important thing. Her life revolved around the kids, and she'd always said that's what fulfilled her, but he supposed she needed more—or something different—these days. He missed the early part of their marriage, when her life revolved around him. It was a selfish feeling, and given the chance to steal her away from their children, he would have declined. But now, as she shared this news, he couldn't help but worry their time together as a couple would be rarer than ever. He'd pray about that later. For now, he was going to enjoy the chicken spaghetti . . . and the way his wife was playfully batting her eyes at him from the other end of the table.

He ate faster.

∾

On the morning of her big day, Darlene climbed out of bed the same time as Brad. She wanted to get ready for her first day of work and still have time to make breakfast for the kids. Brad usually just ate a banana or muffin en route to Houston.

As she curled the ends of her hair, Brad brushed his teeth in the sink next to hers. She hoped he was on board with her new job. Over the last week, she'd sensed that he was worried about the time commitment, even though he did his best to assure her otherwise. Darlene was worried about the time she'd be away from home also. She'd made arrangements with the school for Ansley to have a tutor work with her for an extra hour each day since Darlene wouldn't be home to help her with her homework after school.

"I should be home by five fifteen, in plenty of time to straighten things up and make dinner, and if—"

"Darlene . . ." He spit toothpaste in the sink, then turned to face her. "It's gonna be fine. The kids are older now, and you need to make them help out more anyway." He kissed her on the cheek. "This is important to you, and we will all get by just fine."

She'd been with Brad since she was eighteen years old. He knew her. *Really* knew her. And sometimes she suspected he said exactly what he thought she wanted to hear. But this morning, she'd take it. She was nervous enough without having to worry about her household falling apart because she went to work. And Brad was right; the kids did need to help out more.

"Thank you for saying that."

He pulled a shirt from a hanger and slipped it on. Buttoning up, he turned to her. "If having some extra spending money will make you happy, then I'm happy. So don't worry about things around here."

They'd always stayed on a fairly strict budget, so having some money that wasn't included in those numbers would be a nice perk. "It's not just that. I'll be able to meet some new people too. You have friends at your office, and I'd like to have some relationships outside of just . . ." She turned off her curling iron, put it on the counter, and shrugged. "You know what I mean."

Brad nodded. "I get it. Really. We'll make some adjustments. And when I get home tonight, I want to hear all about your first day."

She still felt the need to justify, if not to Brad, to herself. "My first month's salary will be enough to repair the roof over Ansley's room."

"Honey, I'll take care of that." He sat down on the bed and put on his socks and shoes. "Use the money you make at your job to buy something for you."

She'd never spent much money on herself for clothes, shoes, or personal items. Always on the kids or the house. Not to say she'd let herself go—she'd like to think not. But a variety of nice clothes hadn't seemed essential, even when they were in Houston. "Maybe," she said as she slipped into a pair of black slacks and a white blouse. All her blue jeans were a little too ragged to feel comfortable wearing to work. Maybe that would be first on her shopping list. New jeans.

Brad stood and smiled at her. "Okay, knock 'em dead. I love you." He kissed her and hurried out of the room.

A few minutes later, she was downstairs heating up some leftover blueberry muffins.

"Guess this is what we have to look forward to from now on," Chad said as he eased into a chair at the table. "Leftovers." He chuckled.

"You look nice, Mom." Ansley slid in beside her brother, cutting her eyes at him.

"Thank you, Ansley. Where's Grace?" Darlene put a tub of butter on the table.

"Here I am." Grace walked into the room and slipped into a chair before reaching for a muffin. Darlene noticed her Capri jeans and brown, long-sleeved shirt but decided not to say anything. When the temperatures hit a hundred degrees in another month or two, she was sure Grace would opt for cooler blouses.

Darlene put her hands on her hips. "Now, listen. I don't want this house a wreck when I get home. You're all going to be home almost two hours before me, so pick up after yourselves. And I've left a list of weekly chores on the refrigerator, things like running the sweeper, dusting, stripping your beds, and such."

"You're kidding, right?" Chad said with his mouth full, his dark wavy hair brushing the top of his shoulders.

Ignoring his comment, Darlene said, "And, Chad, you need a haircut." She picked up her purse and keys from the counter. "Ansley, don't forget to feed your chickens when you get home from school."

"I hope they lay eggs soon!"

Darlene smiled, knowing how happy Ansley was that her father stayed true to his promise and bought her four laying hens over the weekend. And one rooster. "I'm sure they will."

"Good luck today, Mom." Ansley stood up and hugged her. Chad ate another muffin.

"Grace, you need anything?"

"No, Mom. I'm fine." Grace tucked a strand of long hair behind her ear. Unlike Ansley, who liked her hair cropped at the shoulders, Grace's hair was almost to her waist.

Darlene let out a heavy sigh. "Okay, then, I'm off. See you all after work." It sounded nice—*off to work*, but she wished the butterflies in her stomach would take a rest.

❦

Grace carried her lunch to the same table she did every day, the one closest to the band hall, the table designated for popular girls, seating for eight. She'd sat with a similar group when she lived in Houston, although their spot at her old school consisted of two tables pushed together for a group of twenty of her friends, guys and girls. Grace had always sat next to Tristan.

She pushed her tater tots around on her plate as the other girls settled into conversation. Nikki talked about going to the senior prom with Dwayne, Glenda asked to borrow Missy's homework, and Jill talked about her prizewinning pig. Although there were many similarities between these girls and Grace's friends in Houston, there were also some distinct differences. Even though Round Top girls got pedicures and enjoyed a trip to the mall, they were also capable of riding horses and raising pigs. Most of them had been on a coyote hunt at some point in their lives and were familiar with the term *cow tipping.* Grace still didn't know what that was.

These girls were all pretty, sought after by the jocks, and in some cases, above doing their own homework. Grace didn't feel like she belonged in the group, but she'd been recruited. Why argue?

Glenda finished copying Missy's math assignment, then leaned across the table, motioning with her finger for Grace to come closer. Grace leaned over her lunch plate as she strained to hear.

"Carter Fritsch is planning to ask you to prom." Glenda's brown eyes bored into Grace's, conviction in her tone, as if this news might cure world hunger or at least save Grace from the dreaded fate of not being invited to the senior prom this year. Grace was only a sophomore, but everyone in the school was vying for a spot. And with only twenty-six boys graduating, only twenty-six lucky girls from all four grades would be chosen.

She thought about Tristan and wondered who he was taking to the prom. In Houston, more than one thousand students would be graduating from her old school, Tristan included. She'd had several of her old friends ask her to attend the ceremony, but she wasn't planning to go. That life was behind her, and visiting would only stir up painful reminders. The day Tristan broke up with her, he'd said, "It's just not working out, Grace. I think we should see other people." She'd tried to reassure him that they would still see and talk to each other after she moved to Round Top, but Tristan had responded, "It's not just that, Grace. I think you have some problems too. You know, like . . . maybe you need to get some help or something."

Grace had thought Tristan understood her.

She'd been told all her life that she was pretty, but didn't one single person understand that looks don't give you a rite of passage into happiness? Grace hurt all the time. Sometimes the ache inside was almost too much to bear.

"Did you hear me?" Glenda sat back and folded her arms across the table. "If I wasn't going with Jake, I'd almost be upset about this."

"I can't go, even if he asks." Grace forced a tater tot into her mouth and chewed, hoping Glenda's comeback wouldn't cause her to choke. She swallowed, then looked up at Glenda, whose jaw hung low.

"Are you kidding me? Everyone wants to go with Carter."

Grace knew she couldn't even consider the idea. "I'll be in Houston that weekend. It's something that's been planned for months."

"What?"

Grace shrugged, not expecting Glenda to push the issue so hard. "Some of my parents' friends, they have this thing, a party . . . every year."

Glenda unfolded her arms and started drumming her fingers on the table. "You'll be the only one at this table not going with someone to the senior prom."

"I know. I hate that it's the same weekend." Grace cringed, knowing her lies only fueled her misery. Her heart ached the way it always did when she didn't tell the truth. She often wondered if it was God's way of letting her know He was onto her.

Glenda nodded to her right as Skylar Brown walked by their table carrying her lunch tray. She was the only girl in their small school who dressed gothic. Black shoes, black jeans, and a black, long-sleeved shirt. "I bet she'd love to go to prom with Carter." Glenda grunted. "Like *that* would ever happen."

Grace watched Skylar for a few moments. She was pretty enough, even with her dark eye makeup and jet-black hair, but Skylar looked more out of place here in the country than she would have at a big school in the city. Grace remembered her first day of school. She didn't have a pencil to take notes in math class. Skylar was sitting next to her and quietly handed her a pencil, never even looking at her. It was a simple gesture, but it stuck with Grace. Skylar glanced in Grace's direction, and Grace quickly pulled her eyes away.

Glenda went on talking about what a mistake it would be not to go to prom with Carter, but her words blurred together as Grace's mind drifted. So many things were wrong with the world. Grace's stomach churned, her heart ached. She knew she had a great family, that Tristan wasn't worth the grief she'd invested in the breakup. But still, she felt unsettled all the time, like a top spinning, faster and faster, vivid colors dancing in her head.

Tops fall over eventually.

The bell rang, and Grace was glad to walk away from Glenda and the rest of the girls. It took everything she had to pretend she was like them. She knew she looked the part, except that most of the other girls were sporting sleeveless or short-sleeved shirts. Grace knew she couldn't get away with the long-sleeved shirts for much longer.

As she walked down the crowded hallway to class, she

thought again about what Tristan had told her when they broke up. She shifted her books on her hip and shook her head. *Everyone has problems, not just me.*

Tristan was wrong. Grace knew her troubles weren't anything she couldn't handle on her own.

Lifting her chin, she made up her mind. She was going to change. Starting today.

Chapter Four

Darlene spent the morning with Myrna, touring the facility and meeting the other four employees.

She'd already met Lindsey during her first visit to the school. Though only eighteen years old, she ran the front office. Myrna said she was proficient and also had a vested interest in the school. Her seven-year-old sister was a student there. There were three other teachers who worked with the students. Two of them had teaching degrees and were recent college graduates. The third teacher was older, maybe Darlene's age, and she had degrees in psychology and teaching. They were all welcoming, but Darlene couldn't help but wonder why Myrna had hired her so quickly without a degree or any teaching experience.

At lunchtime, Myrna led her to the kitchen, a sizable room in the back of the building with a round table and six chairs. Myrna unwrapped her sandwich as Darlene heated up leftover meat loaf and mashed potatoes.

After they both sat down, Myrna asked, "What do you think so far?" Her gray hair was gathered into a bun atop her head, and she was wearing a gray dress that fell just past her knees. Darlene didn't think she'd seen a more matronly-looking woman, and Myrna was a pillar of calm. Even when Lindsey had told her that the toilet was overflowing in the bathroom and flooding the hallway, Myrna had hardly reacted. "If that's the worst thing the Lord tosses our way today, we'll be okay," she'd said with a smile.

"It's a nice facility." Darlene blew on a bite of meat loaf. "I'm anxious to spend time with all the children, especially Cara." After three hours in Myrna's office going over procedures and Cara's routine for the afternoon, Darlene was anxious to get started.

Myrna smiled, and her eyes twinkled as they had all morning while she was showing Darlene around and teaching her about Cara. "Your one-on-one sessions with Cara will start at one o'clock. Then, starting tomorrow, you'll also be in the morning group sessions."

Darlene nodded. "I'm a little surprised that I don't need a degree to do this type of work." She knew she wasn't getting paid much, but she wanted to do a good job, even if she was just classified as an aide. Maybe no one else had applied for the job, and they were desperate for help in this small town.

Myrna dabbed at her chin with her napkin. "I must warn you about something." She paused, sighed. "Cara's father is not the easiest man to deal with. Mae Perkins quit because of him, even though she cared a great deal about Cara."

Darlene knew this had all sounded too good to be true. "Uh-oh," she said as she lifted her fork to her mouth.

Myrna waved a hand in the air. "I'll handle Dave Schroeder."

Darlene swallowed, thought for a few moments. "Did Mae have a degree or experience?" She poked at her potatoes, wondering if she was the right person to be working here.

"Yes, Mae did. You're the first person I've hired without a degree or experience."

They were quiet for a few minutes. Darlene shifted her weight in the chair. "Why *did* you hire me?"

Myrna swallowed the last bite of her sandwich, dabbed her mouth, then locked eyes with Darlene. "Because you're a mother of three teenagers. None of my other teachers have had children. Most have been right out of college, and I know that our small school is just a stepping-stone for them before they move on to bigger and better things." Myrna stood up with her plate and headed for the trash can. She dumped her plate and napkin, then turned to face Darlene. "I just have a good feeling about you, Darlene."

Darlene had been so excited this morning. Now she fought worry. "Tell me about Cara's father. Why is he difficult? Is Cara's mother the same way?"

Myrna leaned her back against the counter. "There is no mother. She was killed in a car accident when Cara was six years old. Dave has been raising Cara on his own."

"Hmm . . ." Darlene stood up and put her dish on the counter. "That must be hard."

Myrna washed her hands and waited for Darlene to do the same. She turned to face Darlene. "We all work with the children in a group in the mornings, then everyone splits off for one-on-one study in the afternoon. Two of the children only come to school in the mornings for group, so that leaves five in the afternoon, one for each of us." She smiled. "I work with my granddaughter, Theresa, most days, but today Theresa will be with Beverly so that I can sit in with you and Cara."

Darlene nodded as Myrna continued.

"There are a few things you should know about Cara before we go into the classroom. As I told you before, she's high-functioning. She is capable of carrying on a conversation, but sometimes she chooses not to. Her own father says she goes days without speaking to him. Other times, she's quite the chatterbox. And her attention span won't allow her to stay on task for long. Our biggest challenge with Cara is keeping her focused. If you find something she likes, she tends to commit herself to it, even if only for a while. She loves crossword puzzles, but rarely finishes one. She seems to enjoy reading, but I don't think she's ever read a whole book."

Darlene was wishing she had pen and paper handy. "Should I be taking notes?"

Myrna snapped her fingers. "Oh, and I almost forgot. Cara only eats white food, no other color." She shook her head and smiled. "Poor Mae brought her a big bag of jelly beans one day, certain that the sweet candy would change her mind about only white foods." Myrna chuckled. "Cara threw those jelly beans all over the room."

Darlene smiled, charmed by this woman who didn't speak about Cara with even a hint of irritation.

"Oh, and you'll need to take off your jewelry. Cara is fixated with it. Not only will she not do anything at all in class if you wear jewelry, but she will want to take it home with her. It's a type of perseveration." Myrna lifted her hands, then pointed to her ears. "You'll notice that none of us have any type of jewelry on."

Darlene pointed to her wedding ring.

"Yes, even your wedding ring will have to be removed."

Darlene couldn't remember the last time she'd taken off her wedding ring. Maybe fifteen years? She wasn't sure it would come off.

"I'm going to go to the ladies' room, then I'll meet you outside the last classroom on the left." Myrna said it in a tone that sounded like they were going to a big concert or a special event.

Darlene nodded, then ran her hand under the faucet in the kitchen, hoping she could slide off her ring.

∞

Every year Brad wondered how they were all going to survive another tax deadline, but at five thirty, Jeannie confirmed that all the returns were in the mail. He loosened his tie, leaned back in his chair, and took a deep breath. For the first time all day, he thought about Darlene and wondered how her first day on the job was going. He picked up the picture of the two of them that he kept on his desk. Their trip to San Antonio a few years ago. They'd stayed at the Hyatt on the Riverwalk, and Darlene was wearing a baseball cap, shorts, and a pink T-shirt as they stood on a footbridge overlooking the river. Brad smiled, wishing he could have bottled all the romance they'd crammed into those four glorious days. Brad's parents had come in from Florida to watch the kids.

Now that tax season was over, maybe he could take a few days off and they'd go on another minivacation. They didn't do that enough. For him, it didn't really matter where, as long as they were together.

He shut off his computer and closed a few open files on his desk, stacking them in the corner. He anticipated that Cliff would be choosing a new partner soon, and Brad hoped and prayed it would be him. Whatever little bit of money Darlene made at her new job, it should be hers to spend on herself, or for extras. Providing for the family was Brad's job. He'd always made a nice living, but his income as a partner would increase substantially. Brad would renovate the old farmhouse into Darlene's own mansion on the hill.

"Jeannie, I'm going. Are you heading home?" Brad picked

up his briefcase, turned off the light in his office, and eased toward his assistant's desk.

"Yep. I'm right behind you. Dan is grilling steaks to celebrate the last day of tax season, and I can already taste 'em."

"We got through it, didn't we?" Brad smiled. "Enjoy your evening. Come in late in the morning if you want." Jeannie had worked for him for many years, and Brad felt like she'd earned every dime they paid her. When he made partner, he was going to push for a nice raise for Jeannie too.

As he walked into the elevator and pushed the button for the lobby, he thought about something Darlene had mentioned several times since they'd moved to Round Top. This seemed like a good time to buy it for her. Now that tax season was over, he'd have time to do a little research and order her that special little something she'd been wanting. A celebration of her new job.

∝∽

By five o'clock, Darlene was a bit anxious about how her own children were faring this first afternoon without her at home. And as good as it felt to be out in the working world, she was having a hard time with not being home when they ran through the door today. She reminded herself that they weren't babies anymore, but she was still glad she didn't have far to drive.

Cara was a lovely girl, and Myrna had spent all afternoon with Darlene and Cara. The first two hours, they worked on simple tasks that helped strengthen Cara's ability to stay focused—reading short stories together, working simple math problems, and practicing hand-eye coordination exercises. From three to five o'clock, they'd focused on communication skills. Cara didn't speak clearly, and she talked fast. Myrna had said it was like her speech couldn't keep up with her thoughts, so when her mind resolved an issue, she just quit talking. Myrna also told her that some autistic children don't like to be touched. Cara was one of those children, although, Myrna said, she showed affection toward her father.

When Cara didn't want to listen anymore, she would hold up her hand and tap all four fingers to her thumb, a hand motion Darlene often made to Brad when she couldn't get off the phone with someone. She'd had to stifle a grin the first time Cara made the motion to Myrna—while Myrna was explaining a math problem.

They'd taken lots of breaks, gone outside to play, and had a snack around three o'clock—angel food cake that Cara's father had sent that morning. Expensive angel food cake. Darlene had noticed the price tag on the outside of the gourmet bakery's box. Twenty-two dollars. It was a good cake, but Darlene would never have paid that much for it.

Darlene had trouble staying focused most of the afternoon too, since she'd spent the entire time either sitting on her hand or tucking her hand under her arm to hide her wedding ring. It was going to take more than a little warm water and soap to get her ring off tonight. She'd taken off her other jewelry, some small silver hoop earrings and a silver bracelet Brad had given her for her birthday last year.

"Cara, I see your father pulling up outside." Myrna peered through a window that faced the front of the building. "Let's clean up our work area and go introduce Ms. Darlene to Dad." Myrna began to stack some workbooks into a pile, but Cara just stared at Darlene. Then, for the first time all day, she addressed Darlene directly.

"Are you going to your house?"

Darlene nodded. "Yes."

Cara stood up when Darlene and Myrna did. Darlene folded her hands behind her back, and she was almost eye to eye with this beautiful twelve-year-old. Cara was tall, taller than Ansley, who was the same age, and her auburn hair was cut in a cute bob that curled under, just slightly above her shoulders. Her sparkling green eyes peeked from beneath wispy bangs.

Myrna had already told Darlene that Cara's mental capacity wouldn't change much. Their job at the school was to help her with basic functions and behavioral tasks. Apparently, when Cara got angry or upset, she became physical—slapping, hitting, scratching, and even biting sometimes. Myrna said her outbursts were few and far between, but she warned Darlene just the same.

"Hey, baby girl." A tall, dark-haired man wearing tan slacks and a yellow polo shirt made his way toward them. Cara walked quickly to him and folded her arms around his waist, then she pulled away and pointed to Darlene but didn't speak.

Myrna took a step forward. "Darlene, this is Dave, Cara's father."

There was no mistaking where Cara got those amazing eyes. Dave looked to be about Darlene's age, late thirties. His light brown hair was cut short, his face clean-shaven. As he approached them, his cologne was a couple of feet ahead of him, a pleasant smell, and surprisingly not overbearing. He extended his hand.

"I'm Dave Schroeder." He didn't smile, and the handshake was brief.

"Nice to meet you." Darlene folded her hands in front of her. "I think we've had a really good day."

Cara was instantly in front of Darlene, tugging on her wedding ring. Hard.

"Oh dear," Myrna mumbled as she took a step toward Cara.

"No, honey, I'm afraid it's stuck on my finger at the moment." Darlene tried to ease her hand away. Cara pulled harder on Darlene's ring until Darlene could feel the points from the small diamonds on her band digging into her finger. Any harder and the girl was going to draw blood. She tugged back, but Cara began to groan, yanking harder on the ring.

Dave put a firm hand on Cara's arm. "Cara, no." Then he narrowed his eyes at Myrna. "Didn't anyone tell *her* about jewelry?" He cut his eyes toward Darlene, then refocused on getting Darlene's hand free. "Cara, let go."

It took several more forceful attempts before Darlene had her hand back. Dave didn't say anything as he ushered Cara out to the car. Cara cried the whole way, looking back at Darlene several times.

"I'm so sorry," Darlene said to Myrna after Cara and her father were out the door. "I was so careful all day long, and then . . ." She shook her head.

"These things will happen, dear." Myrna raised her shoulders, then dropped them slowly. "But I'd probably try to get the ring off tonight if possible." She grinned, but quickly her mouth curled under. "You are coming back, aren't you?"

Darlene had never considered not coming back. "Of course."

"Oh, good. We've run off a few teachers the first day." Myrna pulled the curtains closed in the classroom, and Darlene helped Myrna push in the six chairs around the table. They were the only furniture in the large space. Darlene looked around, noting that the calming shade of baby blue on the walls matched her mood. The walls were also covered with drawings the children had done, giving the room a warm and fuzzy feel. Then she noticed a sign in the midst of all the artwork that she hadn't noticed before.

And all thy children shall be taught of the LORD; *and great shall be the peace of thy children. Isaiah 54:13.*

It brought a smile to her face. At a time when schools were eliminating God from the classrooms, Darlene was glad to see that The Evans School didn't fall into that category.

"I'm looking forward to working with Cara," Darlene said, as much to herself as to Myrna. Maybe Darlene could make a difference, help Cara a little bit. Her own children didn't seem to need her as much these days, except to prepare food and clean their clothes. And maybe Cara didn't really need her either, but being here was a welcome change, and she was going to be the best teacher's aide she could.

After Darlene left the building, she was glad she'd be home in only five minutes. Plenty of time to make dinner and throw a load of clothes in the washing machine. Later this evening she'd try to finish Layla's dress. The alterations weren't anything Darlene couldn't handle, but fear of ruining such an expensive gown had caused her hands to tremble more than once. She'd be glad to get it back to Layla.

When she pulled into the driveway, she saw Ansley walking from the chicken coop with a smile stretched across her face.

"I bet I know what you're smiling about," Darlene said as she closed the car door.

"Yep! Look!" Ansley held out both hands. "Two eggs."

"That's great, sweetie." She wrapped an arm around her daughter. "Guess I better cook something that needs eggs, huh?"

Ansley stopped and frowned. "We can't eat these until after Dad sees them."

Darlene stifled a grin as she nodded. "Okay. Besides, I think I'm going to make beef and cheddar casserole, and that doesn't call for any eggs."

"How was your first day of work?" Ansley walked in the front door and held it open for Darlene. "Are you going to be cranky at night now like Dad?"

"Dad isn't cranky. He's just . . . tired. Especially during tax season. And tax season ended today."

Darlene tossed her purse on the couch and crossed the living room to enter the kitchen. "Where're Chad and Grace?" She pulled a pound of hamburger from the freezer.

"Chad's upstairs. Grace didn't ride home with us."

Darlene stopped pulling the wrapper from the meat. "What? Where is she?"

Ansley shrugged. "She said she'd walk home."

Darlene looked at the clock on the wall. "School was over almost two hours ago. She didn't say why she was staying late?"

"Nope." Ansley added her two brown eggs to a store-bought carton with four eggs left in it. "Wish I would have had these to decorate at Easter a couple of weeks ago."

"You kids haven't wanted to decorate Easter eggs in years." Darlene placed the hamburger meat on a plate and put it in the microwave to thaw.

"That's before we grew our own eggs."

Darlene smiled. "*Grew* our own?"

"You know what I mean."

They were quiet for a few minutes. Darlene cut up an onion. Ansley poked her head in and out of the refrigerator until she finally settled on a piece of cheese.

"I hope Grace is okay." Darlene paused, thought for a moment. "It's almost five miles from the school to home. Maybe I should send Chad to go look for her."

"Good luck with that." Ansley giggled. "Since he's got a girl upstairs."

Darlene's stomach roiled as she spun around. "What?"

"Cindy Weaver. He's been trying to hook up with her since we moved here."

Darlene didn't wait for an explanation of "hook up," but instead moved quickly to the stairs, taking them two at a time. She paused at Chad's closed door and knocked.

"Yeah, come in."

Darlene eased the door open, unsure what she'd been afraid of. She'd never had to tell the kids that members of the opposite sex weren't allowed when she wasn't home—she'd always been home. "Hey," she said as relief washed over her. Chad and Cindy were sitting at opposite ends of Chad's bed with books and papers laid out in between them.

"Hey, Mom. This is Cindy." Chad didn't look up from the book he had his head buried in.

"Hi, Mrs. Henderson." Cindy looked up and smiled, and Darlene silently blasted herself for suspecting that anything other than homework might be going on.

"Nice to meet you, Cindy." She smiled before turning to Chad. "Do you know why Grace stayed after school?"

Chad still didn't look up. "Nope. She just said she'd walk home later."

Darlene folded her arms across her chest, thought for a moment. "Okay, well, if she's not home by six, I want you to go look for her, okay?"

Chad sighed. "I guess."

"It's no problem, Mrs. Henderson. We can go look for Grace. I know where some of the girls hang out after school."

What a nice girl. Darlene smiled again. "Thank you, Cindy. We'll give it another thirty minutes or so. I can see you two are busy with homework."

"Yes . . . we are," Chad said as he finally looked up at her with a scowl.

"Again, nice to meet you, Cindy." Darlene backed out of the room, hesitating for a moment before she closed the door. Cindy was polite, well groomed, and very pretty. She recalled some of the girls Chad had dated back in Houston and shook her head. She was pleased to see him dating a nice girl. Most of Chad's friends back in Houston had avoided Darlene and Brad.

❧

"Wow, that was close." Cindy reached underneath Chad's bed and pulled out her open can of beer. Then she leaned down again and pulled out his.

"Thanks," he said as she handed it to him.

"Your mom seems nice." Cindy took a big gulp from her beer.

Chad tapped his thumb against the can. "Yeah, she's cool." He took a sip. It didn't taste so good anymore. It was hard to forget everything he'd gone through back in Houston. But Cindy Weaver was worth a few steps backward. He had no plans to fall in with the kind of kids he'd been running around with before. They'd snuck out of the house, partied until they threw up, and did things Chad never thought he'd do.

But all that was behind him. Cindy was a straight-A student, one of the most popular girls in school, and she didn't dress all grungy like the kids he used to hang out with. She was pretty. Classy. And she wanted to spend time with him. He'd taken her home from school before, and she lived in a big house close to the square in Round Top. Her father was always working in the yard, and he waved when Chad dropped her off. Mom should be glad he was seeing someone like Cindy.

"We're out of beer." Cindy sat up tall and winked at him, which caused his pulse to pick up, especially when she slid their books aside and moved closer. He'd never kissed her, but the playful way she leaned toward him made him think it must be on her mind too. She touched his cheek and pushed back a strand of his hair, sending shivers up and down his spine. "Hey," she said, grinning. "Do your parents have any booze downstairs you can get your hands on?"

Chad pulled his eyes from hers and rubbed his forehead. "No. They don't really drink. A glass of wine every now and then, maybe."

"Wine will do." Cindy leaned even closer.

"I—I think I better go look for Grace."

Cindy pulled away with a slight frown, but then she smiled. "That's cool." She stood and picked up her backpack. "Can you just drop me at my house before you go look for her?"

"But I thought—" Chad stopped when Cindy raised an eyebrow. "Yeah, no problem. I'll take you home first."

"Great." She walked to him and kissed his cheek. "You're a doll."

Chad was sure he'd remember her soft lips forever. But why was his stomach churning? He recognized the feeling. Guilt.

⸎

Grace picked up the pace as she walked home. She should have left study hall way before now. It was getting late. Mom was going to be worried. She didn't like to cause problems for anyone, especially not Mom. Darlene Henderson was the best mother in the world, and Chad and Ansley had given her enough problems. Grace prided herself on the fact that she never stirred up trouble. She wanted to be "the good child," so she handled her own problems, never dumped her worries on her parents, and made good grades. And staying at study hall today seemed like a good way to make sure she kept doing those things. It also was part of her new plan to improve herself. She held her head high, walked a bit faster, and silently said a prayer for God to give her strength.

She jumped when a car honked from behind her. Stepping farther into the grass, she made room, but the old Dodge pickup slowed to a stop. Grace peered through the open passenger window of the rusted brown truck. *Skylar Brown?*

"Need a ride?" Skylar lowered black sunglasses onto her nose, and Grace grimaced at the amount of black eye makeup Skylar was wearing.

Grace was certain that she and Skylar had never spoken to each other. "Uh, no. That's okay. I don't have far to walk." She forced a smile. "Thanks, though."

"Whatever." Skylar ground the gears as she jerkily headed down the winding gravel road.

Grace started walking again. Skylar's ride must've belonged to her great-grandfather. The engine was loud, and smoke bellowed from a pipe in the rear. But at least it was a ride. More than what Grace had. Hopefully that would change when she turned sixteen soon.

Then there was a loud *pop* . . . and a lot of smoke.

A minute or two later, Grace had caught up to the truck. Skylar stood beside it, staring at it. Then she kicked it. "Well, guess I'm the one who needs a ride now."

"How far away do you live?"

"Far enough that I'm not looking forward to walking."

Grace reached into her backpack and felt around. "Do you need to use my cell phone?" Mom insisted that they all have cell phones now that it was only ten dollars per person on the family plan. Grace pulled out the phone and held it toward Skylar.

"Uh, I have a cell phone," Skylar said, rolling her eyes. "It doesn't work here. I don't know of any cell phones that work along this stretch of the road. But go ahead and check yours."

Grace looked down at the display. "You're right. No service." She stuffed the phone in her backpack and set it down. "You can walk to my house with me and use our home phone. My house isn't too much farther."

"Or I can start walking toward my own house. Eventually I'll get service and can call"—Skylar paused—"someone."

Grace held her hand to her forehead to block the setting sun. "What about the truck?"

Skylar gave the truck another swift kick, her long black hair falling forward. She flipped it over her shoulder. "I guess it'll have to sit here for now."

"Want me to help you push it off the road in case you don't get back before dark?"

Skylar sighed, one hand on her hip. "If you don't mind, that would be great. Let me go put it in neutral and release the brake."

Together they pushed the truck to the side of the road, flattening a group of bluebonnets. Grace was surprised that they didn't have more trouble moving the truck, considering Skylar wasn't much bigger than Grace.

"There's my brother." Grace pointed at Chad's rust-free Chevy pickup coming toward them. "I'm late. He's probably looking for me."

"You're bleeding."

Before Grace looked at Skylar, her eyes darted down to her arm. "Oh, it's no big deal."

Skylar walked closer, and she surprised Grace when she touched her arm. Grace flinched and pulled away. "How long have you been cutting?" Skylar asked.

"What?" Grace felt like her heart would pound out of her chest.

"You heard me. How long have you been a cutter?"

Grace picked up her backpack and swung it over her shoulder just as Chad eased up beside them. "I don't know what you're talking about," Grace snapped.

"Sure you do." Skylar blinked a few times as she took a deep breath. "Let me know if you want to talk."

Grace watched Skylar shuffle down the road in her black army boots, but felt compelled to yell after her, "Don't you need a ride?"

"No." Skylar didn't turn around.

Good. Grace was quite sure of one thing. She had no intention of talking with Skylar Brown about anything.

She crawled in the front seat with Chad, her bottom lip trembling as Chad yelled at her about being late and not calling. And something about Cindy having to leave early.

Grace hated to be late. Or to be yelled at. But she just sat there and listened without responding, gritting her teeth so hard her jaw hurt. Her head felt like a pinball machine, the balls bouncing around, slamming against the side of her brain. And her heart was pounding so hard, she was starting to feel sick to her stomach. *Shut up, Chad! Just shut up!*

She closed her eyes to tune him out, which was nearly impossible, but when she finally did, she envisioned the way Skylar had looked at her earlier—with pity in her eyes. The last thing Grace needed was for a girl like Skylar to feel sorry for her.

There is nothing wrong with me, Goth Girl.

Chapter Five

Darlene eased her chair away from the sewing machine in the corner of her bedroom. She'd taken her time altering Layla's dress, being precise and extra cautious every time she touched it. Standing, she held it high above her head so the bottom wouldn't drag on the floor. "Well, what do you think?"

Brad took off his glasses and placed them on top of the book he was reading before he shifted his weight in the bed. "Looks the same to me." He grinned, having seen the dress several times already.

Darlene lowered the gown. "Oh, ha ha." She carefully slipped it onto a hanger, hooked it on the closet door, and moseyed to her side of the bed. "I never should have agreed to alter that dress." She climbed into bed, fluffed her pillows, and fell back against them.

"You've been sewing since I met you, and the dress looks fine." Brad opened his arm wide, and Darlene snuggled closer. She'd already told him all about her day, heard about his, cooked dinner, cleaned up the kitchen, washed a load of clothes, and made sure all was well with the kids. She just wanted to close her eyes.

"I'm so tired."

"Welcome to my world," Brad said, yawning. "Are you sure you want to do this? Work full-time? I really feel like I have a partnership coming soon."

Darlene kept her eyes closed as she spoke. She wasn't about to tell him that she was missing her children. Brad knew her well enough to know it was true anyway, and she didn't want to fuel his thoughts. This was something she needed to try. A small shot at some independence outside of wife and mother. "It's not about the money." Although the extra money would be nice. "I enjoyed today. It's just going to take me some time to get used to being gone during the day."

"I told you. Make the kids help out more." He kissed her on the cheek. "They're lucky to have you at that school."

"Thank you."

He pulled her closer. "Hey, now that tax season is over, let's get away for a few days. I think the kids would be okay by themselves now, don't you? They're old enough."

Darlene's stomach churned at the thought. She wasn't sure she'd have a good time, knowing her children were unattended.

"I can already feel you tensing up." Brad sighed. "Maybe you're right. They're good kids, but . . ."

Darlene was pretty sure Brad was recalling the events back in Houston with Chad, and Darlene shivered just thinking about them.

It was a long haul for Brad's parents to come in from Florida, and her father-in-law hadn't been in the best of health lately. Since Brad was an only child, Darlene's brother, Dale, was the only sibling between them, and Darlene was pretty sure that having Dale come stay would be just like adding another kid to the mix. She loved her brother, but even at thirty-six, he still played hard.

"Yeah . . . ," she finally said, "and I just started a new job. I can't take time off yet." She nestled into the crook of his arm. "We'll figure out something."

They'd said that for a long time, and they never did figure anything out. She thought about their trip to the Riverwalk, probably four years ago. How great it would be to do that again.

"I guess I'll stop by Layla's on the way home tomorrow and give her the dress." Darlene closed her eyes again, yawning. "I don't know what to think about that woman."

Brad was reading again, and Darlene could tell she better say her prayers before she fell asleep in the middle of them.

"Who do you love?" she asked her husband before she began to thank God for His many blessings.

"You, baby."

The next morning, she hardly budged when the alarm went off until Brad got up, came around the bed, and nudged her. "Work today, baby."

"Oh yeah." She stepped out of the bed, and with her eyes barely open, she grabbed her robe. "I'll go start breakfast."

"Dar . . ." Brad gently grabbed her arm. "Let the kids fend for themselves. There's cereal, muffins, and other stuff they can eat. They don't have to have something cooked."

She yawned. "I guess not."

Forty-five minutes later, she was dressed and downstairs. Chad asked if they'd ever have eggs for breakfast again, and Ansley said she hoped not.

"What's the point of just saving those eggs in the refrigerator?" Chad chuckled. "Unless we're going to save them to egg someone's house."

"Uh—no," Darlene said as she moved toward the coffee. "That's not happening."

"This is weird, you working, Mom. I mean, seriously." Chad talked with his mouth full. "What if one of your poor children needs something during the day?"

Darlene turned around and grinned at Chad's exaggerated frown. "Well, I guess my poor little darlings will just have to figure it out."

"I'll cook eggs one morning," Grace said as she buttered a muffin.

Ansley's eyes widened, but she didn't say anything.

Chad pointed to Grace. "I knew you'd come through for us, Grace."

Darlene pulled her purse onto her shoulder, feeling a bit naked without any jewelry. It had taken effort, but she'd gotten her wedding ring off last night by rubbing lotion on her finger and pulling until she'd thought she might cry. "Lock everything up. And remember to clean up after yourselves, and clothes go—"

"We know, Mom," they all chimed in together.

Darlene picked up her cup of coffee. "Then I'll see you all tonight. Love you!"

⬿∾

Darlene mostly listened the first hour of group session that morning. She sat in the circle, facing Rachel, the teacher Darlene's age with multiple degrees who also led the group. The two younger teachers—Christie and Beverly—chimed in occasionally, as did Myrna. All seven students had come to school that day—Myrna's granddaughter, Theresa, was the youngest at seven, and Mindy was the oldest at fifteen.

Each child had special needs, and Darlene was impressed that the teachers were able to maintain order. And they did it with kindness and compassion. Darlene liked all of the teachers, but into the second hour, she grew particularly fond of Beverly, one of the recent college graduates. A heavyset woman, Beverly had one of those mouths that always seemed to be set in a smile, and three of the children had fought for the chairs on either side of her. Beverly spoke with a slight lisp and often held her hands in a prayer position as she spoke. Not that she was praying—or maybe she was—but her voice was soft, and her comments seemed mature beyond her age. She didn't talk a lot, but when she did, she held the children's attention.

"Mindy, that's a beautiful yellow dress you have on today." Beverly nodded toward the fifteen-year-old to her left. "That color makes me feel cheerful and happy. What does it remind you of?"

Darlene listened as the other children responded with words like *bananas* and *sunshine*. Ten-year-old Tina said yellow reminded her of a driving car.

"They used to live in New York, and her father drove a taxi," Myrna whispered to Darlene.

It was all interesting, but Darlene wasn't feeling like she had much to contribute. She'd noticed that Mindy had begun to twirl her hair between her fingers so hard that it hurt Darlene to watch. Instinctively, Darlene's eyes darted around the room until she saw a small stuffed animal in a nearby crate filled with other toys. She waited until Rachel led everyone in a clapping game that was meant to improve hand and eye coordination. Then she slipped away.

She returned with a furry orange cat, and she put it in Mindy's lap. "I think he needs someone to pet him," she whispered to Mindy, now wondering if she should have just stayed in her seat. But right away, Mindy pulled her hand from around the crumpled mass of her knotted hair and began to stroke the stuffed animal. Darlene remembered when Ansley used to twirl her hair, though not as hard as Mindy. It was something she'd done until she was about nine. Darlene had learned to distract her with something else.

During the last hour of the session, Darlene interacted more with the children and joined in on the discussion. Cara didn't have much to add, but Darlene had caught Cara staring at her a lot. She wondered what was going through the girl's mind, and she was anxious for the one-on-one session with Cara after lunch.

The teachers left for lunch in two shifts, and Darlene took the early shift with Rachel and Beverly.

"That was a great idea to occupy Mindy's mind with a stuffed animal. She didn't twist her hair the rest of the session," Rachel said as she took a bite of her sandwich in the break room.

"My daughter used to do that," Darlene said and felt a flush in her cheeks. She wasn't used to talking about her family with people she didn't know very well. But she missed having other women to talk to. As she ate, she listened to Rachel and Beverly chat and soon realized she didn't have much in common with these women—except their jobs at the school. Rachel was divorced and seemed to have a huge chip on her shoulder about men. Beverly, while sweet as she could be, was at least fifteen years Darlene's junior and newly dating a doctor in town. Christie, who was with the children, along with Myrna and Lindsey, was also young. And of course, Myrna had decades on all of them. But they were lovely women.

Darlene wondered if she'd ever find another friend like Gina, and she was curious about how Gina was doing in her new single life. She made a mental note to give her a call.

After her lunch break, Darlene went to the smaller classroom set up for Cara's one-on-one sessions. Myrna was already inside, sitting with Cara.

"All ready?" Myrna stood up. Cara was working a crossword puzzle. "I'm right in the next room if you need me. Just follow the schedule from yesterday. Consistency is essential." Myrna looked at Cara. "Cara, remember Ms. Darlene?"

Cara didn't look up, but she nodded. Darlene took a deep breath as Myrna smiled, then left them alone together.

Darlene sat down beside Cara and watched her working the crossword puzzle. It wasn't an easy puzzle, and Darlene was surprised how many clues Cara had figured out. She waited, not wanting to interrupt and unsure exactly how to proceed. She glanced at the pile of notes she'd taken yesterday, then at the stack of books and papers between her and Cara. Just as she put a hand on the stack, Cara put her pencil down.

"Are you ready to work on some math problems?" Darlene fumbled through the pile until she found the workbook. She opened it to the page Myrna had marked, beginning where they'd left off the day before. She eased it toward Cara, who didn't look up. Darlene picked up the pencil and offered it to Cara. "Ready?"

Cara didn't move for a few moments, but eventually she took the pencil, did three of the six problems, and put the pencil back down. Darlene checked her answers. All correct. She asked her if she could finish the rest, but Cara shook her head.

The rest of the afternoon was uneventful as they worked their way through the pile. It was interesting that Cara would do some of the work, then would lift her chin and look around the room, as if she was trying to find someone or something. It always took a few minutes to get Cara's attention back on the work. During the communication segment of the class, Cara wouldn't say a word. She mostly just stared at Darlene, and although it was somewhat unsettling, by the end of the hour Darlene had gotten used to it.

Right at five o'clock, the door opened. Darlene was expecting Myrna, but it was Cara's father. Cara stood up and walked toward him. Darlene stacked the papers in a pile, then also stood and moved toward the two of them. "I think we had a good day," she said to Mr. Schroeder.

He nodded, then leaned down and kissed Cara on the forehead. "Did you have a good day, sweetie?"

Cara shook her head. "No."

Darlene's breath caught in her throat. She'd had no indication that things hadn't gone well.

"It was a bad day." Cara spoke quickly and turned to glare at Darlene. Then she pointed a finger at her.

Dave Schroeder scowled at Darlene. "Anything in particular she's referring to?"

Darlene walked closer, glancing back and forth between Cara and her father. "No, I thought things went fine." She locked eyes with Cara, but only for a second before Cara looked away. "Cara, you did a great job on your math problems, crossword puzzles, and the other work Ms. Myrna left for you today. I thought you did a fantastic job." With the exception of the communication segment, Darlene really did think things had gone well. She smiled, hoping for a more positive reaction from Cara. Nothing. "I'm sorry, Mr. Schroeder. Maybe it's going to take Cara some time to get to know me."

"She doesn't like change," he said as he pushed a strand of auburn hair from Cara's cheek.

Darlene wanted to remind him that if consistency was so important for Cara, then he should try harder not to run off her teachers, but instead she nodded. "Tomorrow's a new day."

"Tell Ms. Darlene bye, Cara." Dave immediately moved her toward the door as if he didn't expect his daughter to respond.

"Bye, Cara. See you tomorrow."

Darlene was pacing beside the table in the middle of the room when Myrna walked in. "Well, how did it go?"

"I thought it went fine, but Cara told her father that she had a bad day, so I don't think that went over very well."

Myrna grinned. "Cara is a smart girl. Autistic, yes, but her thoughts are often more organized than you would think."

Darlene tipped her head to one side. "What do you mean?"

"I mean this in the most loving, fondest of ways, Darlene, but if there were such a thing as selective autism, Cara would be the poster child for it. Just now, she told her father she had a bad day because she knows that Dad will take her for ice cream the minute they leave here. And that's all right, I suppose, but our job here is to try to teach Cara the skills necessary for her to function the best she can. Giving in to her every whim doesn't always help her."

"But Mr. Schroeder seemed concerned that she'd had a bad day, and he didn't seem to think she was making it up. You should have seen the look he gave me." Darlene sighed. "I'm not sure he's happy I'm here."

"He's just an unhappy man in general. I didn't know him when his wife was alive, but I've been told that he was very different then. They ran a successful business together, and they were both completely dedicated to Cara." Myrna paused, holding up a finger. "Dave is still very dedicated to Cara and has had a lot of success in real estate, but he's . . . how should I say . . . just rather empty inside, I think."

Darlene cringed at the thought of anything happening to Brad. She was going to add Dave and Cara to her prayer list. "I understand."

"Don't let him run you off, dear." Myrna spoke firmly, then smiled. "Give it time. Like I said, I have a good feeling about you."

"It's only my second day. I know it will take some time."

∝∾

Fifteen minutes later, Darlene knocked on Layla's door. The Versace dress was draped over her arm.

Layla opened the door in her usual attire—jeans, boots, and a work shirt. "Come in," she said with more enthusiasm than she'd shown Darlene in the past. Darlene followed her inside.

"Thank you. Do you mind waiting while I try it on?" Layla asked as she took the dress.

Darlene did mind. She had a family to get home to, dinner to cook. "Sure, I'll wait."

Layla returned in the dress, and once again, it was such a transformation from farmworker to glamour girl. "I think it fits fine. Does it look okay in the back?" Layla turned around.

Darlene wished she could wear a dress the way Layla did. "Yeah, I think it looks great."

"Be right back."

Darlene tapped her foot, glanced at her watch. Layla returned, closing her bedroom door behind her. "Thank you for doing this. I could have taken it to Houston, I guess . . ."

"It's fine. I'm just glad it fit." Darlene smiled. "I better go."

"Why are you dressed up?" Layla inched closer and eyed Darlene up and down. Layla had only seen Darlene in ragged jeans and T-shirts. Now she was sporting a pair of tan Capri pants and a pink and tan blouse.

Darlene glanced down. "Well, I don't know if I'd call this dressed up." She laughed. "But I guess it's dressed up for me. I got a job."

Layla frowned. "Oh. I see."

"I'm working at The Evans School up the road."

The hint of a smile tipped the corners of Layla's mouth. "That's a wonderful facility. What are you doing there?"

"I'm just a teacher's aide, but they're training me. I've never really worked, not outside the home. But my kids are older, and I wanted to do something to . . . maybe make a difference."

Layla sat down on the couch and motioned for Darlene to do the same. Darlene glanced at her watch. She was torn between wanting to rush home to be with her kids and wanting to make a friend in this new town. And this was so out of character for Layla that Darlene couldn't resist taking a few minutes to talk.

"Myrna runs a top-notch school there. I guess you know her granddaughter is autistic?" Layla folded her hands in her lap as she raised an eyebrow.

"Yes."

"Did she tell you that we are trying to open up another wing in the school? We want to make it available to even more children, including lower-income families whose children would benefit from the school but who might not be able to afford the tuition."

Darlene caught Layla's use of the word *we* more than once, and she was surprised by the passion in Layla's voice. "No, I didn't know that."

"Finding teachers in this area is always a problem. I'm glad you're working there."

"I hope I'll be good at it." After today, she had her doubts.

"You will be."

Layla made the statement with such conviction, Darlene wanted to believe her.

"You should attend the gala with me. The proceeds benefit the school."

Darlene put a hand to her chest. "Oh, I couldn't."

"Why?" Layla crossed her legs, frowning, as she kicked a bare foot into motion.

"I—I just . . ." She shrugged. If Layla was wearing a Versace gown, Darlene was sure she didn't have anything in her closet to wear that was even comparable. "I don't really have time to take on anything else."

Layla stood up, almost stomped across the room, and returned with an envelope. "Here, I have an extra ticket, and it would be a shame for it to go to waste. Consider it payment for altering the dress."

"I thought you didn't even want to attend the gala."

"I don't. But I will. Because it's for a good cause. And now I have a date." She raised one thin eyebrow and grinned.

Darlene stood up. "Layla, I'll be glad to donate to the cause, but I can't attend the gala. I've already got a full plate, and—"

"It's on a Saturday night. And if this is a what-to-wear issue, I have at least a hundred more dresses just like the one you altered that you can borrow."

Versace? Darlene had never even tried one on.

"Of course, you'll have to hem it." Layla had transformed into a completely different person in the past few minutes, and even though Darlene had no clue why, she welcomed the new and improved Layla. Maybe they would be friends after all.

"Okay," she finally said as she looked at her watch again.

Brad walked in the door at six thirty, dumped his briefcase on the couch, and walked toward the kitchen, even though he didn't smell dinner. Ansley was putting eggs in the refrigerator.

"Look, Dad. Four more."

Brad smiled. "Ansley, that's great. You do know that we're going to need to start eating them, though, right?" His daughter sighed but nodded. "Where's Mom?" he asked.

"She's not home yet."

Brad looked at his watch. "Where is she?"

"I dunno. Haven't seen her."

"Maybe she hit the grocery store on the way home. What about Chad and Grace?"

"I dunno where they are either." Ansley closed the refrigerator.

Brad eyed the dishes in the sink. "You are all going to have to help more now that Mom is working. You start cleaning the kitchen."

"But those are Chad's dishes. Me and Grace put ours in the dishwasher."

"Well, I'm telling *you* to get that sink cleaned before your mom gets home. I'll get onto Chad when I find him."

Ansley huffed a bit, but she opened the dishwasher—one of the first things they'd added to the old farmhouse when they moved in. "Chad is probably at Cindy's, and Grace is probably in her room."

Brad left the kitchen and headed upstairs. He knocked on Grace's door. When there was no answer, he walked in. Thank goodness one of their children kept a clean room. Grace's bed was perfectly made, no clothes strewn across the floor, and it didn't have that strange odor that Chad's and Ansley's rooms had sometimes.

He bumped into Grace when he walked out of her room. "There you are. Is Chad here?"

"No. Maybe at Cindy's." Grace moved past him and into her room.

"How was your day?" Brad stuck his head over the threshold.

Grace went through life with a peacefulness he wished he had more of.

"Great, Dad."

"Okay, well, if you see Chad come home, tell him to stop leaving a sink full of dishes for everyone else to clean up. And tell him to go check the trough for the Longhorns and make sure they have water." One of these days, Brad would get water piped out to the pasture, but for now, a really long water hose was doing the trick. "Have you heard from Mom?"

Grace shook her head as she sat down on her bed. She pulled a notebook out of her book bag. "No."

"Hmm . . ." Brad went back downstairs. Odd that Darlene didn't bother to call any of them to let them know where she was. It had been a long time since he'd made dinner, but if they were going to eat anytime soon, he figured he'd better start.

He was about fifteen minutes into making hot dogs and French fries when he heard the front door open and close. He finished chopping an onion, then walked into the den.

"I'm so sorry," Darlene said as she met him in the middle of the room. "I took Layla's dress to her, and then we actually started talking, and next thing I knew I'd been there awhile, and—"

"What's that?" Brad pointed to a dress draped over Darlene's arm.

"Oh. This is a dress Layla loaned me." Darlene stepped up on her toes and grinned. "It's *Versace*, Brad. You should see Layla's closet. It's filled with designer dresses. She invited me to be her guest at a gala benefiting The Evans School." She held her breath for a moment. "It's not this Saturday, but the next. That's okay, isn't it?"

"Yeah, that's great. Why didn't you call and let someone

know you were going to be late, though?" He leaned down and kissed her. "I was getting worried."

"I'm sorry. I left my cell phone in the car because I wasn't expecting to be there longer than a minute, but Layla surprised me. Oh, and I invited her to Grace's birthday dinner this weekend, so you'll have a chance to meet her."

"Wow. That's a big turnaround from when you first met her."

"I know. Today she was different, but in a good way." She moved past him toward the stairs. "I'm going to go hang this up. Kids okay? And what's that I smell?"

"Kids are fine, although I haven't seen Chad. And hot dogs and fries."

"Perfect! I'll be back in a minute."

Brad started back toward the kitchen, but turned around when he heard a knock at the door. Through the glass panes, he could see a young woman standing outside. She was dressed all in black.

"Is Grace here?" she asked when Brad opened the door.

He stepped back so she could enter. "Come in. She's upstairs." Brad held out his hand since he didn't know this girl. "I'm Brad Henderson, Grace's dad."

The girl hesitantly latched onto his hand. "Hi."

She didn't look like anyone Brad pictured Grace would be friends with, not that he was judging her by her looks. She just didn't fit the profile of the girls in the youth group or the couple of other girls who had stopped by since they'd moved here. "You can go on upstairs if you want. I'm finishing dinner." Brad pointed toward the stairs. "Third door on the left."

Brad watched her go upstairs in her black work boots, black jeans, and black shirt, sporting jet-black hair and enough dark makeup to scare any parent. He just shook his head and went back to the kitchen where he saw Chad coming in the back door.

"Was that Skylar Brown pulling up to the house?" Chad whispered.

"Actually, she didn't say her name." Brad opened the oven and checked the fries.

"Oh, it's her. She drives that rusty brown Dodge. What's she doing here?" Chad dropped his backpack onto a chair and headed for the refrigerator.

"She came to see Grace."

Chad spun around. "What for?"

"Well, Chad, I really don't know. I didn't quiz her about it." Brad pulled a can of hot dog chili from the cabinet.

"She's a weirdo. See how she dresses, all gothic and everything."

Brad opened the can and dumped the sauce into a pot, wondering what was taking Darlene so long. This was more chaos than he was used to. "You know better than to judge someone by the way they look or dress, Chad."

His son sat down at the table with a glass of iced tea. "Oh, come on, Dad. You gotta admit, she doesn't look like anyone Grace would hang out with."

Brad thought for a few moments. "Grace can choose her own friends."

"Whatever." Chad stood up, picked up his backpack. "Girls like that are trouble. Just sayin' . . ." He shrugged and left the room.

Brad wondered if Chad was referring to some of the girls he hung out with back home. He tried not to think about it as he stirred the chili.

❧

"What are you doing here?" Grace held open her bedroom door so Skylar could come in, then quickly closed it behind the girl dressed in black.

Skylar pulled a piece of paper from a pocket on the front of her shirt, unfolded it, and handed it to Grace. "Since you skipped science class today, Mrs. Telgan paired us together for the science project. Here's our assignment."

Grace took the paper, glanced at it, and put her hands on her hips. "I didn't skip class. I had permission from Mrs. Telgan to retake a math test for Mr. Zahn's class."

"Whatever. Everyone paired up, and I got left with you." Skylar sighed.

Grace pressed her lips together. Not surprisingly, no one chose Skylar as a partner, but she didn't have to sound so perturbed at being stuck with Grace. "So sorry you got *left* with me."

Sklyar shrugged. "Whatever."

Grace struggled with science and math, although she'd still managed to maintain a low A average so far. Skylar was a top student in all her classes. The local newspaper ran the list of honor students when report cards came out, and Skylar's name had been at the top. Maybe because Skylar had no life or friends. Grace studied the assignment for a moment. "The effect of solar activity on radio propagation." She sighed. "Great."

"That's an easy one," Skylar said as she moved across Grace's room toward the pictures Grace kept on her dresser.

"Maybe for you," Grace grumbled under her breath as she sat down on her bed.

Skylar picked up one of the framed family pictures. "Your mom's pretty."

"Yeah." Grace was thinking about the science project. On the downside, she'd have to spend time with Skylar. On the upside, they'd most likely get the best grade in the class.

"You look like your mom." Skylar set the picture down before she turned around to face Grace. "My mom died when I was two."

Grace knew Skylar lived with her dad, but until now, she didn't know if it was because of a divorce or something else. "How?"

Skylar sat down in the chair in front of Grace's small white desk. "Breast cancer."

"I'm sorry." Grace couldn't imagine a life without her mom.

"Yep, as my dad would say, the Lord called her home early."

Most of the kids Grace knew rarely mentioned God. "I'm sorry," Grace repeated.

"I'll see her again someday." Skylar stood up. "Guess I better go. I need to fix dinner for my dad."

Grace stood up too. "Hey . . . why do you—?" She took a deep breath, wishing she hadn't started to ask Skylar the question that popped into her brain whenever Skylar was around.

"What?" Skylar's voice was matter-of-fact. "If you want to ask me something, just ask."

"Why—why do you dress like that, all goth and everything?"

Skylar grinned. "To keep girls like you away from me." Then she lunged at Grace. "Boo!"

Grace jumped, but then she laughed.

"Too easy," Skylar said as she laughed too. Then she shook her head and walked out the door.

Grace sat down on the bed again and leaned back on her hands. Maybe getting paired with Skylar for the science project wouldn't be as bad as she thought.

Chapter Six

On Friday, Darlene was feeling a bit down. She didn't think she'd made much headway with Cara this week. But she was looking forward to tomorrow evening, Grace's sixteenth birthday dinner. Surprisingly, Grace had invited only one friend for the celebration—her science partner, Skylar. Skylar had been to the house the past couple of nights, and she and Grace had stayed upstairs working on their science project until fairly late. It seemed an unlikely friendship, but Grace said Skylar didn't have many friends, so she wanted to invite her. Darlene had asked Layla to join them. And Chad's new friend, Cindy, would be there. She couldn't wait to give Grace her present at the party. She'd certainly earned it.

Darlene looked on as Cara worked through a math problem. Cara hadn't argued about doing the work this week, but every time Darlene had tried to talk to her—about anything—Cara held up her fingers and tapped them to her thumb, signaling yap, yap, yap. Their afternoons had turned into mundane tasks, and Darlene suspected she'd been overzealous in her hopes to somehow make a difference in Cara's life.

And every afternoon, Cara's father had shown up at exactly

five o'clock, asking about Cara's day. Always bad, she would tell her father. He would scowl a bit, then instruct Cara to say good-bye.

Darlene looked at her watch. *Fifteen more minutes.* She had a splitting headache. Her purse was on the chair beside her, so she reached into it and dug around for a bottle of Tylenol, hoping she didn't distract Cara too much. Her flip book of family photos fell out, along with the bottle. She popped open the top, poured two pills into her hand, and tossed them in her mouth, wishing she had a glass of water. As she reached for the flip book, Cara's hand slammed down on hers. Darlene looked at the girl, but Cara only stared at the book as she eased it from underneath Darlene's hand.

"That's my family," Darlene said as Cara ran her finger across the top photo. "That's my husband, Brad, and that's Chad, Ansley, and Grace."

Cara turned to the next photo and gave it the same amount of time, still rubbing her finger across the front. Darlene pointed to Ansley.

"That's my daughter Ansley. She's the same age as you are."

Cara looked up at Darlene, her green eyes glowing, a smile on her face. "You are a mother."

Darlene smiled, surprised at how clearly and slowly Cara had said the words. "Yes, I'm a mother. And those are my children."

"Ansley?" Cara touched Ansley's face in the photo with the tip of her finger.

"Yes, Ansley. She's twelve years old." Darlene paused as she watched Cara's animated expression, her eyes wide. "And you know what? Ansley is raising chickens."

Cara turned to face Darlene, and she giggled. "Chickens? Ansley's chickens?"

Darlene laughed, thrilled to be actually talking with Cara.

"Yep. They are definitely Ansley's chickens. Every afternoon after school, Ansley goes and collects the eggs. Do you like eggs?"

"I like Ansley's eggs." Cara said it so fast that Darlene could barely understand her. Then she said something else Darlene couldn't understand.

"Cara, I can't understand you when you talk so fast. Can you say it nice and slow?"

Cara clamped her eyes closed for a few moments, and Darlene wasn't sure if she was mad or concentrating.

"Take your time, Cara."

"I like Ansley's eggs." Cara pronounced each syllable slowly and clearly.

"Good." Darlene smiled, hoping to encourage her to continue, which she did.

"Eggs are from chickens."

"Yes, they are. And you should see how many eggs we have in our refrigerator. Dozens. Ansley doesn't want us to eat the eggs."

Cara started laughing loudly. Darlene had no idea if Cara understood what Darlene was saying, but the sound of Cara's laughter warmed her heart.

"Well, hello there."

Darlene jumped at the sound of Dave Schroeder's voice. "Oh, I'm sorry. I didn't hear you come in."

"I guess not. So much laughter going on in here." Then he smiled. A first.

He squatted down between Darlene and Cara. "Can you tell Dad what's so funny?"

Cara squealed, something Darlene had never heard her do. Both Darlene and her father winced a bit but they both smiled.

"Ansley's eggs!" Cara yelled as she smiled from ear to ear.

"Ansley is my daughter," Darlene said to Mr. Schroeder. "She's the same age as Cara."

"She's a beautiful girl," he said as he stood up.

Darlene rose also. "Thank you."

"Dad." Cara pointed to the picture. "This is Ansley."

"I see, Cara. You better give Ms. Darlene her photo album so we can let her get home to her family." Mr. Schroeder tried to take the album, only to have Cara squeal, this time with a fire in her eyes.

"It's okay," Darlene said quickly. "She can take it. I have duplicates at home."

Mr. Schroeder flinched. "Sorry. I'll make sure you get it back."

"No problem."

Mr. Schroeder turned to his daughter. "Do you want to tell me how your day was?"

Darlene held her breath.

There was a long silence, then Cara said, "It was good, Dad." She kept her eyes on the photos. "Ansley has chickens."

Dave laughed. "Really?"

Darlene was feeling a bit triumphant. Both Cara—and her father—were laughing. "We're city slickers, I guess you could say. But our youngest daughter was insistent we get some chickens."

"Ansley has chickens," Cara repeated softly.

Darlene picked up her purse. "Mr. Schroeder, I hope you and Cara have a great weekend."

"Dave. Just Dave." He smiled as he briefly touched Cara's arm, nudging her to stand. "Hope you and your family have a good weekend too, Darlene."

She waved as they headed to the door.

It was definitely a good day. And Darlene was looking forward to a good weekend.

79

She was back in the role of homemaker all day Saturday, cleaning and preparing for Grace's birthday party that evening. She'd already baked Grace's favorite cake—yellow with chocolate icing. Ansley was in charge of decorations, and Chad was helping Brad mow and edge the yard. It was hard for Darlene to believe that little Grace was sixteen.

"Honey, are you sure you don't want to invite any other girls from school?" Darlene brushed past Grace in the kitchen. "We told you to invite whoever you want."

"It's fine, Mom." Grace walked to the counter where the cake was.

"No touching." Darlene stood on her tiptoes so she could reach the serving dishes she needed for the appetizers. She pulled two glass plates from the top shelf in the cabinet, then turned to finish the salad. Grace had asked for lasagna, salad, and garlic bread for her birthday dinner. "So you and Skylar must be getting along well."

"Mom, I know she's different, and I know where you're going with this." Grace shook her head.

"Grace, I didn't say anything."

"Well, I can tell by the way you've looked at her every night this week when she came over."

Darlene put her hands on her hips. "Grace, I don't judge people." She cringed inside as she said it, though.

"I thought she was weird at first too. But now . . ." Grace shrugged. "I don't know. She dresses funny, but she's all right."

"Well, we're happy to have her." Darlene checked the pantry to see how many tea bags she had. Plenty. "What do you think about Cindy, Chad's new girlfriend?"

Grace tucked her hair behind her ears, shrugged again. "She's okay, I guess."

"Pretty girl," Darlene mumbled, ashamed of herself for wondering how Chad had snagged such a girl. Chad was a handsome kid, but he was rough around the edges. Cindy was as poised and put together as any seventeen-year-old Darlene had ever seen. Always polite and smiling.

"When do I get my present?" Grace nuzzled up against Darlene. "Huh, huh? When?"

"Right after dinner."

"What? I can't wait that long!"

"Well, you'll have to because it's not wrapped yet."

Grace smiled. "It's a car. It has to be. Chad got a truck for his sixteenth birthday."

"That old clunker?" Darlene forced a frown, but inside she couldn't wait for Grace to see what they'd bought her. "You don't really want something like that, do you? Wouldn't you rather wait until we can afford to get you something decent?"

Grace sighed as she blinked her eyes. "I guess."

Darlene wanted so badly to tell her that they'd been saving for a car for her, and while it was used, it was safe and well made. And it was several notches above the truck that Chad drove. Darlene knew that they would have to help Chad upgrade to a new car before he left for college, but they had another year before that worry came calling.

"I'm sorry, Grace. I promise we will work on getting you a car very soon, but I hope you'll like your present just the same."

"I'm sure I will, Mom." Grace hung her head as she walked out of the kitchen.

That was Grace. She never complained. Which would make it all the more exciting to be able to see Grace's reaction to her gift.

❦

Despite her reservations in the beginning, Layla was starting to like Darlene. She was an attractive gal, though she'd probably never spent a lot of time or money on her own upkeep. She'd just been busy raising kids. Layla found it ironic, yet admirable, that Darlene chose a job working with children. Layla would have thought she would've wanted to be around adults.

Layla was amazed that Darlene didn't seem to want or need anything from her, except maybe friendship. It was a new concept. Everyone seemed to want a part of Layla, which had kept her out of reach for the one person who had needed her the most. Marissa. Layla dreaded going to the Hendersons' for the birthday bash. What a birthday celebration Layla would have had for Marissa for her sixteenth birthday if she'd lived that long.

Layla shivered. Maybe if she'd been more like Darlene, stayed home more, been with Marissa . . .

She buttoned her blouse, then checked her lipstick. For a woman forty-five years old, she knew she'd held up well. Physically. Although she couldn't take all the credit. Money could buy looks. But she did give credit to herself for working hard. Taking care of her land and horses kept her mind from wandering to bad places. She struggled in the evenings, after the sun went down, the house dark, everything quiet. That's when she missed Marissa the most. And Tom.

She thought about Tom sometimes. It was for the best and easier this way. But, oh, how she'd loved him. Not a man before or since made her swoon the way he did.

She grabbed the card she'd picked up yesterday, slipped a check inside, then tucked the gift in her purse. Hopefully she wouldn't be there very long. The memories of Marissa were bound to overwhelm her. She had a bottle of wine ready for when she got home.

⸎

As six o'clock rolled around, Darlene and Ansley finished setting the table. Chad had gone to pick up Cindy, and Brad had gone to pick up the car. As was the rule, the birthday girl or boy didn't have to do any chores on their special day, so Grace was upstairs.

Darlene was surprised when someone knocked on the door early. They'd told everyone six thirty.

"Ansley, go get the door." Darlene laid out the last few napkins around her good china as Ansley skipped to the door.

A minute later, Ansley walked into the dining room with Skylar. "Sorry, I'm early."

Darlene waited for her to explain why she was early, but when she didn't, Darlene just said, "Oh, that's fine, Skylar. Glad you could come. Grace is upstairs if you want to go on up." Then Darlene turned to Ansley. "Honey, go feed your chickens before everyone gets here." She smiled as she thought about Cara.

Skylar walked up to Darlene, her black boots shuffling beneath her. She pushed back a long strand of black hair. "Can I ask you something?"

Darlene tucked her own hair behind her ears. She noticed the small piercing on Skylar's nose for the first time. She was going to pray that her girls never pierced anything besides their ears. "Sure. What's up?"

Skylar pulled a small box out of the pocket of her black jeans, the size of a ring box. She opened it up. "Do you think Grace will like this?"

Darlene leaned closer, then picked up the silver ring with a small angel in the middle. She held the ring up and looked at Skylar. "This is a beautiful ring. I'm sure Grace will love it." Darlene paused as she put the ring back in the box, squinting. "This looks like an expensive gift, Skylar. Are you sure you want to give this to Grace?"

"Yeah, I'm sure." Skylar snapped the lid closed. "It was my mother's."

Darlene brought a hand to her chest. "Skylar . . ." She stared into the girl's dark eyes, unsure what to say, except for the obvious. "You can't give Skylar a ring your mother gave you."

"Why?"

Darlene's jaw dropped. "Because . . . your mother gave it to you." Grace had already told Darlene that Skylar's mother died of cancer when she was two. She couldn't bear the thought of Skylar giving up such a treasured gift.

Skylar locked eyes with Darlene. "I'd really like for Grace to have it if you think she'd like it."

Darlene wondered if Skylar was trying to buy Grace's friendship, but when Skylar smiled, such hope in her eyes, Darlene said, "Yes, I think she'll love it."

"Great." Skylar stuffed it back in her pocket and turned to leave.

"Skylar, there's some wrapping paper on my bed." Darlene pointed to her bedroom. "If you want to wrap it."

"Okay. Thanks."

Brad hurried into the den, breathless. "The car is behind the barn, so don't let Grace go out there."

"Okay, okay." Darlene leaned up and kissed Brad, then cradled his cheek in her hand. "Go get some tea. Rest. Everything is under control."

Brad walked across the dining room toward the kitchen,

but made an about-face when someone knocked at the door. "I'll get it."

Darlene met him in the den, but Brad beat her to the door. He pulled the door open and just stared at Layla through the screen. He didn't open the door, he didn't speak . . . nothing. Darlene looked up at him and wanted to slam his dropped jaw shut. Layla was beautiful, no doubt. *But really, Brad!* She nudged him out of the way and opened the screen door.

"Hi, Layla, come in." She turned to Brad, his jaw still hung low. "Layla, this is my husband, Brad."

Brad smiled but didn't say anything. Then he nodded and abruptly left the room. Darlene would deal with him later.

"It's not much, but we call it home," Darlene said as she motioned for Layla to have a seat in the den.

"It's lovely," Layla said, almost as if she meant it.

"Can I get you something to drink? A glass of tea, lemonade?"

"Tea would be good."

"Be right back." She hurried to the kitchen. Brad was leaning against the counter rubbing his forehead, shaking his head.

"What is wrong with you?" Darlene spoke in a whisper. "I mean, I know Layla is attractive, but that was embarrassing, your mouth hung open and all . . ." She folded her arms across her chest and rolled her eyes. "I mean, really, Brad. You could have been a little more discreet."

Brad moved toward her, grinning like a schoolboy. "You have *no* idea who that is in our living room, do you?"

"It's our neighbor. I told you I was inviting her. It's Layla."

"Layla Jager. That's who it is!" Brad's voice started to rise, but he quickly whispered again. "Doesn't that name ring a bell for you?"

Darlene frowned. "No. What are you talking about?"

Brad chuckled, shrugged. Almost like a crazy man. "Oh, no biggie. We just have an Academy Award winner in our living room. That's all, *Darlene*. How can you not know who she is?"

Darlene didn't move as she tried to absorb what her husband was saying.

"Let me refresh your memory, my dear." Brad scratched his chin. "*Legacy of a Cowgirl, Free Rider, Leaving You on Tuesday* . . . Uh . . . ring any bells yet?"

Darlene didn't move, and her heart was beating out of her chest. Brad was a collector of old westerns, but the light had just clicked on for Darlene. "Oh my. Oh my. Oh my." She put her hand over her mouth.

"She was in her early twenties when she made those movies, but *Legacy of a Cowgirl* won her an Academy Award." Brad lowered his voice. "She kept making movies well into her thirties, even though I don't think they were as successful as those first ones. Then she just sort of fell off the face of the earth . . ." Brad laughed. "And landed in Round Top, Texas, right next door to us."

"I have to take her some tea." Darlene grimaced. "Okay, so she's famous." She pointed a finger at her husband. "Brad, don't you embarrass me. Don't say anything."

Brad held his palms up. "I won't say a word." He dropped his hands, then rubbed his chin for a moment. "Do you know that she's a real cowgirl? I mean, I think she did all her own stunts in the movies, rode the horses, everything. Her father was a huge rancher, and she grew up on a ranch. I never knew where." He snapped his fingers. "I wonder if she's originally from Round Top."

"I don't know." Darlene filled up a glass of tea for Layla. "But that explains a lot." She grinned as she shook her head, thinking of the snake encounter. She walked to the den.

"Here you go." She handed Layla the glass, and now she definitely recognized her from her movies. *Unbelievable.*

Layla took the tea, then stood up when Grace and Skylar came downstairs. At the same time, Chad and Cindy walked in. After introductions were made, they all moved into the dining room. Brad offered the prayer, but Darlene caught him with one eye open, looking at Layla. She shook her head. At least everyone else was too young to know who Layla was.

"Amen."

Brad was practically swooning. Darlene kicked him under the table.

"Ow."

"You pick lasagna every year," Ansley said to Grace as the lasagna was passed to her. She scooped out a small portion as she frowned. "Does this have eggs in it?"

"Are you allergic to eggs?" Cindy asked.

Chad grunted. "No. She's not allergic. She's collecting them."

Darlene cut her eyes at Chad. He just shrugged, shoveling a generous amount of lasagna onto his plate.

After everyone had served themselves, the room went quiet. Darlene glanced around the table, trying to keep her eyes from straying toward Layla, especially since Brad couldn't seem to get his eyes off her. The guests were all eating, except maybe Skylar, who was dissecting her lasagna, peeling the noodles away from the meat and stacking them to the side of the meat sauce and cheese. Darlene kept watching as Skylar forked out mushrooms and other vegetables, also pushing them to the side. When she was done, she had three piles, and Darlene wondered which one she would eat.

"What are you doing?" Chad asked Skylar, smirking.

Skylar shrugged, her cheeks blushing. "I—I just like to eat it this way."

Chad elbowed Cindy, and both of them grinned. Darlene wished Chad was sitting beside her so she could kick him under the table too.

Layla cleared her throat. "I hear it's healthier to eat your food that way." She smiled at Skylar, then began to pick her own lasagna apart.

Darlene had never heard of such a thing. But it was a kind gesture, and Skylar seemed to relax.

From there, the conversation drifted to a girl at school who was pregnant, the math teacher who was having an affair with the PE teacher, and then lastly, Ansley's English teacher who picked her nose all the time. Darlene didn't think she'd ever heard a worse display of improper talk at the table. Layla probably thought they were all a bunch of bumpkins. And Brad was laughing.

"I'm pretty sure this is not how I raised my children to talk at the dinner table." Darlene glanced around. "Don't you have something else to talk about?" The kids paused momentarily, then just kept on talking. She glanced at Layla, who locked eyes with her and grinned. Darlene just shook her head and smiled.

At the end of the meal, Brad spoke up. "If everyone's through eating, maybe it's time for Grace to open her presents." He leaned back in his chair. "I think there might be something out behind the barn . . ."

Grace jumped from her chair and ran toward the door . . . followed by Ansley, Chad, Cindy, and Skylar.

"I'm guessing a car?" Layla helped herself to another piece of garlic bread as the door slammed behind all the teenagers.

"Not a new car. It's a Ford Explorer. Big enough to be safe, sporty enough not to be embarrassed in, and old enough that we could afford it." Darlene waited until Layla finished her bread and laid her napkin across her plate. "Let's go see if she likes it."

Darlene, Brad, and Layla went outside. She could hear the chatter coming from the other side of the barn. A few moments later, Grace emerged and ran toward them.

"Thank you, Mom! Thank you, Dad!" She threw her arms around them both, and Darlene kissed her on the forehead.

"You're welcome, my sweet girl."

An hour later, Grace thanked Layla for the card and check, and she opened the rest of her presents. Chad and Cindy gave her a gift card for Royer's Restaurant in town. Ansley gave her a pink blouse she'd been eyeing at Bealls in La Grange. Her favorite gift—besides the car, of course—was a silver ring that Skylar gave her. There was a beautiful angel on it, tiny and delicate. Even though Skylar didn't mention it, Mom spoke up and said that the ring had belonged to Skylar's mother.

"Are you sure, Skylar?" Grace asked her. She thought about all the time she'd spent with Skylar this past week, and in addition to the science project, they'd talked a lot. About Skylar's family. About Grace's family. And other things that were hard for Grace to talk about.

"She'll keep you safe and strong." Skylar smiled, and they both knew what she was referring to.

"Thank you," she said to Skylar before she turned to each of them. "Thank you all so much."

Grace knew she was blessed with a great family, and now a new friend. And she had a new car. Life was perfect.

Chapter Seven

Darlene snuggled up to Brad in bed later that night. "Do you think Grace had a good birthday?"

Brad yawned. "As long as there was a car involved, she was going to have a good birthday." He kissed her on the forehead. "Yes, I think she had a great day. And your meal was fantastic, complete with a famous guest, who by the way"—Brad's voice rose in pitch—"wasn't anything like you said. I thought she was very nice."

"I bet you did." She teasingly pinched him on the arm. "She's beautiful, no doubt. But I'm telling you, she warmed up to me a lot the other night when I dropped her dress off." She paused. "I wonder why she never told me who she was."

He shook his head. "I don't know. Next Saturday night is that gala, right? Are you going to say anything to her?"

"I don't know. I guess I should. Something like, 'Hey, Layla, I didn't know you were famous.' Is that what you had in mind?" She smiled as she eased away from him, fluffing her pillow as Brad flipped television channels. "I hope you're not looking for a Layla Jager movie."

"Sometimes those movies are on one of the cable channels late at night."

Darlene snatched the remote control.

"Hey, give me that." He reached for it, but Darlene clicked the TV off and put the remote on the nightstand.

~∞~

On Monday morning, Darlene rushed to the front door but turned when she heard Chad coming down the stairs.

"What about breakfast?"

The desperation in his voice should have been amusing, but she was running late this morning. "Chad, eat some cereal. Make some toast. You're a big boy, I'm sure you can find something to eat." She grabbed her purse from the hutch by the entryway.

"I'll get Ansley to make me something, or I'll threaten to eat her eggs."

"Be nice, Chad. I'm leaving." She looked over her shoulder. "I love you. Have a good day."

On the way to work, she thought about what a great day they'd all had yesterday. After church, Brad and the kids had surprised her by taking her to lunch at Scotty and Friends to celebrate her new job. It was Darlene's favorite place to eat a burger in Round Top. The kids had all chipped in and bought her a new purse—one that both Grace and Ansley said would be more stylish now that she was working. Brad said he'd ordered her something, but it hadn't come in yet.

But yesterday's Scripture readings at church had left her feeling a bit unsettled. *Proverbs 31:27—She looketh well to the ways of her household, and eateth not the bread of idleness.*

Wasn't that what she was doing—taking care of her household, not being idle?

But the next part of that Scripture reading made her

question her choices. *Proverbs 31:28—Her children arise up, and call her blessed; her husband also, and he praiseth her.*

Would her husband and children still praise her if dinner wasn't on time, the house clean, clothes washed, and things handled in a way that Darlene had always taken pride in?

Maybe her husband and children should have appreciated her efforts a little more.

She cringed, gripping the steering wheel, as the thought assaulted her. Then came that feeling of being torn between her life as mother and wife . . . and her new venture at the school.

In reality, was she just shifting her motherly duties to a new group of young people, who in essence wouldn't appreciate her efforts either?

So why take on a job outside of the home?

She could say it was for independence—partly true. And she could say the extra income would be nice—also true. But deep down, she knew there was another reason. She wanted Brad to be proud of her. He'd never given her any reason to think that he wasn't proud of everything she'd accomplished as a homemaker—and maybe it was her own hang-up—but the feeling was still there.

She gave her head a little shake. All of the unnecessary analyzing had made it start to ache. Her job was enjoyable. The employees were nice, Myrna was great, and she felt like she was doing something important. So she focused on the mini-breakthrough she'd had with Cara on Friday and refused to let worry bring her down.

The group session flew by in the morning with all of the children and teachers in attendance. Cara disrupted the class several times when she tried to talk to Darlene about Ansley and the chickens. Darlene promised her that they would talk later, during their one-on-one class.

By the time the afternoon rolled around, Cara was talking so fast that Darlene could barely understand her. "Cara, honey . . . slow down so I can understand you."

Cara shook her head hard several times, then tried to start again, but frustration won out and she started to cry. It was the first time Darlene had seen her cry. Darlene reached for her hand, but Cara jerked away and let out a low groan.

"Why don't we try one of your math problems, then we'll talk about the chickens?" She eased the math workbook in front of Cara, but Cara pushed it away and cried harder. "Chickens," was all she managed to get out between sobs.

Darlene thought for a few moments. "Why don't we draw a picture of the chickens? Do you think you can do that?"

Cara sniffled as she nodded.

Darlene was relieved that her crying was easing up. She wanted to hug her like she would anyone who was upset, but Cara didn't like to be touched. Darlene quickly found a pad of paper in the pile of work for the day. She pushed it toward Cara, along with a pencil. "Do you know how to draw a chicken?"

Cara had Darlene's photo album in one hand. She put it down on the table and picked up the pencil. Then she turned to Darlene. "Help me." Darlene was surprised that Cara had spoken slowly and clearly.

"Okay. I can help you draw a chicken." Darlene reached for another pencil, but Cara shook her head.

"No, no, no." She started to cry again.

Darlene put the pencil down. "Okay." She wasn't sure what to do.

Cara pointed the pencil at Darlene's chest, tears streaming down the little girl's cheeks. She said something very fast, but Darlene didn't understand her. She seemed to be repeating the same thing over and over, the pencil still pointed at Darlene.

Darlene had been told that Cara could become violent, and now Cara had a very sharp pencil pointed at her.

"Cara . . . can . . . you . . . talk . . . very . . . slowly . . . like . . . I . . . am?" Darlene's heart was racing, but she didn't move.

Cara put the pencil down and opened her mouth, but no sound came out.

"Just say your words very slowly so I can understand you, and I'll help you with whatever you want."

"Ansley's chickens."

Darlene took a deep breath. "Do you want to draw Ansley's chickens?"

"No." Cara squeezed her eyes shut. "I want to *see* Ansley's chickens."

"You want to see Ansley's chickens?"

Cara smiled, nodding her head.

Darlene thought about how all this had started. If she'd known Cara would become so consumed with the chickens, she would have never mentioned them. "Well, uh . . ."

Cara touched the top of Darlene's hand, her eyes glistening with hope.

"Okay. Let's do all your work, and we'll ask your dad if you can see Ansley's chickens sometime."

Cara eased her hand away. "You are a mother."

Darlene smiled. "Yes."

Cara picked up her pencil and did every math problem Darlene gave her . . . and every lesson for the rest of the afternoon.

Dave eased up to the door of The Evans School, then peered through the glass pane. He'd been coming in the side door that went directly to Cara's room for months. It was easier than coming through the main entrance, and Myrna didn't mind. Darlene was talking to Cara, and his daughter was laughing—just like she was last Friday when Dave had arrived to pick her up. The jury was still out on this new teacher, but seeing her and Cara laughing together brought a smile to his face. He opened the door, closing it behind him. Darlene and Cara turned to face him, both of them still laughing.

"More laughter. That's always good to hear." Dave walked up to Cara, leaned down, and kissed her on the forehead. "Another good day?"

Darlene spoke up as Cara nodded. "We were talking about the chickens again."

Dave had heard about chickens all weekend long, and he'd buy Cara an army of them if she really wanted them. At the moment, though, he was wondering if there was any work getting done. His expression must have shown his concern.

"Cara did all of her work, plus she did some of tomorrow's assignments also." Darlene's blue eyes gleamed as she spoke. It was hard not to smile at her enthusiasm about Cara's progress. But this was only Darlene's second week. What was she going to do the first time Cara threw a fit about something, or if she hummed all day long, or refused to do anything? Dave loved his daughter more than life, but he knew how challenging she could be.

Dave straightened. "Well, it sounds like another good day."

Darlene stood up, then bent at the waist and spoke to Cara. "Cara, I need to talk to your dad. Can you sit here by yourself for a minute?"

Cara didn't look up, but concern filled Dave's mind. Maybe Darlene was already going to quit. Dave recalled the way he treated Cara's last teacher, Mae. Looking back, he knew he had been way too hard on her. And the last thing Cara needed was another change. He followed Darlene as she motioned him to the other side of the room. "What's wrong?" he asked in a whisper.

"Oh, nothing's wrong. I just didn't want to mention this in front of Cara. I didn't want to put you on the spot, but . . ." She tucked her shoulder-length blond hair behind her ears and leaned forward. "Do you think that Cara could come see my daughter's chickens?"

"At your house?" He didn't like the thought of Darlene taking Cara somewhere in a car away from the school, especially since she wasn't familiar with Cara's unpredictable temperament.

"I told her that if she did all of her work we might be able to do that." Darlene smiled, and Dave felt his blood pressure rising.

"So you bribed her?"

Her smile faded, and she bit her bottom lip for a moment. "I guess, in a way. She was so fixated on the chickens, I thought maybe a trip to see them might motivate her."

"I don't think you should have promised her that before you asked me about it."

She hung her head for a moment and sighed, then she looked up at him. "I know. I thought about that the minute I said it, but . . ." She paused, folding her arms across her chest, then grinned. "Since you reward her with ice cream after a bad day, I thought a trip to see the chickens after a good day might be nice." Her mouth spread into a wider smile.

Dave opened his mouth to tell her she was out of line, but then he thought about Mae. Cara seemed to like Darlene, so he didn't want to run her off. But she had a lot of nerve. Even so, it wasn't worth a battle with her right now about his parenting tactics. "I'm not comfortable with you taking Cara away from the school to your house." He paused. "Not yet. You don't really know Cara, and anything can happen. She can be unpredictable."

She pulled her eyes from his, twisted her mouth to one side, then sighed. "I know you're right. I'm sorry I promised her that. It's just that . . ." She bit her lip again and shifted her weight. "I took this job because I wanted to make a difference, and I was just trying to connect with Cara. I really am sorry."

Dave had seen the pictures of Darlene's family. He was curious if she took this job for the money, or if she was telling the truth, that she really did want to make a difference in Cara's life. He just wasn't sure how to pose the question . . . that is, at least not with tact. But this woman was going to be spending more time with Cara than he was, so he decided just to be honest. "Most of the teachers are either here for the money, or this small school is just a dot on their résumé, a step toward a larger facility. Why are you here? Why is it important for you to make a difference in Cara's life when"—he paused, rubbed his chin—"when you have your own family?"

She glanced back at Cara, who was sitting patiently, much to Dave's surprise. Then she turned to face him again. "My kids are twelve, sixteen, and seventeen. They don't need me the way they used to." She smirked. "Except they seem to be suddenly unhappy that they aren't getting a cooked breakfast in the mornings, and they're having to help with the housework." She waved a hand in the air. "Anyway, I've always been a stay-at-home mom, and if I was going to work outside of the home, I wanted it to be doing something besides shuffling papers. Something important."

Dave could tell by the conviction in her voice that she had given him an honest answer, but as was his way, he badgered her one more step. "Are you trained in special education?"

"No. I'm not." She blew out a heavy breath of air. "I know I'm the only teacher to work here who doesn't have a degree or special ed training, and if you don't want me working with Cara, I'd be disappointed but I'd understand."

Dave couldn't believe it when her eyes started to water up. Finally, someone who really did seem to care about Cara's well-being.

"What would you think if Cara and I just followed you to your house and had a quick look at the chickens?"

She brought one hand to her chest, smiling. "I think that would be great."

Dave held up a finger. "But . . . I better warn you. Cara gets focused on something, and then she never lets go of it. Like with jewelry." He glanced at her left hand. "Sorry you're not able to wear your wedding ring around her."

"That's okay." Then she leaned closer to him, whispering, "You know, Cara might have forgotten about visiting the chickens, so we don't have to mention it. She seemed content talking about and drawing the birds. But I wanted to say something to you privately in case she did say something about a visit."

"I think I'll just bring it up. You said she did such good work today, and you did promise her chickens." He grinned and was glad to see Darlene grin back. "We'll follow you to your house, and we won't stay but a minute. I know you want to spend time with your family."

They both walked back to Cara, and Dave told her the news. Cara stood up and hugged him. "Thank you, Daddy." She spoke slowly and clearly, as though she didn't have a care in the world.

"You're welcome, baby."

He looked at Darlene and wondered if she was confused by Cara's calm demeanor because Dave *stayed* confused. But right now, Cara was happy, and that was all he wanted for her. That's all Julie would have wanted too.

≪∞≫

Darlene pulled into her driveway, hoping she wouldn't have to invite Dave and Cara in. There was no telling what shape the house was in, and, she mused, there was always the possibility of someone talking about a nose-picking teacher or some other inappropriate subject. She hoped Ansley's chickens were all in the chicken coop and not running loose like her daughter let them do sometimes.

Chad's truck was here, and so was Grace's new car. Brad should be on his way home. She felt a sense of relief whenever she saw that her teenage drivers were home, especially Grace since she'd just gained her freedom on the roads. As they'd done with Chad, after Grace passed her written test, Darlene and Brad had spent lots of time in the car with her. Both the kids were good drivers, but Darlene suspected she'd worry every time they got behind the wheel.

Dave pulled up behind her in his shiny black Mercedes. She'd show Cara the chickens, then have time to cook dinner. As she climbed out of the car, she could see Layla in the far distance on one of her horses. She still couldn't believe Layla was famous. Maybe she should introduce Dave to Layla. Dave's clothes and car seemed a nice monetary fit with Layla. Then she tried to picture Layla and Cara interacting, and she quickly dismissed that idea. Layla didn't strike her as very maternal.

"Hi! The chickens are over there in the chicken coop," she said as she walked toward Dave and Cara. She saw Dave glance at the farmhouse. "It needs a lot of work. We've only been here two months. It was my grandparents' house."

"I love these old houses," he said, smiling. "Reminds me of when I used to visit my own grandparents. They had an old farmhouse in a rural area outside of Dallas."

"How long have you lived here?"

"Since right before Cara was born. Julie—my wife—and I left Dallas to move here." He paused, his green eyes traveling away from hers. "But she died when Cara was six."

"I'm sorry." Darlene was now in step with him as Cara ran up ahead.

He looked at her again, smiling. "Thanks. But at least I have Cara."

"Chickens!" Cara yelled when she got to the edge of the coop Brad had fixed up. The ten-by-ten-foot cage housed the four hens and one rooster. Each hen had a roosting box filled with hay, and Brad had constructed a wooden perch in the far corner.

"I'm actually rather scared of birds, so I'm glad to see they're in their pen." Darlene glanced at Dave and shrugged. "But Brad promised them to Ansley for improving her grades." She chuckled. "And we are in the country, so . . ."

"Brad's your husband?"

"Yes. He works in Houston, so he usually gets home late."

"Wow." Dave folded his arms across his chest. "That's quite a commute."

"About an hour and a half each way, but he loves it here and says it's worth the drive."

They were quiet for a few moments as they watched Cara studying the chickens. Three of the hens were roosting. The other one scurried around the cage trying to avoid the rooster.

"I should probably get Cara a pet," Dave said as they peered through the chicken wire. "But I can barely keep up with my business and Cara."

"Oh, I understand. We had a dog in Houston. Buddy. We were all very attached to him, but after he died, I told everyone we were going to take a break for a while. Not only did it seem like no one could replace Buddy, but I just didn't want to start all over. The kids promised to feed him, bathe him, and everything else, but I ended up doing most of the work."

Cara threw her head back, laughing. Her auburn hair caught the light from the descending sun as she twisted to face them. "Ansley's chickens!"

"Do you like those, Cara?" Darlene asked as she and Dave moved closer. Cara nodded. Darlene heard the back door slam, so she turned toward the house. "Here comes the owner of the chickens now." Darlene motioned with her hand for Ansley to come their way.

"This is my youngest daughter, Ansley." She put a hand on Ansley's shoulder. "Ansley, this is Mr. Schroeder and his daughter, Cara. I teach Cara at The Evans School."

Dave extended his hand to Ansley. "Nice to meet you, Ansley. That's a great group of birds you've got there."

"Mom hates them. Nice to meet you too." Ansley quickly walked to Cara. "Hi, Cara."

"Ansley's birds . . ." Cara lifted her shoulders and dropped them slowly. ". . . are pretty."

"Want to go in the pen?" Ansley reached down to unhook the clasp on the wire door. Dave stepped forward.

"Oh, I don't know if that's such a good—"

But Ansley was already in the chicken coop, and Cara was right behind her.

"That's Meg, Jo, Beth, and Amy." Ansley pointed to each of the hens she was referring to.

"She'd just finished reading *Little Women* when she got the chickens," Darlene said.

Dave nodded. "And what's the rooster's name?"

"Rocky."

Dave leaned closer to Darlene and whispered, "Is there a Rocky in *Little Women*? I'm not sure I've ever read the book, but just wondering."

Darlene laughed. "Not that I'm aware of."

Ansley turned to Cara as she put her hands on her hips. "Do you wanna feed them?"

Cara nodded, and if Darlene hadn't known better, she would have thought that Cara was just like any other twelve-year-old girl. A quick glance at Dave told her that he was more relaxed than he'd been a minute ago—not as stiff as before, anyway. Darlene had to admit, she'd been a little nervous for Cara to go inside the cage too. Darlene made a point *not* to go in there. But Cara's eyes were bright, and she was smiling ear to ear as she followed Ansley's lead, tossing a handful of feed on the ground. The three roosting hens joined the other one.

"Meg is timid. You can't get very close to her." Ansley tossed some seed toward the brown hen in the corner, but kept an arm out to keep Cara back. "Just throw some food on the ground near her."

Cara did as Ansley instructed, smiling the whole time.

"Now we have to fill up their little trough here." Ansley reached for the water hose. "Here, Cara. Do you want to give them some water? Just pull the trigger and point it at their water bowl, like this." Ansley demonstrated, and Cara took the hose and filled the metal bowl like she'd done it a hundred times.

"They were thirsty." Cara spoke slowly and clearly.

Darlene glanced at Dave. He didn't even look like the same man, his mouth now curled into a full smile. Most of the time, the two lines between his eyebrows were deep, which made him look angry. The result of too much frowning, she assumed. But the lines were faint now.

"That's amazing," he whispered to Darlene without taking his eyes off his daughter. "She's just like . . ."

He didn't have to finish. Darlene knew what he was thinking. "She's a beautiful girl, Dave."

Dave turned to face her. "Well, Ansley is wonderful," he said. "Look how good she is with Cara." He smiled again. "It must run in the family."

Darlene felt her cheeks warm. "Ansley's never met a stranger." She could feel Dave's eyes on her, but she kept her gaze on the girls until she heard tires rolling onto their dirt driveway. "Oh, good. You'll both get to meet Brad. He's early." She glanced at her watch, then lifted her hand to her forehead to block the sun. In the distance, she could still see Layla riding in the far pasture.

Cara and Ansley were tossing more feed to the chickens when Brad walked up. Darlene walked to meet him, then kissed him. "Hey. You're early." They turned and walked toward Dave. "This is Dave Schroeder. He's Cara's father."

Both men exchanged pleasantries as they shook hands.

Her husband towered over Dave, who was still considerably taller than Darlene. Brad's hair was dark, his eyes brown, and her husband had managed to retain his boyish good looks even as his forty-first birthday approached. He had the body of the high school quarterback she'd fallen in love with, and he had classically handsome features. She smiled to herself. Sometimes he still acted like that high school boy. Brad liked everything to balance out at home and at work, but he had a playful side that made him seem much younger than he was.

Darlene figured Dave to be about Brad's age. Cara had his green eyes, which flecked in the sunlight as he talked with Brad.

His olive skin stretched over high cheekbones, and one side of his mouth lifted higher than the other on the rare occasion when he smiled. He always stood straight like a towering spruce, and his massive shoulders filled the green polo shirt he wore. He was a nice-looking man, but . . . uptight. That was the word that came to her mind. She'd been hoping Brad could meet someone here in Round Top to maybe hang out with or play some golf with, but she doubted Dave was going to be that person.

But when she tuned back into their conversation, she was surprised to hear Brad suggesting a round of golf.

"I appreciate the offer," Dave said before he glanced at Cara. "But it's . . . well, hard for me to get away."

"Mom can watch Cara," Ansley said as she and Cara locked up the chicken coop. "She was always the neighborhood baby-sitter in Houston."

"It's true," Darlene said as she smiled. "And I don't mind watching Cara if you and Brad want to go play golf one day."

Dave immediately shook his head. "You watch Cara all day long during the week. I don't want to be a—"

"Dad." Cara tugged on Dave's arm as she pointed back at the bird cage. "Chickens." A smile came to Dave's face. He might be uptight, but it was clear that he loved his daughter.

"I see." He put an arm around her, and Cara nestled against him. He turned to Brad and extended his hand. "It was nice to meet you. I'm going to let you get back to your family." Then he turned to Darlene. "And thank you for letting Cara come see the chickens."

"You are very welcome." Darlene waved. "Bye, Cara. See you tomorrow."

Brad put an arm around Darlene's shoulder and whispered, "Seems like a nice guy." He held up a hand and yelled, "And let me know about that game of golf."

"I will." Dave and Cara got in the car and left.

Thirty minutes later, Darlene had some pork chops baking in the oven, and Brad joined her on the porch. He'd changed out of his work clothes and into a pair of long tan shorts and a gray T-shirt with a NASA emblem on the front. They'd taken the kids to NASA in Houston a couple of years ago. Brad was big into the stars and could rattle on about things Darlene didn't understand. But she enjoyed the time they spent stargazing together, and out here in the country, it was quite a show on some nights.

Tonight, as they settled onto the porch swing, it was way too early for any space shows. The sun was descending on the horizon, and Layla looked like the movie star she once was, her silhouette on the horse pasted against an orange ball behind her.

Brad shook his head as they both watched her cross the field speckled with bluebonnets and Indian paintbrushes. "I still can't believe Layla Jager lives next door to us."

Darlene nudged him with her elbow. "Try not to swoon so much the next time you see her."

Brad pulled her close. "You're the only one who makes me swoon, baby. Only you." He leaned down and kissed her in a way that made her feel like a teenager again.

Thank You, God, for Brad and for blessing our marriage all these years.

❦

As Dave pulled out of the driveway, Cara stared out the passenger window, smiling. He thought about Brad's offer to play golf sometime, and Darlene's offer to watch Cara. He wasn't ready to leave Cara just yet. Maybe as they got to know Darlene better, he'd feel more comfortable about it, but Dave knew Cara was a handful, and he didn't want to discourage a potential friendship with Brad and Darlene. He'd been particularly impressed with Ansley and suspected their other children were equally as pleasant to be around.

Good parents. Good people. At least it seemed that way so far.

He eased back into his seat and stroked his chin. Cara was watching a group of Longhorns resting beneath an oak tree on the side of the road, so Dave slowed down. He watched Cara's face light up, knowing he was a lucky man to have been blessed with someone as special as Cara. "God chooses special couples for special children," Jules used to say.

Lord, I miss her so much.

He missed the laughter of family. Jules used to laugh a lot, even when times were hard. They'd started out with virtually nothing and lived in a small duplex in Dallas in the beginning. But they'd worked together to build their real estate business, then Cara came. She was their everything from day one, and Julie was a good mother.

Darlene reminded him of Julie today.

Brad is a lucky man.

Chapter Eight

"How do I look?" Darlene walked into the den dressed in the royal-blue Versace gown she'd borrowed from Layla. Brad and all the kids were munching on popcorn and glued to the television.

"Wow." Brad sat taller, raising an eyebrow. "I think you better just stay home tonight. This little town isn't ready for you, Dar."

Darlene spun around, showing off her backless dress and hair pulled into a French twist, feeling more elegant than she surely was with her long drop rhinestone earrings. "So I look okay?"

"Uh, yeah." Brad's eyes were fixed on her. "You look gorgeous."

Chad handed the popcorn bowl to Grace. "Mom. That's just *wrong*. Moms shouldn't look like that."

"Be quiet, Chad." Ansley walked up to her mother to have a better look, then whispered, "I think you look like a princess."

Grace joined Ansley beside them. "Mom, you look beautiful."

"That settles it," Brad said with a mouthful. "You're staying home."

"Ha, ha." Darlene picked up the small evening purse she'd found on sale last week. "Now, listen. There's a chicken casserole on the stove. You might need to warm it up. And there's a salad in the fridge."

Brad stood up. "We'll be fine." He kissed her lightly on the cheek, knowing he'd mess up her lipstick if he kissed her on the mouth. "Just go and have a good time." He leaned closer to her ear. "You do look hot, baby."

"No mushy talk," Chad yelled from his spot on the far end of the couch. Then he jumped up and went to the window. "Uh, Mom . . . there's a limo pulling up."

"What?" Darlene's heart leapt as she went to the window. She'd only been in a limo twice. Senior prom and after her wedding. "I can't believe it."

Everyone gathered around the window.

"I can believe it," Brad said before he snickered. Darlene glared at him. They'd agreed not to mention Layla's fame to the kids. Not yet, anyway.

Darlene took a deep breath, said bye again, and made her way carefully down the porch steps, walking on her toes so her heels didn't dig into the rugged terrain between the house and the car. A short man with gray hair, dressed in a tux, was holding the door open. She climbed in across from Layla in the back.

"Champagne?" Layla handed her a glass as soon as she sat down. "My, don't you clean up well."

Darlene accepted the fluted glass, suddenly feeling quite inferior. She'd seen Layla in the gown before, but now, with her hair done, full makeup, and accessories—she definitely looked like someone famous. "As do you," Darlene said, wondering why the need for a limo and champagne when they were only going ten minutes down the road.

"I'm not thrilled about these types of events, but this one is for a good cause." Layla took a sip of champagne.

Darlene nodded. "Yes, it is for a good cause." She carefully leaned back against the seat, taking great care with the Versace gown. "Why the limo?"

Layla shrugged. "I figured you don't get out much and might enjoy it." She grinned.

"Well, I guess you used to travel this way quite often." Darlene smiled as she lifted her glass.

Layla frowned. "I wondered how long it would take for you to figure it out."

"I didn't. But my husband is a huge fan of yours. It was embarrassing the way he acted during Grace's birthday dinner." She sighed and shook her head before grinning. "He's been looking for Layla Jager movies on cable ever since."

"You're not going to act all weird now, are you?" Layla scowled before she tipped back her glass. "I don't go out seeking friends, but I thought you might be a prospect." She winked at Darlene.

"Well, if you don't like calling attention to who you are, why the limo?"

"I told you—for you."

"Right," Darlene said dryly. "You must miss it all sometimes. The fame, riding in limos, and whatever else goes along with stardom."

Layla turned toward the window and stared out into the sunset. "There's a price for it all, believe me."

They were quiet for a few moments. "Well, thank you for inviting me. And for loaning me a dress. I would have never suspected that any organization out here would have such a lavish event."

"Well, there are a couple of people from Houston who organize this event, and they go all out. This is only the second one to benefit the school. It will be a chance for you to meet a lot of the people who live here, ones you might not run into at the grocery store, if you know what I mean."

The comment sounded a bit snobbish, but Darlene let it go. She'd only taken a couple of sips of her champagne when the driver pulled up to Festival Hill. It was a beautiful campus of at least two hundred acres, all dedicated to the performing arts. Darlene, Brad, and the kids had visited the world-renowned Festival Concert Hall and couldn't believe the ornate wood-work inside. It still amazed her that Round Top was home to such a facility. Surrounding it were architectural and horti-cultural wonders, including the Herzstein Plaza, the outdoor gathering area where the gala was being held.

As soon as she stepped out of the car, she glanced around at the other women moving toward the entrance. Most were in floor-length gowns, a few in cocktail dresses, and she spotted a couple of older women in their Sunday best. The men were in suits, and most of those attending were couples. She cupped a hand to her hair, hoping it stayed in place for the night. In the heat of the summer, she kept her hair up, but always in a pony-tail, not anything like the twist she had now.

"There is Chuck Perkins," Layla said as she and Darlene walked toward the steps leading to the plaza. As they stepped onto the red carpet, Darlene could hear a buzz of activity around the corner. "The people throwing this benefit will be glad to see him here. He'll up the auction prices with his bids and also make a hefty donation. He's got more money than God."

"God doesn't have money," Darlene said casually.

Layla stopped and her bottom lip twitched as she spoke. "He doesn't have any *mercy* either."

Darlene stared at Layla for a second, then picked up the pace when Layla did. She knew there were two things not to discuss at a public function: politics and religion. But as the woman in front of them dug around in her purse for her ticket, a Scripture verse flowed into Darlene's head with such ease that it made her shiver.

O give thanks unto the LORD; *for he is good: for his mercy endureth forever.*

Darlene was raised in the church, her kids were raised in the church, and she'd prayed her entire life. She and Brad didn't talk a lot about God; it was just understood. A fact. But every now and then, God would send her a powerful message, a reminder that He was always present.

She thought about the verse for a few moments, then said softly, "Layla, you know God is good and merciful, right?"

Layla stiffened as her eyes rounded into balls of fire. "Don't go getting all religious on me, Darlene. I don't do the God thing anymore."

"Okay. Sorry." Darlene held up one hand, but the second she did so, another verse breezed into her mind: *Thou art my God, and I will praise thee: thou art my God, I will exalt thee.* Guilt flooded over her for giving up on Layla so easily.

As they entered the plaza, Darlene's breath caught in her throat as she gazed around. It had been transformed into a ballroom beneath the stars. People began to swarm around Layla. If Darlene hadn't known she was someone important, she would have figured it out tonight. She watched as Layla lit up the room with her smile and politely greeted everyone, but to Darlene it looked rehearsed, something Layla could turn on and off like a light switch. She didn't introduce Darlene to anyone, and she kept walking as people spoke to her. Darlene followed, and they wound their way between tables covered with white tablecloths. Each had a large vase of red roses in the middle, surrounded by four white votive candles. Six place settings had been laid out, all fine china with crystal and white linen napkins.

"Here's our table," Layla said to Darlene, pointing to a white card with her name on it. Next to hers was a card with Darlene's name. She glanced around. "I need a drink."

"There are waiters walking around. I'm sure they'll get to us." Darlene scanned the area as people continued to come in. On one side of the plaza, a row of tables held the silent auction items, and all around the entire party area were dramatic stone structures, including two waterfalls and a statue of Saint Boniface atop a limestone-and-marble pedestal.

She loved silent auctions, although she always seemed to get outbid at the last minute. Tonight, she had a self-imposed limit of two hundred dollars to spend. Layla said there would also be a live auction after the dinner. That's when the more expensive items would be auctioned off.

Darlene's eyes rested on two stunning ice sculptures, a boy and a girl facing each other. Farther down was a chocolate fountain and what looked to be a variety of desserts. She lifted her chin to see better, but Layla blocked her view as she flagged down a waiter.

"What do you want?" she asked Darlene.

"Uh . . ." She wasn't much of a drinker. Special occasions. That was about it. "Um . . ."

"Bring us both a glass of chardonnay, please," Layla said as a couple walked up to their table, followed by an elderly man.

"Hello, Layla. I guess we're sitting with you." The woman pointed to the man by her side. "I believe you remember my husband, George, and this is George's father, Bob."

Layla said hello, then introduced Darlene. "Darlene, this is Penny Peters, George, and Bob."

Penny gave Darlene an obvious once-over as she extended her hand. Penny shook hands like a girl, as Brad would say. Her husband believed in a firm handshake, even from a woman.

Penny was petite, about Darlene's size, so they both had to look up to see the faces of Layla and the men. Penny turned her attention back to Layla.

"Layla, you look fabulous as always. I don't know how you do it." Penny smiled. Her teeth were as straight and white as Layla's. Darlene knew she had pretty good teeth, but these ladies obviously took things a step further than brushing every day and the occasional whitening strips.

Layla smiled back, the same smile she'd been flashing since they'd arrived, but she quickly turned to Darlene. "Are you ready?"

Before Darlene could answer, Layla turned back to Penny. "Excuse us, Penny. We were just on our way to look at the silent auction items." She latched onto Darlene's arm and coaxed her away.

"Now I'm going to need two drinks. Or four." She rolled her eyes. "I will have Lacy St. John's hide for putting me at the same table as Penny Peters. That woman irritates me to no end, and she's as fake as they come." Layla stopped dead in her tracks and faced off with Darlene. "I don't like fakes. Or liars. Just so you know."

"Okay . . ." Darlene took a deep breath, then let it out as Layla started to breeze between the tables where people were beginning to sit. After a few more interruptions from people who wanted to say hello to Layla, they made it to the auction tables. Making their way down the aisle, they both commented on the lavish offerings. There wasn't anything here Darlene was going to be able to win with two hundred dollars. Almost everything had an opening bid of at least that much.

She thought about the silent auctions she'd been to in the past—for church or the kids' schools or some worthy nonprofit. Most of them had opening bids ranging from five to twenty dollars, with the average selling for around one hundred dollars even if it wasn't worth that much in monetary value. She figured most of these items would go well into the hundreds and thousands.

They saw lots of artwork. Expensive artwork, she thought, eyeing an oil painting depicting the square in the neighboring town of Fayetteville. Done by a local artist, the starting bid was twelve hundred dollars. She swallowed hard and moved on to the next item.

Darlene stayed in step behind Layla, hoping to find something she could bid on. Then, there it was. Layla passed right over it, but Darlene stared at the turquoise necklace and matching earrings. She had a set very similar to this one at home, although hers wasn't real, just costume jewelry she'd picked up several years ago at a boutique in Houston. She lifted one section of the necklace. Much heavier than her fake at home. She thought about what Layla had said, about disliking anyone who was fake, and hoped that didn't apply to a person's possessions.

Opening bid—one hundred fifty dollars. Value—three hundred and fifty. She'd stretch her self-imposed limit if she could get it for that price. She scribbled in her name and the opening bid. Brad had bought her nice jewelry over the years for special occasions, but she couldn't recall ever buying herself something this nice. She smiled, stood a little taller, and followed Layla, who she estimated had put her name on at least five different items.

Layla grunted as she put one hand on her hip. "Look at that. It doesn't even belong here."

Darlene leaned closer. It was a set of handmade cooking mitts, matching towels, and an apron, with an opening bid of one hundred dollars. Overly priced, like most of the items, but clearly crafted with love. "I think it's lovely," she said as she lifted her chin and looked up at Layla. Darlene could almost picture her grandmother making similar items when she was alive.

"You're kidding, right? It's cheap looking." Layla turned toward their table. "I'm going to go get our wine. I'll be right back."

Layla walked off, and Darlene was glad she'd bitten her tongue and hadn't told Layla she sounded like a snob. Layla's comment made her question whether or not she would be able to have a true friendship with the former movie star.

She felt someone close behind her, then a tickle of breath on her neck. "See anything you like?"

She spun around. "Dave! What are you—" She smiled, shook her head. "Of course you would be here. How's Cara?"

Dave had called the school on Tuesday to say that Cara had a bad cold. The next day, he took her to the doctor, and the doctor confirmed that she had strep throat. She hadn't seen Dave or Cara since Monday when they came to see the chickens. She'd helped the other teachers with their one-on-one students the rest of the week.

"She's much better. I stayed with her and worked from home all week."

"Where is she now?" Darlene recalled Dave saying it was hard to get someone to watch Cara.

"With Myrna. She insisted I come, and she's keeping Cara. She was babysitting her granddaughter too since her son and daughter-in-law were invited to come tonight. I'm sure you'll meet them later." He chuckled. "Cara talked about those chickens all week long. She's probably going to drive you crazy."

"Aw, I'm glad she had a good time. And you can bring her to see the chickens anytime you want." She turned to her left when she caught a glimpse of Layla coming toward them with two glasses of white wine. She handed Darlene hers, smiled at

Dave, then leaned in and kissed him on the cheek, followed by a hug. Darlene backed up to give them room.

"Dave, Dave. You are more handsome every time I see you." Layla eased away, glanced at Darlene. "You know Darlene, right? She's one of the teachers at the school."

"She's actually Cara's private one-on-one teacher." He smiled.

"Oh, I didn't know that. Cara's lucky to have her." Layla took a gulp of her wine. Such a nice compliment from Layla, and only minutes ago, Darlene had her pegged as a snob. *Maybe she's a nice snob.* She took a sip of her wine, but lowered her glass when Dave spoke up.

"Yes, Cara *is* lucky to have her." His voice was warm and genuine. Darlene felt her cheeks warm for the second time around him.

"Thank you. Cara is a pleasure to teach."

Layla set her empty wine glass on the table with the auction items. "Penny is waving me back to the table in a very dramatic way. Good grief, I was just there. I guess I better go see what she wants now. Excuse me."

Darlene picked up Layla's empty wine glass, afraid someone would knock it into the kitchen items that Layla thought were so tacky. She eyed the mitts, towels, and apron again. She'd come to check on it later. If no one bid on it, she would give up the turquoise and do it herself. It would be a shame if no one showed appreciation for the craftsmanship and time that went into making them.

"Did you find anything you can't live without?" Dave nodded down the table.

"I bid on one thing. A turquoise necklace and earrings."

"A jewelry junkie?"

"No. I don't ever buy jewelry . . . not jewelry like that." She shrugged. "But I really like that set."

"Then I hope you get it."

"What about you? Find anything you like?"

Dave accepted a glass of wine from a passing waiter, took a sip. "I found a painting that I think Cara would like." He laughed.

"Don't tell me. The painting of the three chickens and the barn, the one down at the end of the table?" She nodded to where she and Layla had just come from.

"That would be the one. And there are a few things I'll be bidding on in the live auction."

Darlene shifted her weight. Her feet were already hurting in the silver heels. "So I guess it's dinner, then the live auction?"

"Yes, then they have a dance. I guess they figure the longer they keep people here, the more they'll drink, and the looser their checkbooks will get." He grinned, then looked toward a small stage at the front of the plaza. A woman was adjusting the microphone. "I suppose we should take a seat."

Dave stepped aside so Darlene could go in front of him. When she reached her table, which was right in the front, she noticed an area between her table and the stage that she assumed would become a dance floor later. She turned to see Dave sitting down beside her.

"How about that?" he said.

Darlene hadn't even looked at the other name after she'd met Penny, George, and Bob. "This is great. It'll be nice to sit next to someone else I know."

He leaned close, put his arm around her, and whispered in her ear, "Penny and George are about as snooty as they come, but George's father is a hoot. You'll love him. He's got a ton of money, and he only hands it out to Penny and George as he sees fit." He nodded at Layla. "And of course, you know Layla. I don't know of anyone with as big a heart as hers. I didn't even think about the two of you knowing each other. I should have. Your farms are right next to each other."

Darlene laughed. "Uh, Layla's house is a lot more than a farm. It's a ranch, an estate. Simply gorgeous."

"Well, it takes time to get our places the way we want them. And Layla, as you probably know, is a hard worker."

Dave still had his arm around her when she twisted to face in his direction. "Can you believe that I had no idea who she was until last weekend when she came to our house for dinner, for my daughter Grace's sixteenth birthday?"

"Really?"

"But Brad knew who she was right away, and I think he's been gaga ever since."

"She's a beautiful woman, inside and out."

That was the second time that Dave had mentioned Layla being a good person. Maybe she'd misread Layla. But why the bitterness toward God?

Dave rubbed his chin for a moment, almost as if he was checking for stubble. "Don't let her fool you. She puts on a big act. I guess it's left over from her days of fame, but she really is as good as they come."

Dave seemed very genuine when he spoke about Layla, and Darlene wondered if maybe her initial hunch had been right. Maybe Layla and Dave would be a good match.

"I heard my name." Layla leaned around Darlene to peer at both of them.

Dave removed his arm from Darlene's chair, and she sat back all the way so they could see each other.

"I was just telling Darlene what a wonderful person you are." Dave finished off the last of his wine. Darlene still had almost a full glass.

"Don't lie to her, Dave."

They both laughed. When Layla went to the ladies' room a few minutes later, Dave put his hand on the back of Darlene's chair again and whispered, "Layla has been through a hard time. Did she tell you about Marissa?"

Darlene shifted her weight in her chair. His face was close to hers as he spoke, and she felt the need to back away just a little. He moved his arm and leaned back.

"Who is Marissa?" she asked.

"Marissa was her daughter."

Darlene's mouth fell open. "I didn't know Layla had any children."

"Marissa died when she was fifteen, drug overdose." Dave ran his finger around the rim of his wineglass and looked down. "No one ever knew if it was intentional, or if Marissa was just trying to get some temporary relief from all that ailed her. Layla told me once that Marissa was bipolar." He paused as he looked back at Darlene. "Layla was never really the same. And it ended her career, although people moved mountains to keep the press away as best they could. But it still got out."

Darlene was surprised Brad didn't know anything about it. And poor Layla. "That's terrible." She paused. "I haven't known Layla very long, and I don't know her very well."

"Well, maybe wait and let her tell you in her own time."

Darlene nodded as she wondered if Marissa was why Layla had said God had no mercy. She couldn't imagine anything happening to one of her children. It was every parent's worst nightmare.

"Marissa is one of the reasons Layla is such a big supporter of the school and wants to see the addition built." Dave eased his chair back. "Oh, excuse me. They are getting ready to start, and I need to go speak with that man over there. I'll be right back." He pointed to a man at a nearby table before hurrying away.

Darlene heard a loud squeak as someone fidgeted with the microphone onstage. A male voice said something about technical difficulties, but she wasn't really paying attention. Her heart hurt for Layla. She wondered if and when Layla would tell her about it. And if she wanted to hear. She thought about Chad, Ansley, and Grace, and said a quick prayer.

Thank You, Lord, for my healthy children.

She just couldn't imagine one of her children harming themselves.

Chapter Nine

Dave chatted with Chuck Perkins for a few minutes while people worked to get the microphone onstage working. Chuck was sure to make a sizable contribution, and he was a good guy in general.

On his way back to the table, he bumped into Lacy St. John, the woman in charge of seating at the event.

"Thank you for my seating request," he whispered with a smile.

"Well, it wasn't easy. That's the best table in the house. I had to bump Chuck Perkins for you to sit there." She frowned, her eyes level under drawn brows.

Dave clamped his eyes shut for a moment and grimaced. "Oops. I didn't know I was taking Chuck's place."

"Well, you did." She folded her arms across a pink strapless gown. "And I hope she is worth it." She glanced toward Dave's table. "And, Dave, *she* is married, so you be careful."

"Lacy, shame on you." Dave shook his head. "It's not like that. She's Cara's one-on-one teacher. I told you that. I just want to get to know her better."

"I know what you told me." She raised one eyebrow. "And you heard what I said."

She breezed by him. He'd known Lacy and her husband since high school. They'd lost touch for five or six years until they all landed here in Round Top. Lacy's husband was still a bit of a jerk like he'd been in high school—Lacy had caught him cheating on her years ago. One thing about Lacy. Nothing got past her. He made his way back to the table just as a woman's voice rang through the crowd from the stage, asking for everyone's attention.

In her opening comments, the emcee encouraged everyone to bid generously on the auction items so that the new wing at the school would become a reality. Dave planned to do just that, and he hoped others would as well. With enough funds, they could hire more teachers and expand the programs to include other children from surrounding areas who also had special needs, including children from lower-income families.

"Enjoy your dinner," the woman said as she finished her speech. "The silent auction will close at nine o'clock, followed by a live auction. Then please stay to enjoy the band and dancing."

Waiters were already bustling around and delivering salads, and a low buzz of conversation ensued after the woman left the stage. Dave shifted to his right so the waiter could place a salad in front of him. Layla grabbed the guy before he could head back to the kitchen, and she requested another glass of wine. He'd need to keep an eye on his friend tonight. She'd probably arrived in a limousine, as she was known to do for these things, but he also didn't want her making a fool of herself—as she'd done once or twice after too much wine.

He'd considered asking Layla out awhile back. Not many single women lived in the area, and she was certainly beautiful. But he'd realized early on that Layla was holding on to a lot of baggage. Not just the loss of her daughter, but after being around her a few times, he sensed she was still in love with her ex-husband, Tom. Nonetheless, they'd become good friends. She respected his crisp reminders that Round Top wasn't Hollywood when her ego occasionally reared its head, and he, too, accepted her frankness when he needed it. Despite her controlling tendencies, she was a warm, loving person.

Penny cleared her throat. "Darlene, I hear you've only been working at The Evans School for a couple of weeks. How do you like it so far?"

Dave glanced to his left at Darlene.

"I love it. I love working with the kids." She turned to Dave briefly. "And I have Dave's daughter, Cara, in the afternoons. She's a pleasure to teach."

When she turned back to Penny, Dave kept his eyes on Darlene. Her royal-blue halter dress showed off a delicate back, and loose tendrils of ash-blond hair swept against rosy cheeks. He wondered if she knew how pretty she was, and if her husband told her often.

"And what's your degree in?" Penny took a sip of wine, her eyes staying on Darlene above the rim of the glass.

"Actually . . . I don't have a degree." Darlene's cheeks reddened a little. "But Myrna and the other employees have been great, teaching me what I need to know to be effective in the classroom."

"Cara likes her a lot," Dave chimed in after swallowing a bite of salad.

"I remember a time when teachers actually had to have a teaching degree to teach. But even substitutes in the public schools don't have to have a degree anymore." Penny shook her head.

As Dave sipped his water, he glanced to his left. A polite

smile trembled over Darlene's lips. He took a deep breath, preparing to choose his words carefully, but George's father, Bob, spoke up first.

"Penny, I don't recall you having a degree," the older man said, dabbing ranch dressing from his chin. He chuckled. "Except maybe a degree in how to shop and spend money."

"Now, Dad . . . ," Penny said as she tried to hide her embarrassment with a tentative smile.

Bob sat taller. "Well, it's the truth."

Penny cut her eyes at George, as if she expected him to muzzle his father. But George just shrugged and kept chewing his salad.

"Penny, that's a beautiful necklace you have on." Darlene changed the subject, a classy move, especially in light of Penny's comment. "Are those emeralds?"

Penny reached up and touched the three-tiered drop around her neck. "Yes, an anniversary gift from George." She batted her eyes at her husband. "Such a sweetie."

Bob coughed, glanced at his son, then shook his head.

Dave leaned around Darlene a little until he could see Layla. She'd been awfully quiet.

"Layla, are you still taking care of your place by yourself?"

She finished chewing before she answered him. "Yes. It keeps me young."

"I don't know how you do it, Layla. You're just amazing." Penny flashed a smile at Layla. "I'd have to hire a fleet of cowboys to take care of a place that size."

"Last thing I need around is a fleet of men." Layla rolled her eyes.

Bob reached for a slice of bread as he coughed again. "Layla, you only need one man. And you know who it is. Just say the word." The older man leaned forward and winked at Layla.

They all laughed, and the rest of the meal's conversation was light and enjoyable. By the time they finished dessert, the band was preparing to start. Dave usually had to force himself to dance once or twice at these events, but tonight his heart beat a little faster in anticipation.

He was well aware that Darlene was another man's wife, and he'd never do anything to mess that up. He just wanted to have her to himself, for a dance.

No harm in that.

∝

Darlene casually walked up to the turquoise necklace and earrings, and her eyes scanned the names and amounts until she got to the last bid. Four hundred dollars. Double the amount she'd planned to spend tonight. She stared at the necklace and earrings, picturing how good they would look with a brown lace blouse she had at home. She tried to recall the last time she'd worn the blouse. But now that she was working, there were more opportunities to wear business casual. She leaned down and tapped the pen to the piece of paper.

"Just do it."

She spun around. "That's the second time tonight that you've snuck up on me."

Dave grinned. "You're easy to sneak up on. You are totally engrossed in your thoughts, which I'm guessing involve a decision about that necklace and earrings."

"Yep. It's over my self-imposed limit, so I'm trying to decide." Brad had never given her grief about spending money. She'd never given him a reason to. She'd always been frugal when it came to buying for herself. Sometimes she splurged on the kids or something for the house, but rarely on something for herself. She smiled at Dave, then leaned down and wrote a bid for four hundred and fifty dollars next to her name.

"Good girl." Dave eased on down the row of tables, as did Darlene.

When she came to the handmade items Layla said didn't belong here, no one had put a bid on them. Except for Layla. Layla had bid five hundred dollars. Darlene smiled.

After she looked at the rest of the items, the emcee made a five-minute last call for the silent auction. Darlene tried to look casual as she made her way back to the necklace and earrings, and her heart dropped when she saw a name underneath hers. Someone named Mary Copeland had bid six hundred dollars. *Oh well.*

A few minutes later, several women scurried to pick up the auction sheets, and Darlene made her way back to the table. Everyone was seated, and they were just starting the live auction. She watched, amazed at the bids being offered, careful to keep her hands firmly in her lap. When it was all over, Layla had won four pieces of artwork worth thousands of dollars. Dave had a beautifully sculpted piece of pottery and three other paintings. And after an intense battle with Layla, he also ended up winning a three-day spa package for two.

Darlene wondered who would keep Cara while he went to the spa. Maybe Dave would feel comfortable enough to leave Cara with her. Of course, there was always Myrna.

Penny and George didn't bid on anything without first consulting with Bob. Several times, the elderly man shook his head, but Penny ended up with two paintings when it was all said and done. Darlene looked at her watch as she yawned. It seemed later than nine thirty, and the band was just getting ready to start.

"Oh, don't start wimping out on me yet." Layla took a swig from her wineglass. "I plan to kick up my heels."

Darlene figured Layla would want to leave as soon as she could, to get away from all of the people who wanted to see her, but with each glass of wine, Layla became more talkative to those she'd snubbed earlier. Even Penny. After a few minutes, the band started playing a lively polka that enticed some of the older people onto the dance floor. Round Top and the surrounding towns had a large Czech influence, and lots of the elderly folks still spoke the language fluently. Dave and Darlene chatted as they watched Layla dancing with Bob.

"I can't quite figure her out." Darlene took a sip of her wine, which was warm now. "I mean, she was a movie star, now she herds cattle. She lives in an amazing house . . ." Darlene giggled. "And she herds cattle. Did I mention that? And she's just . . ." She shrugged. "I don't know. Sometimes she is so strong and abrasive, and other times it's as if you can see clear to her heart."

"She's quite a woman."

They were quiet for a few moments, then the band eased into a slow song. Darlene tried to remember the last time she and Brad had danced. Dave stood up and held out his hand.

"Shall we? Who knows when we'll both get out again for something like this. Let's make the most of it."

Darlene didn't move for a moment. "Oh, I don't know, I—"

"Oh, please, don't force me to dance with Layla. She always steps on my feet," he said, grinning. Darlene wasn't sure what else to say, so she stood up and accepted Dave's hand. He escorted her to the dance floor, which was filling up quickly. They stood in the midst of a crowd of couples beneath a dark sky speckled with twinkling stars. As Dave cupped his arm against her bare back, it felt strange to be dancing so intimately with someone other than Brad, especially someone she barely knew. She kept herself taut against his hold, making sure she didn't get too close.

When the song was over, they walked back to the table and fell into a comfortable conversation about plans for the new wing at the school. Dave was actively involved in every aspect of the planning, and he spoke with a passion about it. Then, in the middle of talking, he reached into his pocket and pulled out his cell phone. "It's Myrna. Excuse me."

He hurried across the room and out the door. Darlene glanced at the clock on the wall. It was nearing eleven o'clock. She hadn't expected to be out this late, and she was yawning when Dave walked back in and sat down.

"Is everything okay?" she asked.

He scratched his forehead. "Yeah. Cara woke up after a bad dream, asking for me, and Myrna knew from past experience that it would just be easier to let Cara hear my voice rather than try to get her to go back to sleep without it. She seemed fine after I talked to her."

"Glad everything is okay," Darlene said. She watched Dave take a deep breath, then glance at his watch.

Darlene turned away to stifle a yawn, hoping Layla would be ready to go soon. She looked around the room, then turned to Dave when she heard him push back his chair. He held out his hand to her.

"One more dance?"

Darlene opened her mouth to decline, but when she saw everyone else at their table move toward the dance area, she nodded and accepted his extended hand.

This time, he held her closer than before and, once, rubbed his hand against her back. But he was right. There might not be another night like this for a long time. She tried to relax into his arms and enjoy the music, but she couldn't ignore the churning in her stomach.

⌖

Beneath the starlit sky, Dave closed his eyes and breathed in the sweet smell of Darlene's hair as he gently eased her closer to him. She felt good in his arms, and it was by far the most romantic thing he'd experienced in a long time.

As they danced, he couldn't help but face his motives. He'd asked to sit next to her because he wanted to get to know Cara's teacher better—this woman spent more time with his daughter than he did. But he knew that wasn't the complete truth. Darlene wasn't just beautiful and good with children, there was something else—a goodness about her, something that intrigued him, made him want to know more about her.

Dave thought of himself as a good Christian man, and these thoughts went against everything he believed in. *Please, Lord, help me to fight this temptation brewing inside of me.*

As the song ended, she eased out of his arms. A few seconds later, a light nearby illuminated her wedding ring. Maybe it was time for him to call it a night.

"I see you yawning," he said as they walked back to the table.

"Yeah, I'm tired." She looked at him and smiled. "But it's been a lot of fun."

Dave pulled out Darlene's chair for her. After she sat, he took his spot beside her and looked around. "I wonder where Layla is. I haven't seen her in a while."

"I haven't either." She leaned forward over the table. "Penny, have you seen Layla lately?"

Penny applied lipstick as she stared at a small compact.

"She was dancing with George earlier, then said she was going to the ladies' room."

"I better go check on her." Darlene excused herself.

Dave looked at his watch. Myrna insisted on keeping Cara overnight, but he always felt unsettled when he was away from her.

A few minutes later, he stood and walked toward the ladies' room, meeting Darlene and Layla as they were coming toward him. "Everything okay?"

"Everything is fine, *Dave*." Layla raised her chin as she smirked at him. He glanced at Darlene. She bit her lip and gave a quick shake of her head when Layla turned to speak to a woman on their left.

He leaned down and whispered in Darlene's ear, "Do we need to get her home?"

"Yes. I think so."

Dave gently pulled Layla by the arm toward him. "Excuse us," he said to the woman she'd been speaking to. He turned to Layla. "I think Darlene is ready to go, and so am I. I'll walk you both to the car."

Layla opened her mouth, but his scowl made her clamp it shut.

"Fine. Let's go." Layla marched ahead of them, smiling to people on either side of her as she walked by.

Dave followed close behind Layla, and when she started to sway, he latched onto her arm. After they exited the plaza, he quickly found the limo in the parking lot. He kissed her on the cheek and helped her get in. Then he turned to Darlene, and without thinking, he kissed her on the cheek too. "I had a great time."

He could have smacked himself. This wasn't a date he was on, and he barely knew Darlene. He stepped aside so she could get in the car.

"Me too," she said as she offered him a strained smile. "See you Monday."

Dave closed the door. *Yes, see you Monday.*

And as wrong as it was, he knew he was going to count every minute until he picked up Cara on Monday afternoon.

❧

Darlene tried to help Layla up the sidewalk to her house, but Layla shook her arm loose. "I'm fine. I don't need you to help me up the walk."

"Okay, well, I just wanted to make sure you were all right before the driver dropped me at my house." She waited until Layla unlocked the door and stepped over the threshold. "Thanks again for inviting me. I had a really nice time." She turned to leave, yawning again.

"No, don't go. Come in." Layla put a hand on her hip. "Have a glass of wine with me."

Darlene knew it had to be close to midnight. "I can't, Layla. We've got church in the morning, and I need to get home."

Layla held up one finger over Darlene's shoulder. "We won't be too long," she yelled to the driver before she looked back at Darlene. "Please."

"Five minutes." She followed Layla in and closed the door behind her. Layla kicked off her gold spiked heels in the middle of the room and kept walking toward the kitchen. Darlene followed, glancing at the clock on the mantel. Twelve fifteen.

She watched Layla pull two glasses from a cabinet in the kitchen.

"None for me, Layla."

"You are no fun, you know that?" Layla filled both glasses and handed one to Darlene. She accepted the glass and watched

Layla shuffle into the large living room where she plopped down on the couch with the carelessness of someone who didn't worry that she might ruin a dress worth several thousand dollars by sloshing wine on it. Darlene, on the other hand, carefully lowered herself onto a wingback chair.

"So you're church people, huh?" Layla chugged half her glass of wine. "I used to go to church."

Darlene shifted awkwardly on the chair. "Well, I don't think having a relationship with God is all about going to church, but I enjoy the fellowship of worshipping Him in a group . . . And I want my children to know Him and understand the Scriptures."

Layla lifted her chin and squinted her eyes at Darlene. "I bet you've never had one bad thing happen to you in your life." She paused, raised one eyebrow. "Have you? I bet your little world has just rocked along without more than a few speed bumps here and there."

The woman was a mean drunk. Darlene thought for a moment. "My life hasn't been perfect," she finally said.

"Well, be careful, Darlene." Layla swayed a bit as she sat up straighter on the couch. She pointed a finger at Darlene. "Because when God decides your life is going too good, He will find a way to humble you, bring you back down to earth, even if it means destroying you. It's what He does when you sin. He takes, takes, takes . . . everything that means anything to you. Then He looks down on you with no mercy, even though you beg on bended knee for Him to stop the pain." Layla was gritting her teeth as she spoke.

Darlene was glad that Dave had told her about Marissa. Otherwise, Layla's rants would have made Darlene feel defensive. Instead, she said softly, "I don't believe that's how God works, Layla. We just can't understand His plan for us. Sometimes bad things happen to good people."

Layla smiled. "Ah, yes." She held her glass up as if to toast. "Everything happens according to *His* will." She stared hard at Darlene as her lips thinned into a cynical smile. "And we just have to live with it. I wonder how strong your faith would be if something rocked your world, something so horrific it snatched your breath away every time you thought about it."

Darlene kept her voice soft. "I know about Marissa, Layla. And I'm sorry."

"Leave it to Dave." Layla crossed her legs beneath the green gown.

Darlene glanced around the room, realizing that there weren't any pictures of Marissa. Or of anyone else. She set her glass on a nearby table and folded her hands in her lap, unsure what to say.

"Marissa loved the flute," Layla said. "She was an aspiring musician and played beautifully by the time she was fourteen. I loved listening to her." She paused, her eyes glassy. "When I was home."

"I'm sorry, Layla." Darlene felt like a failure in her efforts to say something that could make any difference, and she was having trouble keeping her eyes from drifting to the clock on the mantel.

"Go home, Darlene." Layla pulled a clip from her hair and let the wavy tresses cascade past her shoulders. She still looked like a movie star. "Go home to your family."

As Layla chugged the last of her wine, Darlene felt nervous about leaving. She stood. *How should I help her, Lord?* "Layla . . ."

Layla lifted a finely shaped eyebrow.

"Come to church with us tomorrow." Darlene cringed when Layla's nostrils flared. Darlene held up a hand. "Okay, skip church. Why don't you come for brunch afterward? I make pancakes after church, every Sunday. It's our thing. Come have brunch with us."

Layla grinned. "I'm not your charity case, Darlene. As a matter of fact, we're not even really friends."

Ouch. Darlene shook her head. "Fine, Layla. Thank you again for inviting me to the gala. I had a great time." She turned to leave, and she'd walked a few steps when something deep inside her caused her to spin around. "You know what, Layla?" She put her hands on her hips. "I'm making pancakes. And I make the best pancakes in the world. I also make peppered bacon and slice up some fresh fruit. So I will just plan to see you at my house tomorrow at noon." She stared at Layla and raised her chin as her eyes began to water.

Layla just stared back at her with an expression Darlene couldn't read. She waited for her to say something, anything. When she didn't, Darlene walked out, wondering if she'd ever hear from Layla again.

∞

Brad sat on the edge of his bed and peered at the clock again, his emotions vacillating between worry and anger. Why hadn't Darlene called when she knew she'd be so late? She insisted everyone else in the house do it. It was after midnight. He'd called her cell phone twice but no answer. As tired as he was, he wouldn't be able to sleep until Darlene was home. Sighing, he stood up, paced for a few moments, then decided to look in on the kids. He could hear faint music coming from Chad's room, their only child who didn't own an iPod. Chad said he couldn't stand the buds pushed into his ears.

"Sorry. Is it too loud?" Chad lifted his head from the pillow when Brad walked in. His son pointed a remote toward the stereo.

"No, not really. Just checking on everyone." Brad grimaced as he glanced around the dimly lit room. "Really, Chad. How can you live like this?" Dirty clothes and shoes were thrown all over the place, and Brad counted five soda cans on the dresser. "It stinks in here."

"Not once you get used to it." Chad grinned as he folded his hands behind his head and relaxed on his pillow again.

Brad shook his head, left the room, and shuffled down the hallway to Ansley's room. He eased the door open and peeked inside. Both his daughters were sleeping soundly in Ansley's bed, which meant Ansley must've had a nightmare. Grace was good about going to Ansley's room when that happened, although he wasn't sure how Grace endured the chaos in there. Light from the hallway filtered into the room, and although it wasn't as smelly as Chad's, it was just as cluttered. Brad tiptoed to the side of the bed where Grace's iPod lay on the floor. He picked it up, then stepped softly out.

When he pushed open Grace's door, he clicked the light on and smiled. Everything was in place and a floral scent filled the room. *That's my Gracie.* Brad walked to the nightstand, pulled the top drawer open, and dropped in her iPod. He took two steps toward the door but then turned around and walked back to the nightstand. He wasn't one to snoop in his kids' stuff, but something had caught his eye. He eased open the drawer again and eyed the razor blades lying in an open box and the straws beside it.

Brad froze. He knew exactly why kids used razor blades and straws. He recalled his college years and Aaron Turner. The blade cut the drug, and the straws were used to snort it. He and Darlene had never done any drugs when they were young, but plenty of their friends had. Brad suspected Chad might have experimented, but he would have never—in a million years—pegged Grace to be doing drugs.

He sat down on Grace's bed, took several deep breaths, and tried to calm his rapid heartbeat.

Chapter Ten

Darlene eased the bedroom door open and tiptoed in. Brad's eyes were closed and he was sprawled out on the bed, atop the covers, with the TV still going and the light on. She slipped out of her shoes and gently set her purse on the dresser. Holding her breath, she hiked her dress up and moved quietly toward the bathroom.

"Did you forget how to use a phone?"

She spun around. Brad was sitting up, his dark hair tousled as he rubbed his forehead. "I'm sorry," she said as she kept going toward the bathroom. "I had the sound turned off, then I forgot to turn it back on after the gala was over. And there were problems with Layla, but I'll explain in the morning."

After she changed into her nightgown and washed her face, she pulled the pins from her hair and brushed it out. She walked back into the bedroom, hoping Brad would be asleep. She was too tired to go into everything now.

"Dar, it's after one in the morning. I left you two messages." He fluffed his pillows, leaned against them, and pulled the covers to his chest. "You'd be seriously grounded if you were one of the kids."

She hurried to his side. "I know. And I didn't mean to be this late. I have so much to tell you, but can I tell you in the morning? Church is going to come early." She nestled up against him, and he wrapped an arm around her shoulder.

Brad rubbed his hand over his jaw, sighed, then reached over to his nightstand. "I found these in Grace's drawer in her room." He showed her the two razor blades and straws.

Darlene sat up and tucked her hair behind her ears. She stared at the items for several moments. "No way Grace is doing drugs if that's what you're thinking."

"I would have never thought so."

Darlene shook her head. "Nope. Not Grace."

"Maybe . . ."

"Maybe what?" Darlene twisted to face him. "What, Brad?"

"Skylar. Maybe she's getting Grace into something that . . ." He shrugged. "I don't know, Darlene. I mean, Skylar is kind of different."

"She dresses differently, but I don't think Skylar is a druggie. You can't judge her by the way she dresses. And remember how sweet she was to give Grace that angel ring for her birthday?"

"Well then. Explain this." He pushed the blades and straws toward her. "We've known plenty of parents who've dealt with their kids' drug problems. And I think Chad played around with them for a while."

Darlene didn't like to think about Chad doing drugs, and he'd never admitted it, but both she and Brad had suspected it when they were in Houston. "Chad is with Cindy now, and she's a good girl. He's not into any of that."

"I know. I'm just saying that he might have been at one time."

"Maybe. But not Grace. She would never do that. I know my daughter, Brad."

"Well, you haven't been around much the past couple of weeks. Maybe it's something new."

Darlene's mouth fell open. "What's that supposed to mean?"

"Nothing. I'm just saying that you haven't been home much. Maybe Grace is starting to spend time with the wrong crowd."

Darlene eased away from him, turned out her light, and rolled onto her side. "I will talk to her tomorrow, but I know that's not it." She was quiet for a few moments. "And it hurts my feelings that you would blame it on me."

"Baby, no." He turned out his light and snuggled close to her. "I'm not blaming anything on you. I'm just worried about Grace."

"I will talk to her," she said again. There was another explanation, and she'd find out tomorrow afternoon, after church and brunch.

They said good night, and Darlene rushed through her prayers, fearful she'd fall asleep before she finished, and she wanted to be sure to get in some extra prayers for Layla.

And Grace. Just in case.

⸘

Layla woke up Sunday morning with a rotten hangover, still dressed in her formal gown—and with her past life laid out all around her. She'd done this a hundred times before, dumping all the pictures out and crying until she couldn't cry anymore. Pictures of Marissa, Tom, and the three of them together. Reminders of her past that she only faced when she'd had enough wine to temper the pain. Her retreat into a world of beautiful memories would always leave her feeling even more shattered and lost than before. And yet Darlene had wanted to talk to her about *God*?

She picked up a picture of Marissa, the one of her in her pink and white dress, her hair in a ponytail. They'd just gone to a friend's wedding shower, and Marissa was glowing. "I can't wait until I get married," she'd said on the way home.

Layla swiped at a tear, wondering how there could possibly be any tears left.

She and Tom had managed to stay together for several months after Marissa's death, but eventually they turned their grief into anger at one another. They'd been a threesome for so long that being with Tom was a constant reminder of what they'd lost, and she knew he felt the same way. He'd left on a Saturday. They'd spoken a few times, but each conversation ended in tears for both of them. Not only had she lost Marissa, she'd lost the only man she'd ever loved. He'd told her that he couldn't help her until he could heal himself.

If there was a God, He had clearly looked down on her and decided that she'd been given too much. A great career. A wonderful husband. And a beautiful daughter. Maybe God wanted her to pay more attention to the many people around the world who were suffering in worse ways than she was. Or maybe He thought Layla wasn't a good enough mother, wasn't home enough, or put too much emphasis on her career. She'd turned it over in her mind a thousand times. And each time, her conclusion was the same. God was punishing her for something. She just wasn't sure what.

She recalled all the times she'd knelt with Marissa beside her bed to say prayers. Marissa'd had a strong faith. Stronger than Layla's. Why would God take her away at such a young age, such a beautiful person? If the expansion of The Evans School could help one teenager, bipolar or with other challenges, then Layla would keep donating her time and money.

Layla shivered as she recalled the day she found Marissa in her room next to a bottle of pills from Layla's medicine cabinet.

She put Marissa's picture down, got out of her gown, then crawled back into bed. She couldn't bear to have the pictures out in the open, so she kept everything boxed up but nearby, for when she needed to feel Marissa close to her, to remember, no matter how painful.

Despite her feelings about God, Layla knew exactly whose fault it was that Marissa was gone.

And for that, she hated God. And herself.

Darlene served up the last of the pancakes, her mind on two things. Grace and Layla. She planned to talk to Grace after they were done eating, even though she was sure Grace would have an explanation for what Brad had found in her room. As for Layla . . . she kept glancing out the window, hoping maybe she would show up. By twelve thirty, she'd given up hope.

Earlier that morning, while she and Brad were dressing for church, Darlene had told him all about the evening, about Marissa, and about the way Layla begged her to stay for a while after the gala. Brad was understanding and sympathetic, but he'd asked her again why she didn't call.

She'd asked herself that same question.

"I thought you said Layla might come over." Ansley reached for the last piece of bacon.

Darlene glanced out the window again. "I invited her, but I guess she decided not to." She assumed Layla might not be feeling well this morning.

"I can't believe a movie star lives next door." Chad shook his head, grinning.

Darlene put her hands on her hips and looked down at Brad, who had his chin tucked.

"You told? I thought we talked about that."

Brad's puppy-dog eyes grew wide. "They saw her on television last night."

Darlene stifled a grin. Brad's boyish looks never seemed to diminish, and it was hard to stay angry at him. "I'm sure you were looking for one of her movies."

Chad stood up, pushed his chair in. "See, I said she was hot. And go figure . . . she's a movie star."

"I think it's neat how she still rides horses." Grace stood up, then carried her plate to the sink. "And she takes care of that big place all by herself."

Darlene had been discreetly watching Grace all morning for any signs that something might be up, but she saw nothing out of the ordinary. "Ansley, it's your turn for kitchen cleanup." After Ansley grunted, Darlene turned to Grace. "Let's go sit on the porch swing. I want to talk to you about something."

"That doesn't sound good," Ansley said, shaking her head.

"You just clean the kitchen and don't worry about it." Darlene gave a gentle yank on Ansley's short ponytail, then headed out of the kitchen, Grace following. Once they were settled on the swing, Darlene decided to play good cop, bad cop. She'd always been close to all her children, especially the girls, and she knew Brad was wrong.

"Listen . . ." She pushed with her foot until the two-seater gently began to glide back and forth. "Your dad found some razor blades and straws in your drawer, in your room."

"Why was Dad going through my stuff?" Grace twisted in the swing to face Darlene, scowling.

"He wasn't going through your stuff. He was putting your iPod away. But now he's worried that you're doing drugs."

"No way, Mom!" Grace's eyes watered up, and Darlene

reached for her hand, but she jerked away from her. "I can't believe Dad would think that."

"Now, honey, just listen. I know you wouldn't do anything that stupid, but I am wondering why you have razor blades in your room." The straws seemed logical to Darlene. Grace used to have braces, and she often kept straws in her room to drink through, especially after her braces had been tightened. Even after her braces came off a year ago, her teeth were sensitive to cold temperatures, so she continued to use straws.

"I can't believe Dad was in my room, in my things." Grace hung her head and sighed.

"Well, what do you want me to tell him? Are they his razor blades? Where'd you get them?"

"I don't know, Mom. They've probably been left in there from some school project when I needed a straightedge. I have no idea. But I can't believe Dad would think . . ." She swiped at her eyes.

"I think it just scared him. You've got some new friends, and—"

"He thinks Skylar does drugs? Why? Because of how she dresses?" Her voice was sharp and assessing.

Darlene sighed. "Look, I believe you. But I had to ask because Dad was worried."

"Whatever. Can I go now?" Grace stopped the swing with her foot.

"Don't be mad." Darlene nudged Grace's shoulder with hers. "You and I have never had any secrets, so I just wanted to mention it."

Grace got up and went into the house. Darlene shouldn't have said anything, and she should have told Brad he was being silly. She went inside to check on Ansley in the kitchen.

⤴

Grace closed her bedroom door and lay on her bed, tears rising to the surface again. The last thing she wanted was for her father to think she was anything less than perfect. How many times had he said, "My sweet Grace, always a good girl, never giving us any trouble."

She thought about Skylar. Grace's so-called friends wouldn't understand her relationship with Skylar, and Skylar seemed to realize that. She would just pass Grace in the halls without so much as a smile—and Grace still sat with the same girls at lunch. Occasionally, Grace would look over at Skylar and catch her staring, but neither of them ever said anything to each other at school. They talked on the phone, and Skylar was Grace's only friend who came to the house. When Glenda said Cindy told her that Skylar was at the house, Grace told Glenda that it was because she'd gotten stuck with Skylar for her science project.

I'm a terrible person to treat my only real friend like that.

Her thoughts were interrupted when the phone rang. She picked it up without looking at the display, assuming it was Skylar and feeling the guilt.

"Hello."

There was silence for a few moments, then a familiar voice on the other end of the line. "Hey, Grace. It's me."

Grace bolted upright on the bed. "Tristan?" She brought a hand to her chest, hoping to calm her racing heart.

"Yeah. How are you?"

She took a deep breath, tried to sound casual. "I'm great. What about you?"

"Okay, I guess."

Silence again, and Grace was dying to know why he was

calling her. Maybe he wanted to get back together, to invite her to visit him in Houston. He'd finally realized how much he missed her, how much he loved her.

"How's life in the country?" he asked.

"It's okay. How's Houston?"

"Same ol'."

Why are you calling me? It was so good to hear his voice.

"Hey," he said after a few more moments. "I need to tell you something."

Grace's breath caught in her throat. "What's that?"

"I—I just didn't want you to hear from someone else. But . . ."

Her heart started racing. She could tell by his voice that it was bad, and she clamped her eyes shut. "Just tell me, Tristan."

"I'm going to be a dad, and I didn't want you to hear it from some of your old friends."

Grace felt the air leave her lungs. She'd refused to sleep with Tristan, despite his many attempts. She'd only been fifteen. How could he have expected her to do something like that, even if he was a year and a half older? Not to mention that she wanted to be married first. "What?"

"I started dating Jenny Schwartz, and . . . well, she's pregnant. Her parents don't want us to get married, but we are anyway."

Grace was sure she was going to have a heart attack. Tears streamed down her face, but she couldn't say anything.

"Grace, are you there?"

She knew they were young, but she'd always thought that they'd be together. She'd so often pictured Tristan showing up in Round Top, ready to commit his heart to her. They'd go to the same college, graduate, get married, and start a family. And now . . . he'd fathered a child with Jenny Schwartz. Someone

Grace used to call a friend. She held the phone out from her face, stared at it for a moment, then slowly pressed the End button. She gently laid it down on the nightstand.

Somehow, she stood up, then she paced for a moment. An image of the pink collector's pocketknife that her father had given her last year popped into her mind. "Here, in case you run into a snake or critter when we move to the country," he'd said jokingly.

Grace searched for the pocketknife in the top drawer of her dresser. *It hurts, it hurts, it hurts.* And the pain had to stop. It just had to. She finally found it.

She sat down on the bed, raised her blue jean shorts up several inches, and made a small cut across the top of her thigh. The blood oozed, and relief washed over her like a cleansing balm to her soul. She stood, then sliced herself again, deeper this time, drawing a line of blood several inches long. *Thank you, thank you.* Relief. No more thoughts of Tristan. No more regrets. Just relief. She closed her eyes as she stood in the middle of her room, blood dripping down her leg and splashing onto the hardwood floor. She was going to enjoy the moment. One more cut . . . She closed her eyes, breathed deeply.

Less than a minute later, her bedroom door opened, and she locked eyes with Chad. Adrenaline shot through her body like a speeding bullet, her heart beating so hard her chest hurt. *Why didn't I take the time to lock my door?*

"Grace! What are you doing? You're bleeding! What are you doing with that knife?" Chad moved closer to her, his eyes dark and accusing.

Grace froze, her face and ears burning, her body breaking out into a sweat. She'd already lied to her parents about the scars on her arms, telling them she'd had a run-in with a barbwire fence. No lie could fix this.

"Please don't tell," she pleaded. "*Please*, Chad."

Chad pulled the knife from her hand and wrapped his arms around her as she sobbed.

"Gracie, what have you done? What's going on?"

Chapter Eleven

It went against Chad's better judgment—which, he admitted, wasn't always the best—to keep Grace's secret, and the only reason he'd agreed was because his sister said she'd never done anything like it before and now knew it was stupid. It had been the result of a phone call from Tristan. *If I could get my hands on that guy . . .*

Tristan was a scumbag who'd tried to sleep with any girl he could in Houston, and Chad had never wanted Grace around him. She was way better than Tristan, but Grace had been madly in love with him, so he could understand—sort of—why she went all nuts. *But cutting herself?* That was crazy, and Chad didn't get it. But he'd been through his own stuff, so who was he to judge? He figured the best he could do was be there for Grace.

Later that evening, he talked to Cindy about it.

"Man, I'm just really worried about her."

Cindy sat down beside him on his bed. Chad was still surprised that his parents allowed her in his bedroom, but Cindy was the epitome of the perfect high school girl, the one every parent hoped their son would date. Beautiful, classy, straight As, polite, and involved in every civic function available. *Right.*

Cindy sipped from a McDonald's cup that had more in it than Diet Coke.

"Here, want some?" She pushed the paper cup in his direction, and he had to admit, the rum and Coke tasted good. "Yeah, I'd be worried about Grace too. I mean, I've heard of girls doing that, and it's crazy." She took the cup back and took a swallow.

Even though Chad thought Grace's behavior was a little nuts, he didn't like hearing Cindy say it. "Well, she said she's not going to do it again."

Cindy shrugged. "Ya never know. I've also heard about girls who go to cutting parties. They have a few drinks and everyone cuts. It's supposed to be like a high or something."

Chad recalled the way Grace was crying—so hard that she couldn't breathe. His sister hadn't cut herself as recreation. She was devastated. "No, it's not like that with Grace. She was super upset."

"Well, I hope no one finds out about this . . ." Cindy cringed. "She'd be ruined in this small town."

Something about Cindy's tone left Chad uneasy. "Well, don't tell anyone then."

Cindy sipped on her drink, shrugged again, and didn't look at him.

"Cindy, did you hear me? I told you this in confidence. Don't tell anyone about Grace."

"I won't, but things like this tend to get out." She flung her hair over her shoulder, the hint of a smile on her face.

Cindy didn't seem so beautiful in his eyes anymore. "It's late. I should take you home."

"It's not late. It's only seven o'clock." Cindy pushed her lips out in a pout, something he used to think was cute. "Oh, I get it. You're mad." She leaned over and cupped his cheek with her cold hand. "Don't worry. I won't tell anyone about Grace."

Moving closer, she kissed him on the mouth, lingering, waiting for a response, but her touch didn't give him the heady sensation he'd expected. Instead, her lips felt as cold as her hands . . . and her heart. She hadn't showed one ounce of compassion for Grace.

"No, really. I've got stuff to do. I better take you home." He stood up, and Cindy slowly did the same.

"Okay," she said as she picked up her books.

Chad hurried her out the door.

Please, Lord, don't let Cindy tell anyone. And please, please don't let Grace do anything like that again. But Chad had decided that if she did it again, he was telling his parents.

Then a name came to mind. Every goth kid he'd ever known was into something weird. Did Skylar introduce her to cutting?

∞

Grace knew it was no coincidence that she kept bumping into her brother on Monday. Normally Chad avoided her at school, but he was around every corner today.

"I'm fine, Chad," she said as she closed her locker and found him standing beside her. "So quit following me around."

"I'm just worried, Grace." Chad pushed a longer strand of his dark hair behind his ear. "I know you're flipped out about Tristan, but I just . . ." He hung his head and sighed. "I don't want you hurting yourself."

"Hush." Grace brought a finger to her mouth. "I told you that I'm never going to do it again, Chad. So let it go." She stomped off, rounded the corner, and ran right into Skylar.

"Hey, Grace. I thought maybe I'd come over today after school, and—"

"Today's not good." Grace kept walking, surprised that

Skylar asked to come over. She wasn't sure why Skylar even wanted to be friends with her. She picked up her pace. *Skylar is a loser.* And she was going to keep telling herself that until she believed it.

Truth was, Skylar was probably the best friend she'd ever had. The only person who really understood her. There'd been a time when she thought Tristan was that person, but apparently she'd been wrong.

She felt the fresh wound rubbing against her blue jeans, and the pain comforted her, distracted her from other feelings she couldn't face right now. But Grace was smart enough to know that she had to keep such frustrations bottled up. Good girls didn't go all crazy and act nuts.

She heard Skylar call her name, but she walked faster until she ran into Glenda. She locked arms with her, forced a smile, and glanced over her shoulder at Skylar. The last thing she needed was another lecture from Skylar. Because Skylar would know . . . what she'd done.

She just had to get through this one thing. Then she'd stop for good.

Dave looked at his watch as he hurried to his car. He'd closed a sale on a big ranch outside of Warrenton, and as was usually the case on a million-dollar deal, there had been problems— issues with the inspection that had almost caused the buyers to back out. Now he was late picking up Cara.

Ten minutes later, he pulled into the parking lot at The Evans School. He put the car into park, then tapped his thumbs against the steering wheel. He'd spent all of the prior day convincing himself that whatever his infatuation was with

Darlene, he needed to get over it. She was a married woman, Cara's teacher, and she deserved nothing but respect from him. He reminded himself to keep things professional between him and Darlene. She was Cara's teacher. Nothing more. He twisted his mouth from side to side for a few moments, then decided it would be best to limit his contact and conversations with Darlene as much as possible.

A minute later, he entered Cara's classroom and saw them sitting at the table together. Darlene was wearing a pink blouse. *She looks beautiful in pink.*

Dave shook his head, then smiled at Cara and Darlene.

"Cara had a good day," Darlene said.

Dave walked to Cara like he did every day, kissed her on the forehead. "That's great." He was having trouble keeping eye contact with Darlene. He never should have danced with her at the gala.

"Tell Ms. Darlene bye, Cara." He nudged Cara toward the exit, praying his daughter would just come along with him without incident. And she did. They were almost out the door when Darlene's voice rang through the classroom.

"Dave?"

He turned around, forced a smile. "Yeah?"

Darlene hurried toward him, then handed him a folder. "Cara forgot this. It's some pictures she drew for you today."

Dave's hand brushed Darlene's as he accepted the folder. "Thanks." He paused. "Okay, well, we'll see you tomorrow."

❧

Darlene walked to the window, pulled back the blind, and watched Dave and Cara drive away. She was glad that Dave seemed to be pulling back, focusing on Cara and her studies, limiting chitchat. She'd worried over the weekend, even felt a little guilty about dancing with Dave. There was something a little too intimate about the way he'd held her, and she shouldn't have allowed it.

She'd spent all yesterday afternoon trying to cuddle up to Brad on the couch while the kids were off doing their own things, but she'd been outdone by the remote control. Maybe guilt had fueled her attempts, but either way, she just wanted to be close to Brad.

As she drove home, she wondered if taking this job had been a mistake. Even though everyone seemed to be doing just fine with her working, she knew she was missing out on some of the kids' day-to-day stuff, and she had less time for Brad because she was catching up around the house on nights and weekends. In fact, she was exhausted by the time she crawled into bed at night.

But she loved working with Cara and the other children. She felt needed. Something she hadn't felt in a while from her own family—that is, until they no longer had breakfast on the table in the mornings, then they needed her. She smiled. Perhaps *taken for granted* was a better way to describe her feelings, but she knew there probably wasn't a mom on the planet who didn't feel that way.

She pulled onto Layla's drive, glad the gate was open. She parked in front of the house and hopped out of the car. After draping the Versace carefully over her arm, she started up the front steps. Layla opened the door before she could knock.

"Why are you bringing that dress back?" Layla said, folding her arms across her chest and frowning.

"Because it's yours." Darlene shifted the dress from one arm to the other. "I didn't have it laundered, but I'd like to. I just wasn't sure if it needed special handling."

Layla shrugged. "It doesn't matter." She swung the door wide, motioning for Darlene to come in. Darlene stepped inside, and when Layla turned to close the door, Darlene noticed Layla's usual cattle-herding garb. Sweat mixed with dirt stained her shirt, and one of her blue jean pant legs was tucked into a brown work boot.

Layla turned and headed for the kitchen. Darlene followed and watched as she pulled a jug of water from the refrigerator and began gulping down mouthfuls.

"Why in the world don't you get someone to help you with this place, Layla?" Darlene laid the gown over a chair in the kitchen.

Layla ran her forearm across her forehead and caught her breath. "Because this keeps my mind busy and my body in shape." She rolled her eyes. "Not that it matters much these days." She nodded toward the dress. "Just keep it."

Darlene's eyes widened. "Uh, no . . . but thank you." She couldn't imagine Layla giving her a dress worth thousands of dollars. "I let it out so it will fit you again."

Layla picked up the dress, cast it across her arm like an unwanted burden, then walked through the living room and to her bedroom. She opened the door and tossed the dress inside. Darlene bit her lip so hard she thought it might bleed. She should've just kept the gown.

"Thanks again for letting me borrow the dress and for inviting me to the gala."

"No problem." Layla started walking toward the door, and Darlene obediently followed, knowing it was her cue to leave. Apparently she'd been right—she and Layla were not going to be friends. Layla would've hit her in the butt with the door, but before it was completely shut, Darlene swung around and held out her hand, the door pushing Layla backward a bit.

"Layla, I was wondering if you'd like to come for dinner tonight." She gritted her teeth, but something deep inside her beckoned her to reach out to this woman. *Give me strength, Lord.*

Layla blinked her eyes a few times, mouth dropped. "Uh, thanks. But I can't."

"Okay, just asking." *I tried, God.* Relief washed over her. Layla was unpredictable, kind to a fault sometimes and rude as all get-out other times. She gave a quick wave as she turned to leave. "Bye."

"Darlene?"

She took a deep breath and spun around.

Layla had her arms folded across her chest again. "I can't come for dinner, and I'm in a hurry because I have a very sick cow out in the far pasture. I don't think she's going to make it, and I'd like to be with her."

Darlene stammered, "Anything I can do?"

"No. Just wanted you to know why I can't come to dinner." Layla took a step back inside and closed the door.

On the drive home, Darlene kept asking herself why she even wanted to be friends with Layla. But she knew the answer. Layla was a good person deep down. And she needed a friend.

❧

Over the next several weeks, everyone settled into a chaotic routine. After school was out for the summer, Darlene had to run the household like a dictator from a remote location, often texting her children throughout the day to remind them what needed to be done at home.

The washing machine had bounced across the mudroom, dislodging the pipe and flooding the area last Tuesday. Before that, Ansley's rooster, the infamous Rocky, had pecked the UPS man on the leg, drawing blood. The deliveryman had shown up at The Evans School to chat with Darlene about it. Another snake had made its way into the house, a grass snake no bigger than a pencil, but Chad had hacked it into pieces with a kitchen knife, further marring the wooden floor.

Darlene was just glad that Chad had snagged a part-time job tending Clydesdales at a nearby ranch. He wasn't home to help out as much as his sisters, but at least he was occupied and earning a little spending money. Brad had been working later and later in an effort to make partner.

The house was a wreck most of the time, and when the kids did clean it, it wasn't anything like Darlene would have liked. And she was tired most of the time. But as she watched Cara working a crossword puzzle—the third one she'd finished in the past week—she knew she was making progress. And the extra money was building up in savings. It wouldn't be long before she could cover the floors with new hardwood.

"Great job," Darlene said after Cara eased the crossword puzzle in front of Darlene. She quickly scanned her answers, then moved it to the side. She was reaching for a book Cara had been reading when Cara touched her hand. It was the second time this week that Cara had touched her. "What is it, sweetie?"

"You are the best mom ever."

Darlene stopped breathing for a moment. Cara had spoken slowly and clearly, but the way Cara was gazing into Darlene's eyes made her nervous. "Thank you. I hope my children all think so too." She forced a smile as her chest tightened.

Cara still had her hand on Darlene's. "You are my mother now."

Darlene eased her hand out from under Cara's and twisted in her chair to face her. "Cara, I'm your *teacher*, and I am so proud of the work you've been doing . . . But I'm not your mother, honey."

Cara shook her head so hard Darlene was sure it had to hurt. "No! You are my mother now!"

"Cara, listen to me." Darlene paused, hoping she could make Cara understand. "You are very special. Do you know how special you are?"

Cara's bottom lip trembled as she leaned forward and put her head on Darlene's chest. Darlene was so shocked that she didn't move for a few moments. Then she slowly wrapped her arms around Cara. She was still holding Cara when Dave walked in.

"What's wrong?" He hurried to them, his eyebrows narrowing as he looked at Darlene. "Did something happen?"

"No, everything is fine," Darlene said as Cara pulled away, ran to her father, and hugged him.

"Was it a good day?" Dave kissed Cara on the top of her head, but his eyes were on Darlene.

She, Cara, and Dave had settled into a comfortable routine. Every now and then, she'd catch Dave staring at her in a way that made her slightly uncomfortable, almost in admiration, but she assumed it was because she and Cara were making such great progress.

Today, she was worn out and hoped Cara would tell her father it was a good day, as it had been—until Cara's confusion about Darlene's role in her life. She was wondering if she should mention the incident to Dave when Cara nodded and told her father it had been a good day.

Dave smiled. "I was surprised to see Cara in your arms, but I see now that progress is being made." He gazed into Darlene's eyes for a few moments. "Thank you. For everything."

Darlene nodded, knowing she was blushing. "Cara is a great student."

Dave instructed Cara to say good-bye, and they left. Darlene wanted to take some time to think about Cara's comment before she decided if she should mention it to Dave or Myrna. Even though she didn't want Cara to be confused, it warmed her heart that she and Cara had grown so much closer.

She left right after Dave and Cara, and as she drove past Layla's house, she realized she hadn't seen Layla since she'd dropped off her dress. Sometimes she felt guilty for not making more of an effort to be friends with her.

When Darlene pulled into her driveway at home, she wished she could wave a magic wand and have dinner on the table, the clothes folded, and the house clean. She climbed out of the car and noticed Brad's car in the driveway too. *Hmm . . .*

As she opened the door, two aromas mingled into a heavenly scent that she recognized—the lemony fresh smell of a clean house and dinner in the oven. She kicked her shoes off and ran to the kitchen, noticing the spotless den along the way. Brad was stirring something on the stove.

"I do have a fairy godmother!" She ran over and wrapped her arms around him. "What are you doing home so early, and what happened to my house?" He leaned down, and she gratuitously kissed him several times. "And what do I smell?"

"I'm home early because I felt like doing something nice for my wife. The house is clean because I threatened the children. And this is pot roast with carrots and potatoes because you know that's all I know how to cook. Besides hot dogs." He winked, and Darlene didn't think she could love him any more than at that moment.

"You are the best husband on the planet," she said, meaning it. She stood perfectly still for a moment, then cupped a hand to her ear. "It's too quiet in here."

"Kids are all upstairs watching television and being very quiet like I told them to be."

Darlene grinned. "Really?"

"Oh, and I told them they could all go out to eat pizza Friday night if they'd just keep it down for a while this evening."

She pulled out a kitchen chair and sat down. Brad set a glass of tea in front of her.

"Thank you." Darlene slumped down in the chair, took a sip of the tea, and sighed. "I'm so tired tonight."

Brad put the lid on the roast, then took a seat across from her at their breakfast table in the kitchen. "Then maybe you should quit."

Darlene sat taller. It was okay for her to consider her options, but she didn't want Brad considering them for her. "No, I love my job, and the extra money is nice."

Brad reached over and squeezed her hand. "As for the money . . . it's no longer a concern. Feel free to do all the renovations on this house that you want." His eyes twinkled as he spoke.

"Oh my gosh. You got partner!" Darlene bounced in her chair. "Didn't you?"

Brad's smile broadened. "Yes, my dear. I did."

She jumped from her chair and into his lap. "I knew you would." She threw her arms around his neck and kissed him all over his face. "I'm so proud of you."

He cupped her cheek, kissed her on the mouth. "So now you can quit, and things will be back to how they used to be."

Darlene fought the tinge of bitterness that crept into her heart, suddenly not sure if she wanted things to go back exactly as they'd been. "I don't know . . . it would be hard to quit. I mean, I know I'm tired, and everyone has to pitch in around here, but . . ." She shrugged. "It makes me feel independent."

"I didn't know that you didn't feel independent before. Have I ever told you what to do or not do, what to spend, or anything else?" Brad rubbed his chin as he cocked his head to one side.

"No. That's not it." She shrugged again. "I don't know. I'll think about it." She thought about the money she'd been saving for the floors. Maybe even whisk Brad away for a weekend. There had to be someone who could at least check on the kids. Layla's name came to mind, but . . .

"Whatever you decide." Brad kissed her again, tucking her hair behind her ear. "I just want you to be happy."

"I know. And I am." She thought about how disappointed Myrna would be if she quit her job after just two months. And what about Cara?

"Maybe everyone would appreciate me a little more around here if I wasn't working—now that they've had a taste of what it's like when I'm not here." She nudged Brad playfully, although she was serious.

"We've always appreciated you." He eased her off his lap and walked to the stove. After lifting the lid off the roast, he leaned down and inhaled through his nose. "Not bad, if I do say so myself."

Darlene pulled her blouse loose from her slacks, then stretched her arms above her head. "I'm going to go change clothes, then I'll—"

A bloodcurdling scream from upstairs made her gasp midsentence. She couldn't move for a moment. Then another scream.

"Mom! Dad! Come quick! Hurry!" Ansley's voice sounded panicked.

Darlene was ahead of Brad as they both darted up the stairs. Her heart was in her throat.

Chapter Twelve

Ansley stood in the hall outside of Grace's room, crying. Darlene pushed past her younger daughter and into the room, Brad on her heels. Chad was sitting beside Grace on the bed, and Darlene knelt down in front of her.

"Gracie, baby?" Darlene's mouth moved, but hardly any sound came out as she eyed the blood on Grace's powder blue shirt. Her baby girl's hands were covered in blood. Tears were streaming down both her cheeks. Darlene looked down and saw the gashes on the inside of Grace's thighs, slightly below her white shorts, which were also splattered bright red.

"Who did this to you?" She grasped Grace's shoulders. "Tell me!"

"Oh, dear Lord in heaven," Brad said as he pulled Chad out of the way and sat down beside Grace. "Gracie, baby girl. What happened? Who did this?"

Darlene didn't take her eyes from Grace as she told Ansley to hurry and get some wet cloths. "What happened?" She glanced back and forth between Grace and Chad. Grace couldn't catch her breath, so she turned to Chad, who was also crying.

"She—she did this to herself, Mom." Chad swiped at his eyes.

"What?" Brad glared at his son, then looked back at Grace.

Darlene touched Brad on the leg. She could feel him trembling. When Ansley walked back into the room carrying a wet rag, Darlene asked everyone to leave. Brad started to argue, but he finally took Ansley and Chad by the shoulders, and they all went downstairs.

Darlene took a deep breath as she sat beside Grace on the bed and began to clean her wounds. She silently prayed and thanked God that Grace's wounds weren't deeper. She might have scars, but she didn't need stitches. She left once to get antibiotic ointment, and when she returned, Grace was still crying just as hard as when she and Brad had first walked in. Grace just kept sobbing and saying how sorry she was, over and over again.

"It's okay, sweetie. It's okay." Darlene was repeating herself too, but she didn't know what else to say. Her main focus was on comforting Grace, even though her mind was spinning. Why would her beautiful daughter do this to herself?

Four fresh cuts ran along the inside of Grace's thighs, and on the top of her legs, smaller wounds were scabbing over, making it heartbreakingly clear that this was not the first time Grace had done this to herself.

After she finished applying the antibiotic cream, Darlene couldn't control the flood of tears that poured down her cheeks. "Why, baby? What made you do this?" She blotted her eyes, thinking maybe she should have let Brad handle this. But she couldn't bear to leave Grace yet. Grace was so hysterical. She just kept shaking her head and apologizing. Darlene felt helpless.

After a while, she convinced Grace to lie down, and Darlene stayed with her until she fell asleep. She stared at her daughter, unsure of what to do. Where to go? Who to call? Why had Grace done this? Darlene felt like she might vomit.

Brad eased the door open, his eyes bloodshot. Darlene put a finger to her lips. "She's sleeping," she mouthed.

Brad motioned for her to come out into the hall.

"Chad said he knew she'd done this once before, but never this bad."

"What?" Darlene lowered her eyelids as more tears gathered in the corners of her eyes. "Why didn't he tell us?"

"I've already torn into him, Dar. He was just trying to keep a promise to Grace to not tell."

"Keep a *promise*?" She hung her head and started to cry again, then whispered, "Why would Grace try to kill herself, Brad? Why? Why?" She fell into his arms, muffling her cries against his chest, gripping his white shirt until her knuckles throbbed. She'd never felt like more of a failure in her entire life. Forcing herself away from him, she stared into his eyes. "What do we do?"

She needed him to be in charge. Darlene didn't have the strength. But when he just shrugged and shook his head, Darlene spoke up. "We need to call someone. A counselor, a psychiatrist, someone like that." She dabbed at her eyes, knowing she needed to pull it together. For Grace's sake.

Brad shook his head right away. "No. Let's talk to her more after she's slept. I don't think we need to involve anyone else." He paused. "It's a small town. Everyone would hear about this."

"I don't care!" she fired back in a loud whisper.

"Well, I bet Grace would care." Brad's tone was equally as defensive. "I doubt she wants her friends at school to know about this." He held up a finger at Darlene, the way he often did with the kids. "Just wait. Don't do anything yet." Darlene pushed his finger away, brushed past him, and darted down the stairs two at a time.

She was in front of Chad in a matter of seconds. "How dare you know something like this and not tell us."

Chad sniffled but held his chin high. Ansley was crying,

and Darlene could hear Brad coming down the stairs. "Ansley, go upstairs and sit with your sister until I come get you."

Ansley nodded but was crying too hard to speak. Darlene turned to Chad again. "Tell us what is going on. Grace has done this before?"

Brad put a hand on Darlene's shoulder. "Ease up, Dar."

She spun around with the fury of a woman whose child was in danger. "Don't tell me to ease up." She turned back to Chad. "Tell us."

Chad's face was blotchy and wet. He wiped his nose with his hand. "I only know of one time."

"Don't you think that's one time too many?" Darlene's voice rose an octave as a tear rolled down her cheek. "When?"

Chad's voice squeaked. "Not that long ago, and she promised it was the only time and that she'd never do it again . . . I'm sorry, Mom." Chad's bottom lip quivered as he blinked back tears.

Brad stepped up beside Darlene. "It's okay, son. Go up to your room." Once Chad was upstairs, he turned to Darlene. "This isn't his fault."

She faced off with him, her insides feeling like a volcano about to erupt. "I didn't say it was his fault." She hung her head, then looked back up at him. "I just need some answers, Brad. I don't understand why our beautiful little girl would cut herself up like that. Why would she do that?"

Brad put a hand on his hip. "She's not trying to kill herself. She would have slit her wrists if she were planning that. I know a guy—"

Darlene didn't hear the rest. She recalled the razor blades that Brad had found in Grace's room. "Oh, Brad. That's what she was planning then. The razor blades." Darlene started to cry again.

"Honey . . ." Brad rubbed his forehead for a few moments.

"Did you hear what I said? I know a guy at work whose daughter did this. Grace was not trying to kill herself, but something is definitely wrong if she's cutting herself."

"What's wrong?"

He raised his shoulders and dropped them slowly. "I don't know. But according to Paul, his daughter did that for a while, and then she just stopped. Some kids think it's cool to try."

"Brad, Grace doesn't look like a teenager who tried something cool and decided it wasn't for her. Clearly she's done this before, and she's hysterical!"

"Well, you're hysterical too! Maybe you need to calm down to be able to help your daughter."

Darlene was sure her blood was beyond boiling, but she knew Brad was right. She took a deep breath, held it for a while, and blew it out slowly. "I think we need to find someone for Grace to talk to."

"You and Grace are close. You should be the one to talk to her after you've both calmed down." He reached out to her, but she backed away.

Brad threw up his hands. "Okay, Darlene."

She put her hands on her hips. "What does that mean?"

"Don't you think we need to work through this together?"

Darlene grunted. "Uh, usually I take care of things while you're at work."

Brad hung his head, shook it, then looked back up at her. "I'm going to let that go because I know you're upset. We've always worked through everything together where the kids were concerned."

Not true. She glared at him. "I'm going upstairs to be with Grace."

She wasn't even to the staircase when she heard Brad mumble, "Maybe if you'd been here, not working . . ."

She stopped dead in her tracks.

"I'm sorry, Dar. I didn't mean that."

She could hear Brad coming up behind her, but the damage was done. She bolted up the stairs two at a time.

❧

Grace woke up, and it took her a few seconds to decipher why her mother was lying next to her on the bed, facing her, but with her eyes closed. It was dark outside, her room lit only by the Tinkerbell night-light she'd gotten when she was four. Then everything came rushing back to her, and panic took over. She felt like she couldn't breathe, like someone was choking her, like an elephant was on her chest. "Mom," she managed to whisper.

"I'm here, baby." Her mother jerked up, then wrapped an arm around her.

"I can't breathe. I'm sorry. I can't breathe." As the memories of earlier flashed in her mind, she didn't know how she was going to survive this. Her parents would never get over this, and neither would she. *Stupid, stupid, stupid me.*

Her mother pushed the strands of tangled hair from her face. "Everything is going to be all right, Gracie." Mom kissed her on the forehead and pulled her closer. "Take a deep breath. Mommy is here. You're going to be okay." She kissed her again.

Trembling, she tried to do as her mother said, but the air in her lungs spewed forth in shallow gasps mixed with sobs. Mom tightened her hold and rocked back and forth. After a few minutes, Grace felt less panicked. Mom eased her away.

"Grace . . ." Her mother smiled, despite her red, swollen eyes. "You listen to me." Her voice was firm, but soft and comforting. "There is nothing this family can't get through."

She paused, brushed a hand through Grace's hair again. "But, honey, can you tell me what made you do this?"

Grace shrugged, knowing she couldn't tell her mother her true feelings. She'd never understand how one pain could so completely override a larger pain, give comfort despite the hurt. "Some girls at school used to do it," she finally said. "And I know it's wrong, Mom. I'm never going to do it again."

Her mother kept her gaze fixed on Grace, and it was hard to tell if Mom was buying it.

"Do you want to talk to someone about this?"

Grace's heart leapt in her chest. "No. You mean like a psychiatrist?" She shook her head. "No, Mom. I don't need to talk to anyone. I'll just stop. I promise." Her eyes began to fill at the thought of having to lie down on a couch in a shrink's office.

"Okay, baby. We'll see." Her mother kissed her on the forehead again, then stood up. "Are you hungry? I think we both missed your father's pot roast."

Grace had heard everyone fighting downstairs earlier, and she didn't want to face anyone right now. And she didn't want to eat. "I'm not hungry."

Mom tilted her head to the side like she did sometimes when she was thinking. "Well, I'm going to bring you something up here, in case you change your mind." She blinked back tears, and Grace felt ashamed. "Grace . . . we're going to get through this. God will get us through this, okay?"

"There's nothing to get through, Mom. Really. I tried something I shouldn't have, and I didn't like it." *Please, God, forgive me. Help me.*

"Grace, this wasn't the first time, though, and—"

"I know, Mom. I know." Grace slapped her hands to her knees as she swung her legs over the side of the bed, cringing from the pain of her fresh wounds. "I messed up! I shouldn't have done it. How many times do I have to say I'm sorry?" The tears came full force, and Grace knew she shouldn't talk to her mother like that. But Mom had a way of pushing until she heard what she wanted to hear. Didn't Grace just assure her that it wouldn't happen again?

"Okay, baby." Mom held up one hand as her own eyes welled with tears. "We can talk more later."

Great.

"Do you want me to stay up here with you tonight?"

"No." She sniffled, wishing more than anything that her mother would just leave. "I just want to be alone."

"Okay."

Her mother had almost closed the door behind her when she peeked her head back in. "Grace?"

She raised an eyebrow.

"Skylar didn't have anything to do with you doing this, did she?"

"No, Mom." She rolled her eyes. *If you only knew what a good person Skylar is.* Grace thought about the way she'd treated Skylar. And felt another wave of self-hatred.

"Okay." Her mother paused, tears in her eyes. "Do you know how much I love you?"

"With all your heart." Grace choked the words out. *And I'm so sorry for what I've done.*

Mom blew her a kiss. "Yes, with all my heart. No matter what."

Please just go, Mom.

❧

Brad spit mouthwash into the sink, then stared at himself in the mirror. *Lord, why is this happening?*

He'd waited years to make partner. It should have been a day to celebrate. Instead, a war of emotions raged within him at the realization that he and Darlene had somehow failed one of their children. He pulled a white T-shirt over his head as he searched his mind for clues as to why Grace would harm herself like this. She was the middle child. Did she not get enough attention?

He walked to the bed, sat down, and tried to think. They'd never had any problems with Grace. The door to the bedroom opened. A tense, drawn face greeted him, and Brad swallowed hard.

"How is she?"

Darlene's bottom lip quivered as she stood in the middle of the bedroom. "I don't know. She said it was just something she tried and that she'd never do it again." She sat down in the rocking chair in the corner of the room, her fingers tensed in her lap. "But I think there's more to it than that. She needs to talk to someone, Brad. A professional."

Brad rubbed his forehead, sighed. "She said she'd never do it again, Darlene." He locked eyes with his wife. "Maybe we just need to trust her." His fears matched his wife's, but he didn't want his daughter's reputation ruined in this small town if there wasn't going to be another incident. Being a teenager was hard enough without the added label of "mentally ill." "The minute she steps foot into a shrink's office, this whole town will know about it."

"I really don't care." Darlene's lips barely moved as she spoke. "I'm only concerned with our daughter's well-being."

"Like I'm not?" Brad stood up and walked toward her. "I'm just as worried as you are, but I don't want us doing anything rash either. We need to think about this." He put a hand on his hip. "Let's just sleep on it, and we can talk tomorrow."

"I'm calling someone tomorrow." Darlene stood up, brushed past him, and went into the bathroom. Brad followed.

"So you're just going to make that decision on your own? Did you even ask Grace what she thought? We're not in Houston. You know how everything is public knowledge around here. The local psychologist is probably a classmate's father, uncle, or grandfather."

Darlene turned to look at him through the doorway of the bathroom. "Brad, our daughter is in trouble. She's not old enough to make decisions about what is best for her. We're her parents. That's our job!"

"Yelling isn't going to help." Although Brad felt like hollering at the top of his lungs too.

"Well, neither is pretending that it didn't happen." Darlene threw her hands up in the air. "Brad, she's got cuts all over her legs, and I'm sure those scars on her arms aren't from barbwire. She's already lied to us. Do you want her to hurt herself again?" Tears started to pour down Darlene's face. "Our beautiful Grace. Why would she do this to herself?" She raised her head and dabbed at her eyes.

Brad couldn't keep the tears from forming in his eyes again. There was a long, brittle silence before Darlene spoke again.

"And since this is *my* fault for not being here to supervise *my* children, I will handle it."

Brad hung his head, shook it. He was surprised it took her this long to bring up his comment. "Dar, I shouldn't have said that. And they are *our* children. We'll handle it together. We don't need to be fighting about it, we just need—"

"Actually, I've been thinking about quitting my job. I'm going to give notice tomorrow."

"Don't do that because of what I said."

"I'm not." She turned toward the sink and turned the water on. "I need to be home for my children."

Brad knew this was a direct repercussion of his earlier comment, her attempt to lash out at him. Didn't she realize he was hurting too? "Whatever. Quit then." He turned to head back to the bed, his head splitting and his heart filled with worry about Grace.

"Yeah, whatever," she said, slamming the bathroom door.

He crawled into bed.

Congratulations to me for a long-awaited, well-deserved promotion.

It was possibly the most selfish thought he'd ever had, but it had surfaced just the same.

Darlene leaned her head all the way down to the sink and let the tears fall again, hoping the running water would drown out her sobs. Brad wouldn't have made the comment if he didn't at least believe it to be partly true. Maybe if she'd been home, she would have noticed a change in Grace, possibly prevented this from happening.

Even though she felt bitter about having to quit her job, losing her independence, and leaving the students—especially Cara—her own kids were more important. And Grace needed her.

She washed her face and brushed her teeth, all the while thinking about how hard it was going to be to give notice to Myrna. But the vision of Grace's legs, the blood on the bed, in her lap, on her clothes . . . Darlene shivered.

As she climbed into bed, she stayed far on her side. This wasn't Brad's fault. She wasn't sure if it was her fault. But one thing she knew for sure, she needed to find out more about this cutting and get Grace some help. No matter what Brad thought.

⋘⋙

At breakfast, no one said much, and Brad left early for work. Grace almost acted like nothing had happened, and she seemed to be trying to lift everyone's spirits. She joked with Chad, who didn't react much. And she offered to take Ansley shopping on the square in Round Top later that afternoon. It was unusual for all the kids to be up so early during summer break, but they'd been waiting to watch the space shuttle on television this morning. Darlene was glad to see that Grace had gotten up for it.

She'd already instructed Chad to keep an eye on Grace, thankful that he didn't have to work today, and even though her insides churned, she knew she had a responsibility to go to work. But maybe Brad was right. Maybe Grace was just trying something out, and it would never happen again. Her intuition told her otherwise, though.

Chad reached for the last cinnamon roll, and Darlene blew them all a kiss. "See you tonight." She glanced at her son. "Call me if you need me." He nodded, and with much anxiety, Darlene left for work.

⋘⋙

Myrna took the news much better than Darlene expected, probably because Darlene had told her the truth about Grace, despite Brad's worries. Myrna also gave her the name of a psychologist who specialized in "these types of troubles," as

Myrna had called it. Darlene had offered to give two weeks' notice, but Myrna told her that she would combine her grand-daughter's one-on-one study with Cara's until she could find Darlene's replacement, insisting that Darlene needed to stay close to Grace and get her some counseling.

When she'd voiced her concerns about the children at the school, especially Cara, Myrna said that God would guide them all. At the mention of God, Darlene realized that she hadn't said any prayers last night, for the first time in as long as she could remember. Too much on her mind with Grace, but she knew that Grace's situation was even more reason to reach out to God for guidance.

Myrna thought it best not to say anything to Cara or Dave today, although Darlene felt terrible that she'd just stop com-ing after today, never showing up to teach again. When Dave showed up at five o'clock to pick up Cara, Darlene could hardly look him in the eyes.

"Glad it was another good day," Dave said after Darlene gave him a report on Cara's accomplishments for the day. He offered a weak smile, and Darlene thought again about how Dave had opened up at the gala, then shut down afterward. Sometimes she still wondered what she'd done to cause him to run cold again. Not that it mattered, she supposed. Today was her last day. "We'll see you tomorrow." He reached for Cara's hand, and together they left the classroom.

Darlene's whole body felt like a lead weight. She wouldn't see them tomorrow. Or the next day.

God be with you, Cara.

And please be with Grace and our family.

Darlene walked down the hall to tell everyone good-bye. She knew in her mind and in her heart that she needed to be with Grace right now, but Brad's comments, his blaming her, rang in her mind, as if he accepted no responsibility for Grace's actions.

All she'd ever wanted to be was a good wife and mother. Was it so wrong to seek just a little bit of independence outside of those two roles?

Apparently so.

Chapter Thirteen

Grace held the nails in a small pouch, handing one to her father each time he asked for one. Normally she wouldn't have offered to help her father repair the fence, but she was desperate to talk to him without anyone around. It had been two weeks since she'd been caught cutting herself, and she hadn't done it since then. But her mother was on a mission to get her to see a shrink, like she was a crazy person. Mom had made her an appointment for next Tuesday.

Her father had worked late every night that week, so she hadn't had a chance to talk to him privately. Today, though, he was working on repairs around the farm, starting with the fence.

"Dad?"

"Huh?" He wiped sweat from his brow, then adjusted a fallen board back into place. "Another nail, please." He held out his hand without looking at her. She pulled a nail from the pouch and handed it to him. Across the pasture, Layla was riding one of her horses. Grace waved, and Layla waved back. She hadn't seen Layla in weeks, but she knew her mother had visited her. Mostly her mother was hovering over Grace, making Grace feel like she was suffocating. She wished Mom had never quit her job. Grace had cured herself of the cutting. Now she just had to convince her father.

"Daddy, please don't let Mom take me to a shrink."

Her father finished hammering the nail into place before he looked up at her. "Grace, maybe it's the best thing for you to talk to someone."

"No, Dad. I stopped. It was a stupid, dumb thing to do, and I haven't done it since. Please don't let Mom take me on Tuesday. *Please*."

He locked eyes with her for a moment as sweat dripped from his forehead. It was already a hundred degrees, and it wasn't quite July yet. They were all going to melt come August.

"Grace, I don't know . . ." He shook his head. "Your mother really thinks that it would help you to talk to someone. Don't you think it might feel good to talk about your feelings, to maybe understand what's going on in that beautiful head of yours?" He playfully tapped her on the forehead. She smiled, but was no less committed to getting him on her side.

"Dad, I feel great. Better than I have in a long time. I was so sad when I found out about Tristan. I'd heard other girls talking about cutting themselves to make themselves feel better, and I thought maybe it would work for me. But it didn't." *God, forgive me.*

Her father put a hand up to block the early-morning sun rising above the colorful pasture filled with wildflowers. "Are you sure, Grace?"

She touched his arm. "Yes, Daddy. I'm sure. Please talk Mom out of taking me." Grace had heard them arguing about this several times, and she knew she needed to weigh in on her father's side of the argument. "I'd just die if anyone around here found out that I went to a shrink. I couldn't stand for everyone to think that I'm crazy. I might as well just die if that happened."

"Grace, don't say that." Her father kicked a board into place, then reached his hand out to her for another nail. "Your mom said the counselor is in Eagle Lake. That should be far enough away to keep it private. I can understand how you don't want this to get out, but having said that—it's nothing to be embarrassed about. Sometimes we all need someone to talk to."

"I talk to God." It was the truth. How could he argue with that?

"And that's good. But I still think—"

"Dad, I can't go! *Please!*" Her eyes started to water up, and even though she knew it would soften her father, the tears came without force. She really couldn't stand the thought of trying to explain something that she didn't totally understand herself. And she truly was scared to death that people would find out. She'd heard Glenda and the other girls bash people who had far less significant problems than Grace had. "Please just talk to Mom."

Her father put his hands on his hips and faced her. "Grace, are you sure you feel okay now? And that you don't have an urge to hurt yourself anymore?" He cupped her cheek. "We just want to do right by you, Grace, to take care of you."

She put her hand on his. "I know, Dad. But if you want to help me, please get me out of this appointment. It is causing me so much stress, and I'd be way better if I didn't have to worry about it."

He leaned over and kissed her on the forehead. "Okay, munchkin. I'll talk to your mom."

Over the years, Grace had told him that she was much too old for that endearment, but at the moment, it was music to her ears. She'd won him over. "Thank you, Dad." She reached her arms around his waist. He kissed her on the top of the head.

"You're welcome, baby."

⸎

It was early evening when Brad cornered Darlene in the kitchen. He wrapped his arms around her waist while she was loading the dishwasher. Things had been strained between them since their argument about Grace. And instead of fewer hours at work, his new position was demanding more hours, so he really hadn't had a chance to talk to her much. She was quiet, and he knew she missed her job. And she was worried about Grace.

"Let's go to dinner tonight, just the two of us." He twirled her around until she was facing him. "We haven't had a date night in a long time."

"That sounds good."

It was nice to see her smile. She was the love of his life, and while they might not always agree on everything, he couldn't stand it when they were distant. "Where do you want to go?"

"It doesn't matter. I can make something for the kids ahead of time, or—"

"Or they can just make a sandwich. They'll survive one night without a hot meal."

"I guess so."

Brad needed to talk to her about Grace, and maybe a relaxed atmosphere and a nice restaurant would make it easier for them to communicate.

"Why don't we just go to Joe's Place in Fayetteville?" she asked as she eased away from him and started the dishwasher. "We won't have to get dressed up, and a steak sounds good."

"Wherever you want to go is fine with me. I'm going to jump in the shower." He leaned around her, kissed her on the cheek.

Thirty minutes later, he started down the stairs in a pair of blue jean shorts and a white T-shirt. He'd heard the doorbell, and Darlene was opening the front door as he stepped onto the landing. Brad was surprised to see Skylar. Grace's friend hadn't been to the house in a long time. He waved to her as she walked past him and toward the stairs, then he glanced at Darlene, whose brittle smile didn't fool Brad. They both waited until Skylar was upstairs before they said anything.

"Do you think everyone will be okay for an hour or two?" Darlene's eyes searched his.

"Yes." Brad knew that Darlene's worries about Skylar mirrored his own. It was wrong to judge the girl by the way she dressed, but they were both so worried about Grace, everyone was a target for blame.

Grace heard a knock on her door and put down the book she was reading. When she opened her bedroom door, she was surprised to see Skylar, especially after the way Grace had treated her at school. Skylar had called a few times, but Grace hadn't called her back. "Hey."

"Hey. Just wondering if you were okay."

She didn't deserve a friend like Skylar. "Yeah, I'm fine." She stepped aside so Skylar could come in.

"Whatcha reading?" Skylar nodded to the book on Grace's bed.

"It's a novel. A story about the Amish."

Skylar grinned. "Really?"

"Yeah." Grace liked reading about the Amish because of the peaceful lives they led. It was an escape from her problems, but she didn't feel like explaining. She felt like crying. She'd been horrible to Skylar, and yet here she was, acting like nothing was wrong.

Grace sat down on her bed, and Skylar sat down beside her. Grace noticed light roots in Skylar's jet-black hair. She wondered what Skylar would look like with her natural hair color and without the dark makeup and black clothes.

"So I just wanted to see what's up." Skylar shrugged, and Grace fought the tears threatening to spill.

"I—I . . ." Grace blinked a few times. "Why are you here, Skylar? I mean, I wasn't exactly nice to you before school let out."

Skylar grinned. "I didn't notice."

They were quiet for a few moments, then Skylar spoke up again. "I was just kinda worried about you."

All of Grace's defenses kicked in. "Why? I'm fine." She got up from the bed, walked over to her dresser, and stacked some books in a pile. "I've been reading a lot." She shrugged, straightening the books. "It's not like you can find a job around here."

"Tell me about it. I applied everywhere I could think of, but in these small towns, there isn't much need for summer help. And it's not like my truck could take a lot of extra driving to another town."

"I've only been able to get some babysitting jobs, but at least it's something."

"So . . . how long have you been cutting again?"

Grace spun around. "I haven't done that in a long time."

"How long?"

"So you just came over here to grill me about it? I should have never told you in the first place."

"Then why did you?"

Grace grunted. "Because you figured it out."

Skylar lowered her head, frowning.

"Don't look so bummed. After my parents found out, I

swore it off for good. So if you came over here just to talk about that, then—"

"Your parents found out?" Skylar lifted her head and locked eyes with Grace. "What happened?"

This was the last thing Grace wanted to talk about, but maybe she could have some closure with Skylar on the subject if she just spilled everything. She told her the entire story, and Skylar listened without saying anything.

"So anyway, my dad is taking my mom to dinner tonight, and he said he would try to talk her out of taking me to a shrink."

"Maybe a shrink wouldn't be so bad."

Grace slapped her hands to her hips. "You quit on your own. So can I."

Skylar shrugged. "Okay. But not everyone can."

Grace walked back over to her pile of books, straightened them again. How presumptuous of Skylar to think she was better than Grace. "I can do it on my own too, and I don't need to tell my feelings to some doctor while lying on a couch."

"Well, I had a reason to stop."

Grace folded her arms across her chest. "Oh really? So what was the reason?"

Skylar took a deep breath and avoided Grace's eyes. "It's complicated."

"I've got time." Grace's words were choppy and unsympathetic as she sat down on the bed.

Skylar slapped her hands to her knees, then stood up. "You know what? I have to go pick up some medicine for my dad. Wanna ride along?"

Clearly Skylar wasn't going to share any details at the moment, and Grace realized that she didn't know much about Skylar's life, except that she lived alone with her father. "Is he sick?"

"Yeah, kind of." Skylar walked toward the door. "It sure is hot to drive to La Grange to pick up his medicine." She turned around and faced Grace, an exaggerated pout on her face. Grace knew Skylar didn't have any air-conditioning in that beat-up truck she drove.

"I'll take you." Grace found her purse, dug for her keys. "But can we just talk about something else?"

"Sure."

Skylar followed Grace down the stairs.

⤬⤬

Darlene ordered the small T-bone steak, a baked potato, and a salad. Brad ordered the same, but got the larger version. It was a much-needed, relaxing break. Until Brad got around to a conversation he'd evidently wanted to have the entire time.

"Grace really doesn't want to go see the counselor. She wanted me to talk to you." Brad sipped on a cup of coffee, keeping his eyes on her above the rim.

"Well, she's going."

He put his cup down, shook his head. "So she's going, and that's it? I don't have a say and neither does Grace?"

"Why are you ruining this night?"

"I'm not. I'm trying to talk to you, Dar, but when it comes to Grace, it's your way or no one's. I'm not sure she needs counseling."

Darlene stared at him for a few moments. "My way or no one's? Really, Brad? Because I don't see it that way at all." She and Brad never used to talk to each other with such sarcasm and flat-out ugliness. She tried to keep things in perspective, knowing they were both worried about Grace. "Something caused Grace to cut herself like that. More than once." She glanced around, lowered her voice to a whisper. "Our beautiful daughter has cuts on her arms and legs that might leave scars for the rest of her life. Do you want her to keep doing that?"

"Of course not. But I don't want to push her over the edge either. She is terrified and stressed about that appointment on Tuesday. I'm just saying maybe give her some time. And she doesn't want people to find out."

"*She* doesn't or *you* don't?" It just came out, and even though it was what she was thinking, Darlene wished she hadn't said it.

Brad stiffened as the lines across his forehead deepened. "Okay, Darlene. I can see that this isn't even open to discussion. You've made up your mind." Brad pointed a finger at her, and she was tempted to slap it away, but she folded her hands in her lap, not wanting to draw attention to their table. "But if you push Grace over the edge with this appointment, it's on your conscience. Counseling isn't for everyone." He wiped his mouth with his napkin. "You ready to go?"

Without waiting for her to answer, he scooted his chair back and stood up. *How dare you.* "You know I only want what's best for Grace," she whispered from behind him as they walked to the counter to pay. "And I can't believe you don't see that she needs some help. Did you see her legs?"

Brad didn't answer, just paid the bill. Darlene waited until they got to the parking lot before she said anything. "So if Grace goes to the counselor and it doesn't work, it's my fault. If she doesn't go and she hurts herself again, then it's your fault. Can you live with that?"

He pushed the key remote, pulled open his door, then glared over the roof at her. "Why does it have to be someone's fault? Why can't we just work together on this?"

"You already said it's on my conscience if this pushes her over the edge!" Darlene slapped her hand against the hood.

"Ultimately, you want me to make the decisions so it's not on your conscience. And I know you don't want anyone around here to find out because *you* don't want to be embarrassed."

"I'm through talking to you about this tonight." He slammed the door when he got in.

Darlene didn't want to get in the car, but it was a long walk to the house.

And it turned out to be a silent drive home.

Ten long minutes later, Brad pulled into their driveway. "Where's Grace?" Darlene jumped out of the car before it even stopped completely and hurried toward the house. After she checked Grace's room, she opened Chad's door without knocking.

"Mom! Can't you knock?" Chad was sitting on his bed, legs crossed beneath him, watching television.

"Where's Grace?"

"She went somewhere with Skylar."

"Where?"

Chad hit a button on the remote, pausing whatever he was watching. "Something about getting some medicine for Skylar's dad in La Grange. She said she'd be back by ten."

Darlene glanced out the window at the orange hue in the sky, then looked at her watch. It was only seven forty-five. A short dinner with her husband.

"She's fine, Mom."

Darlene glanced around Chad's room, trying to distract herself from worry about Grace. "This room is a mess."

"Don'tcha love it?" He snickered.

"No, I don't," she said as she backed out. "I'd be scared to sleep in here."

Darlene went downstairs, heavy steps to match her heart. When did she and Brad start talking to each other like this?

When did they start to play on opposite teams? They'd had plenty of fights over the years, but something was different about this one. Possibly fueled by their fears about Grace. Why was there a need to blame someone? They hadn't treated each other this way when Chad got into trouble in Houston, so why now?

She sat down on the couch. Ansley was out back, probably with her chickens again. No sign of Brad, so she assumed he'd gone upstairs to get ready for bed. She leaned her head back on the couch, fighting tears.

Darlene knew exactly why she was lashing out at Brad. She was angry at herself for not being there for Grace. This *was* her fault.

⚮

Skylar kept her promise during their ride to La Grange and back—no heavy conversation. Instead, they'd talked about places around town to eat, things to do, and then they landed on Skylar's college plans. Grace felt bad that she hadn't asked Skylar more about her life, especially since Skylar was always interested in Grace's life. Grace spun the angel ring on her finger as Skylar talked.

"I had to go to school all last summer and the first part of this summer to be able to graduate after this next year."

Grace and Skylar were both going to be juniors when school started—or so Grace had thought. "So you'll really be a senior this year?"

"Yeah."

"Why'd you do that? Do you hate school that much?"

Skylar turned to her right and stared out the window of the car. "The sooner I get a degree and a good job, the sooner I can make things better for my dad."

Grace had assumed Skylar hadn't been around because Grace had been ugly to her before school was out. Instead, she'd been working hard so she could graduate early. Grace wanted to ask her what the hurry was, but then she thought about the medicine they'd just picked up for her father. She swallowed hard.

"So what college are you going to?" Grace turned when Skylar told her to, the road leading up to a shack far off in the distance. *Surely Skylar doesn't live there.*

"I want to go to UT, A&M, or Texas Tech. Ms. Long at school has been helping me apply for scholarships and awards, and I've won a few for essays and stuff." She shrugged. "Ms. Long says my grades are good enough that I should be able to come up with most of the tuition."

Grace slowed down when her tires hit huge ruts in the dirt road. There was nothing but a forest of trees on either side of them and a dilapidated house in the distance. "Chad will be a senior this year, but then he's planning to go to UT." She twisted to face Skylar. "Wow. My grades are pretty good, but I doubt they're good enough to get awards or scholarships."

"Your parents can probably pay for you to go wherever you want," Skylar said matter-of-factly as she stared forward at the house coming into view.

Grace was speechless, and she was struggling not to quiz Skylar about her living arrangements. *How could anyone live here?* The yard on either side of the grayish-white house looked more like a forest than a yard, with weeds as high as the porch and a worn path leading up to the front door. Paint was chipping, and part of the porch on the left side had fallen in completely. Grace's house was a mansion compared to this.

"So what's wrong with your dad?" Grace asked as she put the car in park, hoping she wouldn't have to get out. Skylar's house was on the way back from the pharmacy in La Grange, so Skylar asked if they could drop the medicine off before they picked up her truck.

"He's got bad arthritis. It's been so bad lately that he hasn't been able to work much." Skylar opened the car door but didn't turn to face Grace. She hung her head for a moment. "You don't have to come in if you don't want to."

Grace felt a hollow ache in her stomach, but despite her own reservations, she didn't want to hurt Skylar's feelings. She pushed open the car door. "I'd like to meet your dad."

Skylar's eyes widened as she smiled. "He loves visitors. It's hard for him to get out much. Hopefully he won't talk your ear off." There was a bounce in her step as they moved toward the rickety porch steps. "I'll tell him we can't stay long." She pointed to their left. "Watch your step."

It was almost completely dark now, and there was nothing but woods surrounding them. Grace felt like she was in a scary movie. But that all changed the moment she stepped into the small den. A bear of a dog met her in the entryway, wagging his tail, and the air smelled like liver and onions cooking. Grace was the only one in her family who ate liver and onions, so her mother never made them. She'd only had the dish a few times: at a friend's house, at her grandparents' house years ago, and at Luby's restaurant in Houston. There was no mistaking the distinct smell of really strong beef—and sautéed sweet onions.

"Hello, there." A tall, thin man with hardly any hair grimaced as he stood up from a worn recliner to greet her. He looked much older than Grace's father. "You must be Grace." His hand shook as he extended it to her. When Grace gently latched on, he put his other hand on top of hers. "I'm Jack. Welcome to our home. Are you hungry?"

She thought about the casserole her mother had left on the oven. Her parents probably weren't even home yet, and she'd told Chad she would be home by ten. Plenty of time, and just the thought of liver and onions made her mouth water. "Yes, sir."

"It's liver and onions," Skylar said as she pet the large, shaggy dog. "Most people don't like it."

"Oh . . ." Grace ran her tongue along her upper lip. "I love liver and onions."

"Then you just sit yourself down and I'll bring you a plate." On shaky legs, Skylar's father moved out of the room.

"Daddy, I'll get it. Sit down." Skylar turned to the dog. "Enough, Bear. Go lay down."

Skylar's father waved her off. "Nah, I'll get it. Be right back."

Grace looked around the house as sweat dripped from her forehead. A window air-conditioning unit struggled to cool the small room, and the wooden floors were covered with worn throw rugs. She glanced at the two recliners and the small television with a long antenna, then spied a bookcase on the opposite wall. It was filled with odds and ends, only a few books, and lots of pictures of Skylar. Grace wandered that way.

"Is this your mom?" Grace picked up a picture of a woman holding a baby. She had wavy brown hair and bright blue eyes, and she was wearing a peach-colored dress and white shoes.

Skylar was still trying to get Bear to settle down, but she finally sidled up to Grace. "Yeah. That's my mom."

"She's pretty." Grace put the picture back, then turned around when Jack walked back into the room. He handed Grace a big plate of liver and onions.

"Thank you." Her mouth watered as she accepted it, breathing in the wonderful aroma.

"Sit down here and talk to me a spell." Skylar's father motioned for Grace to sit in one recliner while he sat in the other. As Skylar left the room, Grace lowered herself into the chair and put her plate on her lap. In between the two recliners was a TV tray covered with a small lamp, lots of pill bottles, a glass of water, and a box of tissues.

Skylar returned with two more plates of food and gave one to her father before sitting on a small couch. Now that everyone had their food, Grace took a bite of the liver and onions, and it was possibly the best she'd ever had. Despite how small their house was, something about it was warm and inviting—even with the loud window unit, the television blaring, and Bear jumping on and off the couch. Skylar gently pulled Bear by his collar until he was lying at her feet on the floor. She rewarded him with a piece of liver.

"Bear thinks he's one of us." Skylar smiled, and Grace nodded, her mouth full of food. She swallowed and took another big bite.

"Jack . . ." She felt funny calling Skylar's father by his first name. "This is the best liver and onions I've ever had."

"Well, Grace, we're mighty glad to have you for supper. We don't get lots of company out here." Jack shifted his weight, reached for a Kleenex, and blew his nose. "And Skylar has said such nice things about you."

Grace avoided his eyes, undeserving of the comment. She glanced at Skylar but quickly looked away.

"So how are you likin' small-town living after living in Houston?" Jack scooped up a piece of liver with his fork.

"I like it." She pushed her food around on her plate for a few moments. "I mean, it's different. I guess it's taken some time to get used to."

"The country is a good place to grow up. Things are too fast in the city. Everyone's in a hurry." Jack shook his head, and Grace thought about the Amish book she'd been reading.

Grace was away from city life, kind of like the Amish. Why couldn't she feel the kind of peace that they had?

Grace polished off the rest of her food.

"Gracious. You do like liver and onions, don't you?" Jack laughed, then pointed to Skylar. "Go get your friend some more, honey. Poor girl looks like she hasn't had liver and onions in years."

"I haven't." Grace smiled as she put her plate in Skylar's outstretched hand. "No one in my family likes it, so my mom doesn't make it." She shook her head. "And that's a shame. Because I love it."

"Well, I'm going to make sure Skylar lets you know the next time we have it. You're welcome anytime."

"Thank you, Jack."

As they ate, she and Skylar talked with Jack for a while. He enjoyed watching sports, and even though Grace didn't understand most of what he was talking about, she liked listening to him. He seemed happy to have company, and Grace couldn't help but like him.

"Where's your room?" Grace asked as she helped Skylar take their dishes to the kitchen.

"Just down the hall."

Grace followed her around a corner, down a small hallway. They turned into a room on the left, and Grace swallowed hard. It was almost like a giant closet with a small twin bed, a nightstand, and clothes hanging on a rack by the door. All dark-colored clothes. It should have been the most depressing room on the planet, but like the rest of the house, there was something welcoming about it. *Maybe it's the smell of that amazing liver and onions.*

Bear strolled in, jumped on the bed, and rested his head between his front paws.

"Bear . . ." Skylar pointed her finger at him and shook her head. "Not your bed."

The dog didn't move, but Grace could tell that Skylar hadn't expected him to. They sat down on each side of him, and Grace glanced around at the framed pictures on the walls, mostly of Skylar and her father. A couple of them were taken long ago and had a little girl in them—probably Skylar—with her mother. Skylar looked completely different in all the shots, wearing bright colors, her hair a dark blond. She was much younger in most of the photos, except for one of her and her father that was taken recently, and Skylar looked to be holding an award of some sort.

"So what kind of work does your dad do?" Grace turned to face Skylar as she petted Bear.

"He's an electrician. When he's able to work, he subcontracts for Tony Belton's company." Skylar leaned down and tied the laces on one of her army boots. "I'm going to get out of this town, get a degree, and then get a good job. First thing I'll do is get Dad a better house and make sure he has enough money for his medications. Sometimes I know he's gone without . . ." Skylar sat up again. "For me."

Grace thought for a moment. "Doesn't he have insurance?"

Skylar shook her head as she tucked one leg beneath her on the bed. "He gets some assistance . . . you know . . . from the government."

Grace didn't know, so she asked the one burning question in her mind. "Did you start cutting because of your dad's problems?"

Grace hated to bring up the subject, but she couldn't help but wonder if Skylar had felt some of the same things Grace did.

"No, I *stopped* cutting because of his problems." Skylar tucked her hair behind her ears. "He never knew anything about it. It started a couple of years ago. I didn't really have any friends, didn't fit in, and . . . I just tried it one day." She paused, then rolled up her black, long-sleeved shirt, and Grace gasped as she eyed the deep scars, much worse than Grace's. "But as good as it felt at the time, I knew it was out of control. It was getting harder and harder for Dad to get around, and if anything had happened to me . . ." She rolled her sleeve back down. "I just stopped one day."

Skylar ran her hand down Bear's back, and they were quiet for a few moments.

Grace wondered when she'd started to feel like her life was out of control. "I hope my dad can talk my mom out of making me go to that appointment with the shrink on Tuesday." She reached over and rubbed Bear's head.

Skylar leaned back against the pillow on her bed. "If I could have, I think I would have talked to someone. Maybe I would have been able to quit sooner. But . . ." Skylar sighed. "We didn't have the money for something like that and—" She frowned, locking eyes with Grace. "I'm not saying that to make you feel sorry for me or anything. I'm just saying . . ." She shrugged. "I think you should talk to the shrink."

Grace cringed. "I just can't. I don't understand it, so how can I explain it to someone else? And it would be weird to have someone all in my head. Not to mention embarrassing."

"That's why you should go, since you don't understand it. I never really understood it either."

"But you stopped on your own."

Skylar shrugged again. "Yeah. But I would have talked to someone if I could have. Instead, I read everything I could about it." She was quiet for a few moments. "You know, I think it's probably how an alcoholic feels, or a drug addict needing a fix. The cutting was a release. I think it gave me some sort of control over my own body when I couldn't control anything else in my life. It was like a high, but with highs . . . you always come down."

"See? I don't need a shrink. I have you." Grace smiled and silently said a prayer that she wouldn't have to go to the psychiatrist or psychologist—or whoever it was—on Tuesday.

When Skylar didn't say anything, Grace stood up and walked the few steps across the room to look closely at all the pictures on the wall. She'd realized what it was about Skylar, her father, and this place that she liked. The pictures, the smells, the kindness in her father's voice. Even Skylar seemed warmer in this space. It was a home, filled with love, just like what Grace had. *Just goes to show that it's not the size of the house. Just what's in it.*

"You'll figure it out," Skylar said. "But I don't have the answers."

Grace wasn't sure anything would work for her, although she was proud she hadn't cut in a long time. "I think I've stopped anyway." She lifted one shoulder, dropped it slowly. "I haven't done it in weeks."

Skylar didn't say anything.

"I guess I should take you to get your truck at my house." Grace stood up and Skylar did too. But instead of moving toward the door, Skylar unzipped her black pants and slowly pulled them down to her knees. Standing in her underwear, she looked at Grace as tears formed in the corners of her eyes.

Grace gazed upon the deep scars that ran down Skylar's legs, and Grace was sure she would never cut herself as badly as Skylar had. She'd never do that. *Never.* Her heart was beating out of her chest. She looked up at Skylar as a tear rolled down Skylar's cheek.

"Go see the counselor, Grace. Don't wait as long as I did."

She started to cry. "What guy is ever going to want to be with me like this?" She pulled her pants back up as the tears fell.

Grace wrapped her arms around Skylar and held her tight. "Someone will love you for the person you are, Skylar, and you're a beautiful person."

Skylar eased away, dabbing at the black makeup smearing under her eyes. "Promise me you'll go to that appointment."

Grace looked at her pink tennis shoes and shook her head. "I can't. I can't talk about it."

Skylar reached for Grace's hand, then squeezed as she closed her eyes and lowered her head.

"Dear Lord, please give Grace the strength and courage to face her fears, knowing that You are by her side all the time. She needs You, Lord."

Grace started to cry so hard, she couldn't stop. She'd been praying, but hearing Skylar doing it on her behalf touched her beyond words.

Maybe there was hope for her after all.

Chapter Fourteen

Darlene sat at the far end of the couch from Brad, thumbing through a magazine while her husband channel surfed. With every click of the remote, she wanted to yank it from his hand. She glanced at the clock on the wall. Ten minutes until ten. Chad and Ansley had been upstairs for about thirty minutes, and now she just needed her third child to come walking through the door safe and sound.

An invisible shield of anger divided her and Brad, tension so tight Darlene wished he would just go to bed. Logic told her that fear for Grace had fueled their argument at the restaurant, but Brad's blaming her only added to her own guilt. Maybe if she hadn't been working, spent more time with Grace—maybe it wouldn't have happened. She wanted to broach the subject again with Brad, but she was too tired. And worried about Grace.

Five minutes later, the front door opened. Darlene tried not to let the worry in her heart show on her face. "Hey. How was Skylar?"

"Fine." Grace walked toward the stairs. "I'm going to bed."

Darlene glanced at Brad, wondering if he was thinking what she was. Darlene worried now every time Grace went upstairs to her room. She was about four steps up the stairs when she turned around.

"Oh, Dad . . . I know we talked earlier, but I just want you both to know that I'm okay about going to that appointment Tuesday."

Darlene looked at Brad, then back at Grace. Brad spoke up before Darlene had a chance to.

"I think that's great, honey. What made you change your mind?" Brad pressed the Pause button on the remote.

Grace shrugged. "I don't know. I'm just okay with it now." She turned and went upstairs.

"Well, you got what you wanted," Brad said after they heard Grace's bedroom door close.

Darlene didn't say anything. She didn't have the energy for another argument that Brad was clearly provoking, and the most important thing was that Grace was open to visiting with the psychologist.

"I'm gonna go get a shower." Brad put the TV remote down and left the room.

Darlene picked up the remote control and searched for anything that might take her mind off the pain she felt in her heart.

∞

Brad stayed in the shower longer than usual, hoping the warm water would ease the tension in his neck and shoulders. He hated when he and Darlene fought. It didn't happen often, but when it did, most arguments were about the kids. This time Darlene had hit a nerve. She was right when she said Brad didn't want anyone to know about Grace. Partly he was protecting Grace from the ridicule she'd surely get from her classmates.

But he also had to admit, her actions made him feel like he'd failed her somehow.

He couldn't understand why anyone would inflict pain on themselves unless there was something seriously wrong with them mentally, and that thought terrified him. He was hoping this would just go away on its own.

He knew in his heart that Darlene was right to insist that Grace see a professional, but Brad could still recall his visits to see a counselor when he was eleven. Dr. Mathis. A plump woman with silver hair and red reading glasses. He'd gone because he'd had bad dreams—actually, terrible nightmares that used to make him run into his parents' room.

But all he could remember was feeling like he was crazy because he had to go to a counselor. And that Dr. Mathis tried to put notions into his head that simply weren't true. She'd insinuated that his family life was a wreck. Not true. Tried to convince him he'd been bullied at school. Again, not true. And the list went on. It seemed to Brad that she needed to justify her fee by finding a cure for his sleep disorder. She never did. And for a long time, his mind had reeled with all the possibilities about what might be wrong with him. One day the nightmares just went away on their own.

He knew Grace's situation wasn't the same, but he could still remember Dr. Mathis and how much he dreaded those visits. He just wasn't a big fan of psychologists, and he didn't want to put Grace through that.

As he turned off the water, Darlene walked into the bathroom and began her ritual. He resented the fact that she'd said he didn't want Grace to see a psychologist because it would embarrass him. Did she think he was that shallow, that concerned with what people thought? Maybe he was.

He stepped out of the shower, dried off. Darlene didn't look up. He thought about the ways they used to make up, years ago. Things seemed simpler then. Tonight he doubted there would be a make-up session. And that was okay. He was tired. And tomorrow was church.

∞

Tuesday morning, Darlene was surprised when Brad stayed home from work and said he was going with her to take Grace to see Dr. Brooks. It was going to be a long morning since Dr. Brooks had blocked out two hours for their first visit.

They'd had pancakes as usual on Sunday after church. Then, on Monday, while Brad was at work, Darlene and the kids had cleaned out the attic. In addition to boxes they'd stored up there after moving in, there were crates and other items left from when Darlene's grandparents lived there.

Grace had claimed a vintage lamp that Darlene could remember from her great-aunt's house when she was little. She had no idea how it had gotten into her grandparents' attic. Chad had found some old records of hers and Brad's from high school. And Ansley had wanted some old photo albums to keep in her room.

Darlene's attic find was a small jewelry box. She'd almost missed it since it was mixed in with her grandfather's old work clothes. The gray slacks and matching shirts brought back memories of when Darlene would visit. For over thirty years, her grandfather had driven a tractor for the county, mowing long stretches of grass along the highway. When he got home, her grandmother would make him sit in a chair on the porch, and she'd carefully pick off any ticks that had hitched a ride home with him. Darlene smiled at the recollection. Most of the time, she and Dale were running around the yard capturing fireflies in a glass jar as their grandmother worked on their grandpa on the porch.

But the small wooden jewelry box wasn't something she ever remembered seeing. It had only one item inside—a delicate sterling silver necklace with a dove pendant. She couldn't recall her mother or grandmother ever wearing that piece of jewelry. Her first thought had been to give it to Grace since Ansley wasn't very fond of jewelry, but she hadn't wanted to risk hurting Ansley's feelings. Darlene had put the necklace on right away, knowing the dove was symbolic of the Holy Spirit and hoping it would give her strength. The dove's wings were tarnished, though, so as soon as she could find her silver polish—probably in an unpacked box in the den—she'd give the necklace a thorough cleaning.

There had been lots of reminiscing that afternoon. Then they'd finally gotten down to actually cleaning out all the trash and things they didn't want. It had been a good day with the kids. It was a shame Brad couldn't have shared the experience, but he rarely took off from work—with the exception of this morning.

They still hadn't said much to each other since their dinner at the restaurant, and Darlene knew that today would likely bring on even more tension. She'd been praying that Dr. Brooks could fix whatever was wrong with Grace and keep her daughter from hurting herself.

Not long after they arrived at the office, they met with Dr. Brooks for an introductory session. She wasn't anything like Darlene had pictured in her mind. She was dressed in blue jeans and a white button-down blouse that hung loosely around her hips, and her dark brown hair was pulled back into a tight ponytail. Tiny silver loops hung from her earlobes, and Darlene could feel some of her anxiety lessen in the woman's presence. *That must be her intent.*

During this first part of their appointment, Darlene had filled out paperwork, and they'd talked about family history and the purpose for Grace's visit. They'd also discussed patient confidentiality, which was something Darlene had wondered about. As it turned out, Brad and Darlene had a legal right to information about Grace's therapy sessions because she was a minor, but they opted for Grace to keep the visits confidential. Dr. Brooks said that was fine unless Grace showed imminent signs of harm to herself or others. At that point, both Grace and Darlene had teared up, but somehow they got through the first part of the appointment. Next, it would be Grace's turn to talk with the doctor alone, but first they took a fifteen-minute break.

Grace and Darlene went to the ladies' room and got a drink of water, then returned to the waiting room to sit with Brad until Dr. Brooks was ready for Grace. Her hands shaking, Grace sat between Darlene and Brad. Darlene would have given anything to swap places with her daughter. Nothing hurt a parent more than seeing their child suffering, but this paled in comparison to walking into Grace's room and seeing her hands, sheets, shirt, and shorts covered in blood.

She closed her eyes for a moment but was jarred back to the present when Dr. Brooks called Grace's name.

"It's gonna be fine, Grace," Brad said as Grace stood up. "We'll be right here if you need us."

Brad pressed his lips together, and Darlene thought he seemed more uptight than Grace. She reached for her daughter's hand and squeezed. "Your dad's right, baby."

Grace moved slowly toward the open door, and once it closed behind her, the minutes began to tick by. With every second, Brad became more and more agitated. He shifted his weight constantly, aimlessly flipped through magazines without reading anything, and if he let out another exasperated breath, Darlene thought she might snap.

"It's been over an hour," he finally said, tossing a magazine onto the nearby table. He leaned his head back against the wall and sighed.

"I'm sure everything is fine." Darlene was antsy enough without having to worry about Brad.

He glared at her. "You don't know that."

Darlene didn't want to argue. She was worried about Grace, but she believed she was in good hands. Myrna wouldn't have recommended someone she didn't think would be good for Grace.

She and Brad were quiet for a while. Darlene reached up and stroked the dove between her fingers. "Maybe we should pray."

Brad's eyebrows narrowed, his voice defensive. "I do pray. All the time."

"I know . . . I just—just thought maybe we could pray together. Now." Except for prayers before meals, she couldn't recall her and Brad ever praying aloud together. Darlene had prayed aloud with the kids at bedtime when they were young, but even the children had taken to saying their own prayers. Or at least she hoped they did.

"Yeah, I guess we can." Brad bowed his head, and Darlene swallowed back tears before she began.

"God, please lay Your healing hands on Grace and help her to lean on You during these troubled times. She's so young, Lord, so . . . so precious to us." Darlene bit her bottom lip, overcome with emotion. She was glad when Brad took over.

"Dear Lord, please be with our baby girl. Wrap Your loving arms around her, and help her to heal. Please give Darlene and me the knowledge and strength to be good parents to all of our children. Amen."

"Amen." A tear rolled down Darlene's cheek, and when she glanced at Brad, he looked the other way. But she'd seen his watery eyes.

A few minutes later, the door slowly opened. Darlene could tell that Grace had been crying, but she mustered up a weak smile anyway. "Don't look so worried. I'm okay." She edged closer. "Dr. Brooks wants to see you both in her office." Grace sat down beside Darlene. "I told her it was okay to talk to you about everything."

"Are you sure, honey? Because you can keep this between just you and Dr. Brooks." Darlene put a hand on Grace's leg.

"I'm sure, Mom."

Darlene noticed that Grace's hands weren't shaking as she reached for a magazine. When Darlene and Brad hesitated, Grace spoke up again. "I promise. I'm fine."

Darlene and Brad stood and walked down the hall, back into the large room with dark blue couches and wingback chairs. Darlene had noticed earlier that the room was painted a soothing powder blue, almost the same color as the classroom at The Evans School. She took a deep breath and focused on the scenery outside the windows. One wall was almost entirely windows, and through them, she could see a field of wildflowers and Longhorns.

Dr. Brooks asked them to take a seat on the dark blue couch as she sat in one of the wingback chairs across from them. She crossed her legs, set her pad and pen on a table next to her, and smiled. "Grace is a lovely girl."

Darlene and Brad forced smiles and waited for her to go on.

"I know that Grace's cutting has stirred up a lot of emotions and worry for both of you, and I'm going to do my best to answer your questions and try to explain to you why I think Grace is doing this."

Darlene held her breath as she nodded.

"Let me start out by addressing the biggest fear I often hear from parents." She smiled, glancing back and forth between Darlene and Brad. "Cutters are rarely trying to kill themselves. I'm not going to say it hasn't happened, but not one of my patients has fallen into that category, and I've counseled a lot of kids like Grace.

"Cutting is usually triggered by intense feelings that the person can't express in ways that the rest of us do. Some of us yell, some cry, or maybe we go for a run, or eat a gallon of ice cream." She paused, again glancing back and forth between Darlene and Brad. "When a person can't express these feelings of anger, hurt, frustration, or even shame, they feel like they are out of control, and the only way to regain control for some of them is to cut. It's a release for them and a way to focus on something besides the things that are hurting them in other ways. Does this make sense?"

Darlene nodded, even though it didn't make much sense to her at all.

"What is hurting Grace so badly that she feels the need to do this?" Brad shook his head. "I just don't get it. Is it because of her breakup with her boyfriend back in Houston?"

Dr. Brooks smiled, something Darlene now wished she would quit doing. "Things started before the move, but seem to have worsened due to the breakup with her boyfriend and anxiety about relocating."

Darlene put a hand to her chest as she wondered how long Grace had been able to keep this a secret. Her eyes filled with water, and she turned to Brad and said the first thing that came to mind. "I wasn't working then, Brad, so my two months' working outside of our home didn't cause this."

"Darlene, I never said this was your fault."

"Yes, you did."

"I never said it was your fault—it just came out that way, and—"

"Darlene, Brad . . ." Dr. Brooks interrupted. "This is not your fault. I've seen plenty of cases of abuse, alcoholism, and neglectful parenting that have triggered this, but I don't sense any of that from Grace. She just can't express her feelings and"—she paused, glancing back and forth between them—"Grace wants to be perfect. She doesn't want to disappoint anyone."

Darlene felt her heart beating in her chest as guilt flooded over her. How many times had they called Grace their perfect little girl? She lowered her forehead into her hand, dabbed at her eyes.

"So it is our fault." Brad rubbed his forehead, looking down. "We've somehow been bad parents." He turned to Darlene. "You were home with her most of the time. Didn't you notice anything?"

Darlene stopped breathing for a moment, then spoke slowly and steadily, hoping to cut him to the core. "And you were never home. Not to mention that you have always told her how perfect she is. It's hard always living up to your expectations."

Brad's face turned bright red, but Dr. Brooks interjected before he could speak.

"Okay, folks. We're getting off track here. Our goal is not to place blame, but to help Grace deal with the pressures in her life in some other way besides cutting."

"How can cutting yourself until you bleed make you feel better? Why would anyone do that?" Brad's voice was hoarse, his tone critical.

Dr. Brooks uncrossed her legs, placed her elbows on her knees, and leaned her chin on her hands. "This is more common for girls. Usually it starts out as an experiment, or maybe even because other girls at school are doing it. But if the person is able to mask other emotional pain by cutting, it can become a habit. And habits are hard to break. But we are going to work with Grace, let her know that no one expects her to be perfect, and that there are other ways to release the stress she feels in her life.

"Grace is going to have some scars, both emotional and physical, but her willingness to stop is a huge plus. Some of the young ladies I treat don't have a desire to quit. They're just here because someone found out and forced them into my office. Grace seems to sincerely want to stop."

Darlene coughed, sniffled. "Is she—does she—have anything mentally wrong with her?"

"Your aunt Helen was schizophrenic." Brad shifted on the couch to face Darlene.

"That doesn't mean anything," Darlene snapped.

"No, it doesn't," Dr. Brooks said. "Although a history of mental illness can play a part in some cases. With Grace, recent events in her life led to depressed emotions that she didn't know how to cope with, which led to some difficulty adjusting in Round Top." She sat taller. "I'd like to see Grace once a week, and I think we can work through this. She won't be cured overnight, but we have to reprogram her to understand that no one expects perfection and that there are other ways to deal with her emotional pain."

"What emotional pain?" Brad's voice was louder than before. "She broke up with the guy, but prior to that, what emotional pain has she had? Something we don't know about? She's had a loving family, a good home, good grades, and she's a beautiful girl. I still don't understand."

Darlene wished Brad would just shut up, even though she was having some of the same thoughts.

Dr. Brooks stood up and walked to her desk. She put on a

pair of black-rimmed reading glasses, then flipped through a calendar book on her desk. "I can see Grace at this same time next week?"

Darlene nodded, and Dr. Brooks leaned down to write in her book. She pulled the glasses off and looked back and forth between Darlene and Brad. "This can be difficult for parents to understand." She paused. "And sometimes blaming each other can cause problems within the marriage. Are the two of you available to visit with me next week as well?"

"No." Brad stood up, smoothing the wrinkles from his slacks. "Really. Our marriage is fine. We're just a bit freaked out by all of this."

"I understand." Dr. Brooks walked around her desk. "If you change your mind, I'm available. The most important thing right now is to encourage Grace to talk about her feelings. It won't be easy at first because she is so used to hiding them from everyone. But she seems to have a wonderful support system." Dr. Brooks paused. "And her friend Skylar has certainly helped to set her on the right path."

Darlene stood up and edged closer to Dr. Brooks. "Skylar?"

Dr. Brooks folded her hands in front of her. "Yes. She's a former cutter, and she recognized the signs with Grace. She's been encouraging her to stop and to seek counseling. She sounds like a special young woman, and Grace is lucky to have her as a friend."

Darlene wanted to run out the door and hug Skylar's neck, then apologize profusely for all the times she'd tried to blame Skylar for Grace's behavior. She turned to Brad.

"Maybe it wouldn't be a bad idea for us—"

"No. We don't need counseling." He turned to Dr. Brooks. "Thank you for working with Grace. We'll do what we can on our end."

"What if she does it again? Cuts?" Darlene asked. "Do we call you? Try to talk to her? Are there signs we can watch for?"

Dr. Brooks touched Darlene on the arm. "You can call me anytime, day or night." She turned and pulled a business card from a holder on her desk. "My cell phone is on this card. And in the meantime, allow Grace to express her feelings, and don't be surprised if she begins expressing them in ways that you aren't used to, possibly yelling or acting out in other ways." She paused, touched Darlene on the arm again. "The cutting won't stop overnight. I'd love to be able to tell you that it won't ever happen again, but it might. Just stay close to her, talk to her."

Darlene nodded. "Thank you."

As they left Dr. Brooks's office, Darlene had two things on her mind. Her daughter and the distance she felt from Brad.

⌘

Three days later, Darlene tried to coax Grace into going grocery shopping with her, knowing that she wouldn't succeed.

"Mom, I hate grocery shopping."

Darlene opened the refrigerator and took inventory of what she needed. She counted seven dozen eggs and shook her head. "Remind Ansley that eggs do eventually go bad if we don't eat them."

Grace giggled. "I will." Her laughter was music to Darlene's ears.

"Sure you don't want to come shopping with me?"

"Mom." Grace threw her hands in the air, then quickly dropped them to her sides. "You have to quit hovering over me. It's bugging me. Just go to the grocery store. Skylar is coming over later, and we're gonna just hang out and watch movies."

Darlene was happy to hear that. "Okay, when Chad gets up, tell him to take out the garbage before he leaves for work, and Dad wants him to mow the grass when he gets home." She grabbed her purse and turned to Grace. "Why hasn't Cindy been around?"

"Chad said it didn't work out between them."

Darlene sighed, feeling a bit guilty that she thought her own son had chosen above him. "I hope Chad isn't too upset that Cindy broke up with him."

Grace sat down at the kitchen table and grabbed a banana from the fruit bowl. "She didn't break up with him. Chad told her he didn't want to see her anymore."

Darlene raised an eyebrow. "Really?" She hoped Chad hadn't fallen into the wrong crowd again. Cindy had seemed like such a nice girl. "Okay, well, I'm off. I have to go to Walmart in La Grange, then to the grocery store, so I'll be awhile. Are you sure—"

"No, Mom. I don't want to go. Everything will be fine."

Darlene forced a smile, feeling somewhat better that Skylar was coming over.

Thirty minutes later, she was at Walmart comparing prices on toilet paper when Dave rounded the corner, pushing a basket, alone. She hadn't seen him since her last day at work.

"Hi, Dave. How are you?" She smiled. "How's Cara?"

She tossed a twelve-pack of toilet tissue into her cart and waited. A muscle flicked in Dave's jaw—a withdrawn, congested expression settling on his face. Darlene swallowed hard and braced herself.

"I knew I would eventually run into you somewhere." Dave folded one arm across his chest and stroked his chin with his other hand, a bitter edge to his voice. "How are you?"

Darlene was pretty sure he didn't care one bit how she was.

"I'm okay. I'm sorry about having to leave The Evans School. I miss Cara."

"She cried every day for a week. It was confusing for her. She didn't understand why Ms. Darlene just vanished, abandoned her."

It stung, and Darlene knew she deserved it. "I wanted to tell her good-bye, but Myrna thought it might make matters worse."

"Maybe you could have warned *me*, though. Would that have been so hard?" He shook his head. "Why did you even take that job if you were only planning to stay for a couple of months? These kids get attached to their teachers. I know I was hard on Mae, but I thought I'd let you have the reins with Cara, and Cara had been doing well. They still haven't replaced you. Myrna is teaching her granddaughter and Cara. But I guess you did what you had to do." He paused. "Anyway, take care." He edged his basket past her.

Darlene swallowed back tears, not wanting to cry in front of him, but she wanted him to know that Cara and her schooling had been important to her. "Dave?"

He turned around but didn't say anything.

"I'm sure Myrna will find a suitable replacement. And I hope you and Cara are doing well." Despite her best efforts, she blinked back tears and turned away from him.

He walked a couple of steps until he was at her side again. "Why are you crying?" His voice sounded tight, like he was holding his breath and the words were strangling him.

"I just feel bad about the way I left. I didn't know what else to do. And . . ." She put her hands up to her face, and it was as if all the tears she'd been holding back wanted to escape at one time. She swiped frantically at her eyes, then raised her chin. "I'm so sorry. I'm so sorry for everything. Please give Cara my

love, unless you think it will upset her. But I really do miss her."
Another tear scrolled down her cheek, and she hurried to push
her basket forward. A firm hand caught her by the arm.

"Hold up."

She kept her head down since she couldn't seem to control
her emotions.

"What's going on with you?" Dave's voice was softer. She
looked up at him.

"It's—it's my daughter Grace." She paused and took another
breath. "She's . . . well, we've . . ." She dabbed at her eyes and
waited for a woman and her young son to pass by them and
move out of earshot. "Grace has had some problems."

Dave let go of her arm and was quiet for a few moments.
"What kind of problems?"

It wasn't his business, nor his concern, but she owed him
some kind of explanation. "She's—she's been . . ." Darlene took
a deep breath, blinked her eyes several times. "She's been hurting herself. Cutting herself." She locked eyes with him. "Please
forgive me for abandoning Cara like that, but my daughter is in
trouble, and I have to stay close to her."

He didn't say anything for a moment, just stared at her.
Then he hung his head for a few moments. When he looked
back up at her, he said, "We make all kinds of sacrifices for our
children. I knew you loved that job." He took a deep breath.
"I just couldn't understand why you left. I'm so sorry to hear
about Grace."

She lowered her head again. "Thank you."

He gently put his hand on her arm as he stepped closer to
her. His touch was so tender, she wanted to fall into his arms.
Into anyone's arms. Brad had been so distant, and she needed
to be held. She'd thought about going to see Layla, but it had
been awhile since she'd seen her. And Layla didn't seem to be

the nurturing type anyway. Darlene wished her parents were still alive. She needed some mothering. When Dave pulled her into his arms, she cried on his shoulder for a few moments, long enough to get his blue shirt damp and feel ridiculous about her behavior in the middle of Walmart. She eased out of his comforting arms, took a deep breath, and quickly glanced around to see if anyone had seen her display. "I better finish my shopping," she said as she fished around in her purse for a tissue. "Wow. Dave, I'm so sorry. I don't know what's wrong with me."

"Let's get out of here," he said softly. "I think you need to talk, maybe someone to listen, or . . ." He gazed into her eyes, a sympathetic smile on his lips. "Or just a shoulder to cry on for a while."

Darlene looked past him at a woman turning the corner and heading toward them. "I don't know." She lowered her head, swiped the tissue over her eyes.

"Nothing like a good cup of coffee and having someone to listen when we feel down. How 'bout it?"

She glanced at her cart, and the last thing she felt like doing was finishing her shopping. "Okay."

He picked up her purse, handed it to her, then guided her by the elbow down the aisle. Then they were out of the store and in his car.

⚮

Dave pulled into the parking lot of Latte on the Square in La Grange. At ten in the morning, they'd missed the coffee crowd, and it was still too early for lunch. There was only one woman in the corner of the small restaurant when they walked in. Dave escorted Darlene to a table in the opposite corner, farthest from the door, as his mind spun with conflicting thoughts.

Before she'd left her job at the school, he'd avoided anything more than report-like conversations about Cara. Ever since the gala, he'd known he was in dangerous territory. He was attracted to everything about the woman. Maybe he should have been relieved when she'd quit her job, but it had been hard on Cara. And he'd resented her—not just for hurting his daughter, but because he'd started to fall for her in such a short period of time. But now she needed a friend. Dave knew he could be that for her. He understood the instinct of keeping your child safe, and having to do whatever it took to ensure it.

He spent the next hour listening to Darlene talk, the most harrowing part being when she and her husband found their daughter covered in blood in her room. Then she told him about the counseling session. And about her husband's reactions.

"I think, as men, we feel out of control when something is wrong with a loved one, like we should have been a better father, husband . . . or man." He watched her take a sip of her coffee, glad she wasn't crying. She'd cried through most of her story, and it was breaking Dave's heart to see her like this. But she seemed better now, and he wished he had advice that would help her.

"Brad is a good man, a great provider. But I think you're right. He feels like a failure sometimes." She bit her lip for a moment. "When he's not blaming me for this."

"Darlene, I'm sure he's not intentionally blaming you." In strange new territory, Dave felt the need to defend Brad, even though he was having inappropriate thoughts about the man's wife—maybe *because* he was having those thoughts. He'd never cheated on his wife, nor been involved with a married woman. Despite his feelings, he reached over and touched her hand. "And you shouldn't blame yourself either."

She eased her hand out from under his. As she should have. "I guess I better go home. I hate to leave Grace for too long. I mean, I'm sure she's fine. I just . . ."

"I think we both left half-full baskets at Walmart." Dave smiled and was glad to see that she did too.

"True. I guess I should finish shopping."

They walked to the car, and Dave took her back to the store.

"I have a meeting, so I'll have to finish my shopping later," he said as he pulled in front of the entrance.

"I'm sorry you were busy hearing about my problems and didn't get to do your shopping."

He couldn't tell her that there was no place he would have rather been, so he simply nodded. "No problem at all. I hope things get better for your family." He was racking his brain about how he could see her again. Cara had finally stopped talking about Darlene, so he couldn't use his daughter as an excuse. It might be a setback for Cara. But the thought of not seeing Darlene again caused him an unfamiliar pang of anxiety.

"Thank you. For everything." She smiled, then closed the door.

Dave watched her walk inside until she was out of sight.

He knew he was going to find a way to see her again.

Dear Lord, help me.

❧

Brad tapped his pen on his desk, glanced at his watch. It was already seven o'clock. If he left now, he wouldn't be home until around eight thirty. He'd left the house early this morning, completed more work than he expected any of his associates to do in a day, and still he felt like it wasn't enough.

Logically, he knew he was trying to overcompensate for the

way he'd been treating Darlene and the situation with Grace. Darlene was sad, needed comfort. And Grace just needed her dad to act normal. Since Tuesday, he could hardly face Grace without a knot forming in his throat, and he didn't have the emotional strength to comfort Darlene. Which, in the end, left him feeling like an even bigger failure.

But here he was. Still at work. And not wanting to go home and face anyone.

His prayers had been heartfelt, asking the Lord to guide him, help him to be a better man for his family. He thought about how he and Darlene had prayed together at the counselor's office. He'd often prayed at church, at night before bed, and silently during the day. But never with his wife.

He twirled his pen between his fingers as he pondered why that was. They'd prayed aloud with the children when they were young. Why didn't he ever pray aloud with Darlene?

When no answers came to mind, he figured he would bill out a couple more hours, then maybe he'd be ready to head home. He opened a file on his desk, the most complex corporate tax analysis he had, and buried his head in it.

By the time he took a break, it was nine o'clock. He flipped open his cell phone and dialed home. Darlene answered quickly, as if she'd been waiting for his call.

"Hey. I'm just now getting ready to leave work. I had some stuff I needed to finish." He looked out his window into the darkness, a mirror of his heart. "But I'm leaving now."

"Okay. I'll keep your dinner hot."

Darlene assured him all was well with Grace, but the conversation was strained. Just like every word they'd spoken since Tuesday.

Visions of his precious daughter covered in blood haunted Brad, and he'd even started having bad dreams again, after all these years. Usually he was running . . . trying to get to Grace . . . She was covered in blood, and Brad never could reach her. Last night, his entire family had been covered in blood, and he couldn't get to any of them. Darlene was screaming for him to help them all.

He picked up his keys, shut everything off, and closed the door behind him.

Grace picked up her Amish book. She'd been waiting for her dad to come home, and he'd finally pulled in the driveway at almost eleven o'clock, even later than last night. She'd hugged him, tried to be as cheerful as possible so he'd know she was fine, then she'd come upstairs.

She wondered if her parents were fighting. Actually, they didn't seem to be speaking much at all. Grace knew it was her fault. The images of her parents' faces when they walked into her room the night they'd caught her haunted her several times each day. The last thing she'd ever wanted to do was to cause worry for her parents, to disappoint them.

She thought about what Dr. Brooks had said. "Everyone disappoints and is disappointed throughout their life. It's how we cope with these downfalls that counts." Then she went on to say that no one was perfect, and those kinds of expectations were unrealistic. In her mind, Grace knew all that. She tried to absorb herself in the story she was reading, but she couldn't focus.

After tossing the book aside, she lay back on her bed and stared at the ceiling. She wanted to be the best she could be, and upsetting her parents, causing them to fight . . . that was only making things worse. She knew she couldn't cut. If her parents found out, they'd go over the edge. But as her anxieties welled inside her, so did the urge. Just one tiny cut, one moment of relief, her mind in another zone, away from everything.

Tears were building, and her heart was beating against her chest. She reached over to her nightstand, hands trembling.

And she called Skylar.

Chapter Fifteen

Darlene almost fell out of the pew when Layla walked into church the following Sunday. Every eye was on the ex–movie star as she glided down the aisle in a fitted ivory dress, her long, wavy blond hair flowing freely past her shoulders. She slid into the pew beside Darlene.

"Oh, don't look so shocked." Layla pushed back a strand of hair from her cheek. "I was hungry for pancakes." Then she frowned. "And where've you been anyway?"

"I've been around, Layla," Darlene whispered. "You tend to give a person the impression that they're bugging you, so I stayed away."

"Really? I give that impression?" She grinned. "Well, I missed you."

Darlene stared at Layla for a moment. It had been weeks since she'd seen her, and she was wondering why Layla had decided that church was the place to make her appearance.

"Tom called. He's coming for a visit this week." Layla smiled broadly. "I'd prayed about it. About us—Tom and me."

Darlene's jaw dropped and her eyes widened.

"Yes, Darlene. I've been very angry at God, but I decided to reach out to Him." She paused, raised her chin. "And now today I've come to thank Him."

Darlene was just glad Layla was in church and happy. "I think that's wonderful," she said, with the realization that her own prayers had been slipping away from her. It was unintentional, and every time she thought about it, she lifted up prayers on the spot. But her ritualistic prayer offerings seemed to have gone by the wayside in the evenings. She'd been tired, scared, restless, sleepless, and—if she allowed herself to admit it—a bit guilty about confiding her personal family issues to Dave. Brad wouldn't have appreciated it, and she'd never kept anything from him before.

But Dave's tender touch came at a time when her own husband wasn't giving her the time of day, and when she needed it the most.

Then why was she backing off from prayer? She, and her family, needed God more than ever. She thought of the brief prayers she and Brad had said at the counselor's office and realized that she needed both God *and* family, and she wanted to combine them more through prayer. She reached up and touched the dove on her necklace.

After church, Layla followed them back home, and the woman ate more pancakes than Chad. Ansley's eyes bulged as she watched Layla load her plate with syrup.

"You like Mom's pancakes, huh?" Ansley stuffed a bite into her mouth.

"Yes, your mom is a good cook. Well, I mean, I guess she is. She never invites me for dinner, even though I'm over there in that big house all by myself."

"Layla!" Darlene grinned as she put her fork down. "That is not true. Don't lie to my children." She pointed around the table at Grace, Ansley, and Chad. "Listen up. Make sure you hear." Then she turned to Layla. "I'm making chicken-fried steaks and mashed potatoes tomorrow night, Layla. Would you like to have dinner with us?"

Layla grinned. "Of course, Darlene. How nice of you to ask."

Everyone laughed, even Brad. Darlene pointed a finger at Layla. "You've turned me down in the past, but now we have witnesses. So we'll see you at seven tomorrow night."

"I love chicken-fried steak."

Later in the evening, Darlene and Layla sat on the front porch swing. Darlene told her everything about Grace, the counselor, and even how distant she and Brad had been.

Layla was quiet for a long time before she said anything, then she turned to Darlene with tears in her eyes. "You're a good mother, Darlene. And Brad is a good father. And together you're good. I think everything will be all right." Then she did the totally unexpected. She reached over and squeezed Darlene's hand. "You did the right thing by quitting your job. Grace needs you now. Maybe more than you know."

Darlene worried that Layla was also talking about Marissa, so she changed the subject. "So tell me about Tom. When will he be here?"

Her face brightened. "Wednesday."

"Do you think you'll get back together?"

Layla smiled. "Maybe." She turned to face Darlene. "I made no secret that I have been more than angry at God. But I don't know . . ." She shrugged. "There was a time in my life when I reached out to Him all the time. So I tried to bury those angry feelings, and little by little, I started to pray again. And something inside of me began to change. Next thing I knew, Tom called. Do you think that's a coincidence?"

"No. I believe God answers our prayers. And when He does, we're grateful. But when He doesn't answer our prayers, for reasons we can't possibly know, then we tend to feel abandoned, even bitter." As Darlene said the words, she wondered if she, too, had been a bit bitter at God lately—about Grace and about the tension between her and Brad.

"Well, He answered my prayers in a big way when Tom called." Layla's voice had taken on an airy tone. "Did I tell you that Tom's the only man I've ever loved?"

"No. But I think that's wonderful. Brad is the only man I've ever loved too. I can't imagine being without him."

They rocked back and forth in the swing for a while, the night sky filled with stars. Layla finally spoke in a soft voice.

"I'm sorry I'm not a better person, Darlene. I liked you from the moment I met you . . ." She paused, grinning. "As you scuffled around with that stupid snake under your bed." She was quiet for a moment. "But most people don't want to be friends with me just to be friends. They usually want something. I guess when you stopped coming around, I realized you didn't really need anything from me." She nodded toward the house. "You have everything you need right inside those walls."

Darlene was quiet. She swallowed hard. "What I need is a friend. Things with Brad are maybe a little worse than . . ." She took a deep breath.

Layla didn't question her, but grabbed her hand again and squeezed. "There's something you should probably know. When I make a *real* friend, it's a friend for life." Before Darlene could answer, Layla let go of her hand, then stood up. "So now we're friends."

"For life." Darlene stood up too. She thought about her friendship with Gina back in Houston, but their relationship had revolved around the kids and their activities. Darlene hadn't confided in Gina about personal family matters. She missed the companionship, but once Gina's divorce was final,

Darlene realized that their friendship wasn't likely to last. "I've never really had a close woman friend who I could confide in. I wonder why that is."

"Women are catty. Most of us anyway. And a lot of times we don't play well with others."

Darlene really didn't think she fit into that category, but she was curious why she'd never had any close girlfriends. Then she realized why. Brad had always been her best friend. She'd told him everything.

∞

Layla ate dinner with Darlene and her family the next two nights, then from Wednesday on, Darlene noticed a white car parked out front. Tom, she was sure.

When Darlene saw that the car was gone on Saturday, she went to Layla's.

"Well?" she asked when Layla opened the door.

"It was wonderful. We talked a lot." She motioned for Darlene to follow her inside, and the first thing Darlene noticed was that Layla had put framed photographs all around the house. She picked up one of Layla standing next to her daughter in a pink dress.

"It looks very nice in here, Layla." Layla had never looked more radiant, as if she could step onto the big screen without missing a beat. Darlene wondered if she would ever try to make a comeback.

Layla grimaced. "Your eyes are puffy, and you look old." She studied Darlene's face for a moment longer. "How is everything going? Did Grace go to another counseling session? Those are very important. I wish that—" She stopped, sighed. "Anyway, sit down."

Darlene touched the deep circles underneath her eyes as she sat down on the couch. "How old do I look?" Without waiting for an answer, she went on. "I think Grace is doing better. The counselor said it was a good session, and her friend Skylar has been coming around a lot. She's good for Grace too." Darlene laid her head back against the couch. "School starts back next week, though, and I'm worried about that. But I have to trust that God is paving the way for Grace and that she's getting better."

"What about Brad? Things better there?"

"No." Darlene closed her eyes. "We're just distant. It started with all this about Grace, but now we just can't seem to reconnect. And I can't figure out why."

"Men. A difficult bunch." Layla tucked her legs underneath her at the opposite end of the couch. "I think God is giving me a second chance at happiness. I'm not sure why. But I feel so much better. And not just because of Tom. I don't really know what's going to happen with Tom and me, if too much time has passed or not . . . but I feel better inside. Does that make sense?"

Darlene nodded. "Yes," she said, even though she hadn't felt the peace that Layla spoke of in a long time. She missed Brad more than ever. They were civil, respectful of each other, but very quiet. Darlene wanted more than ever to wrap herself up in his arms, in his love, and for things to get back to normal between them. But something inside her kept him at bay. And Brad wasn't making any huge efforts for them to be close again either.

❧

The following Thursday, Darlene was making her weekly Walmart run when she ran into Dave again.

"We've really got to stop meeting like this," he said, shaking his head.

"Hi, Dave."

"I've wanted to call and check on you, but I don't have your cell number. How's Grace?"

"She doesn't say a lot. If you didn't know what was going on, you wouldn't think she had a care in the world. But her counselor said they're making progress, and to the best of our knowledge, she hasn't hurt herself again."

"Well, thank God for that."

Darlene tucked a strand of hair behind her ear, knowing she must look a mess in her gray shorts, faded T-shirt, and flip-flops. "How's Cara?"

"Well . . ." He narrowed his brows.

"Oh no. What's wrong?"

"No, nothing's wrong. Cara just . . . well, she shocked us." Dave smiled.

"How so? Something good, I see."

Dave leaned his head back and to one side. "I think I can show you better than I can tell you. Do you have five minutes after you finish your shopping?"

"Sure."

"I'll meet you at your car, help you unload, then we'll take a drive. It won't take long, and I'd really like to show you what Cara has done."

"Well, I can't imagine, but I can tell that you're very pleased, so I'd like to see." She glanced at the list she was working from. "Two more items, so when you finish up, I'll see you outside."

Ten minutes later, Dave met Darlene at her car. They unloaded all her items, nothing perishable since she preferred to shop at the grocery store for actual food, and once they were done, they walked over two rows to Dave's car.

"Where are we going?" Darlene buckled up as sweat dripped down her face. August in Texas was brutal, and this summer was no exception. She glanced down again at her baggy shorts and T-shirt, then tightened the band on her ponytail. She was a wreck.

"We're going to my house," Dave said as he pulled out of the Walmart parking lot.

Darlene's stomach quivered for a moment, but then she realized that she had nothing to be anxious about. A few minutes later, they pulled up to an iron gate—similar to Layla's—and Dave pushed a remote on his visor. The gate slowly opened. Dave eased his car down the gravel driveway, and Darlene's eyes widened when Dave's house came into view. She should have guessed from his expensive car and clothes, the private fees he paid for Cara to attend The Evans School, the items he'd bought at the gala . . . Dave was wealthy, and his enormous house was evidence of that.

"I got a really great deal on this property since I'm in the business," he said, almost as if apologizing. Darlene wondered what he must have thought about their partly restored old farmhouse. Layla had made several comments about it, things she'd change or add. But that was just Layla. Dave was too nice to have said anything.

In front of her, a massive white-brick house hugged a circular drive with lavish flower beds of summer blooms. The driveway curved around a grassy area sporting a fountain. Its water spilled into a small fishpond.

"Wow. This is beautiful." She let her eyes drift around the grounds. There was a red barn with the traditional white X on the doors. It looked freshly painted. And there was what looked to be a gardening house.

"That was Julie's greenhouse," he said as he pointed to

the structure. "I don't have a green thumb to save my life." He nodded toward the flowers filling the flower beds around the house. "I paid Bargas Landscaping to put those flowers in."

"How many acres do you have?"

"Four hundred and sixty, but most of it is leased to Bill Walsh to run his cattle on. Taking care of me and Cara is about all I can handle." He pointed to his left. "All those Longhorns are Bill's."

Darlene stepped out of the car, feeling even more under-dressed than she did before. Dave was perfectly put together, as always, in his tan khaki shorts and a white button-down polo shirt. *Does the man ever even sweat?* Darlene dabbed at her forehead as she followed him up to the front door.

The entryway was gorgeous, a large chandelier hanging overhead, and to the left was a large granite hutch with a display of pictures. Darlene picked up one of the pictures. "Is this Julie?"

Dave flipped a light on, then walked closer. "Yes."

"She's beautiful." Darlene studied the women's exquisite features, her long dark hair, stunning blue eyes.

Dave's hand landed on Darlene's as he reached for the picture and looked at it for a moment. "Yes, she is." He gazed at the photo for a few moments before giving his head a quick shake. "Come on in. Make yourself at home. I'll get us something cold to drink."

Darlene looked around the massive living room and wondered why he and Cara needed all this space, but the property was in a prime location and beautiful. If he could afford it, why not?

Dave returned a minute later and handed her a glass of iced tea. She took several large gulps before she asked, "So what did you want to show me?"

"Oh. Cara's paintings."

"Paintings?"

Dave motioned for her to follow him down a long hallway. He walked into a room on the left that reminded Darlene of Grace's room. Lots of pink. Hanging on the wall was a picture of a chicken, not painted in traditional colors, but in unusual shades of red and blue speckled with white dots. Darlene knew nothing about art, but if someone had told her the piece was worth fifty thousand at an art gallery, she would have believed them. It wasn't just the vivid colors, but the expression on the chicken's face, almost as if the bird was staring right through her. "Dave, that's amazing. When did she do that?"

"Last week. She still brings home pictures that she's drawn at school, and some of them are really good. So I bought her a starter set of acrylics, and this is what she came up with." He smiled. "I couldn't believe it. So I bought her more paints." He waved with his hand. "Follow me. I've got one in my study and one in my bedroom too."

They walked into a large room with an oak desk, a large bookcase, and a sliding glass door that led out into a garden with another small fountain. Dave pointed to a framed painting of a house that hung on the wall. It was in the same color scheme as the chicken, but this was almost abstract. Darlene studied the painting, surprised at Cara's abilities. Cara's pencil drawings at school had been good, but nothing like this. She'd often heard that autistic children sometimes possessed a special talent, but most did not. Perhaps Cara was just now discovering her hidden passion for art.

"And the last one is in my room."

Darlene followed Dave into his bedroom, which felt a little strange, a little too intimate, like the way she felt at the gala when they were dancing. But she looked where he was pointing. Hanging above his dresser was another framed painting.

She edged closer, unable to take her eyes off it. "Dave . . ." She reached up to touch it, then stopped and just stared in disbelief. She turned to face him. "It's *you.*"

He walked up beside her. "Yeah. Isn't it amazing?"

"Cara has real talent," Darlene said as she looked at the intricate details of Dave's face set against a background of various shades of green. "How did she . . . I mean, wow." She smiled. "Her drawings were always good, but who would have thought she could paint something like this? It's beautiful. Truly amazing."

When he didn't answer, Darlene turned to face him. He was staring at the painting also. "Yeah, I just couldn't believe it." After a while, he snapped out of the trance he was in and turned to face her. "Come on. I'll show you the rest of the house."

Darlene waited until he was closing the door behind them before she glanced at her watch. Brad had asked her to sign for a package today, but she knew UPS always came between four and five. It was just three o'clock.

Four bedrooms, three and a half bathrooms, a sunroom, media room, and game room later, the tour was complete.

"It's gorgeous," she said as they walked back into the living room.

"Thanks. I thought about selling it after Julie died, but this is the only home Cara has ever known, so it just makes sense to keep her where she's comfortable." He motioned for Darlene to sit. "So when does school start?"

"Monday." She took a deep breath. "I'm always glad for summer so I can have time with the kids, then I'm always ready for them to go back to school. But I'm—" She stopped, brought a finger to her lips.

"You're worried about Grace." Dave sat down beside her on the couch, turned to face her.

"Yeah. I am. And I know I've got to quit hovering over her so much." Darlene grinned. "She told me to quit doing that. But it's hard. I want to be with her every second now just to make sure that she doesn't . . ." She raised one shoulder, forced a smile. "I'm sure she'll be fine."

"What about Brad? Things better?"

"Well, it's not any worse." The moment the words slipped from her mouth, she regretted them. Her relationship with Brad was none of Dave's business, yet she was already guilty of involving him in it. "I mean, we're okay."

Dave crossed one leg over the other and rubbed his chin for a few moments. "Marriage is hard, no doubt. But I'd do anything to have one more day to be with Julie, even if we spent the entire day fighting."

His comment put things in perspective. She couldn't imagine her life without Brad.

They were quiet for a few moments, then Dave sat taller. "Hey, I have a proposition for you."

"What?" She blinked her eyes a few times as she felt her cheeks warm.

"Relax, Darlene." He chuckled. "Maybe proposition wasn't the right word. I was going to ask you the next time I saw you if I could bring Cara to see the chickens. She mentioned them for the first time recently, and I thought it would be a nice treat for her. And I think enough time has gone by that she won't cry when she sees you." He paused when Darlene dropped her chin. "I didn't say that to make you feel bad. You know what I mean."

"You can bring Cara to see the chickens anytime." She looked up at him and smiled, relieved to hear that the proposition involved Cara.

"That would be great. Otherwise, I'll be forced to buy some chickens, and I'm not excited about that idea."

Darlene looked at her watch, then stood up. "Oops. I've gotta go. Brad is expecting something from UPS, and maybe I won't miss the delivery guy if we hurry. It's the last few days of summer, and I have a feeling my children might be running around enjoying it and not home to accept the package."

"Sure." Dave rose also, reached into his pocket for his keys, and motioned her toward the door.

❦

Neither Chad's nor Grace's car was in the driveway when Darlene got home, so she hurried inside to the designated note spot on the counter. *Went to Skylar's. Love, Grace.* And *Riding horses at Layla's. Love, Chad and Ansley.* The second note was in Ansley's handwriting, and Darlene cringed at the thought of either of her kids on a horse. To her knowledge, they'd never ridden before, but surely they were riding under Layla's supervision.

But she was glad Grace was at Skylar's. She'd looked by the front door and in the mailbox and hadn't seen anything from UPS. She wondered if she'd missed it. When she'd asked Brad what he was expecting, he'd just said, "Something I ordered online." She suspected it was the gift he'd mentioned when they went to dinner to celebrate her new job.

As she sat down on the couch, she couldn't shake the feeling deep in her gut, and she finally allowed herself to admit it: Dave Schroeder was hitting on her. It had been so long that she almost didn't recognize the signs, but the way he looked at her, talked with her . . . the way he'd held her at the gala.

Guilt wrapped around her so tightly she couldn't breathe. She put her hand on her chest as she stood up and walked across the living room, resolved that she would never allow herself to be alone with him again. If he brought Cara to see the chickens, that was fine, but that was it.

Hurry home, Brad.

She wanted to wrap her arms around him, tell him she was sorry about the words they'd had and the distance between them lately, then spend the rest of the evening together.

But no sooner had the thought crossed her mind than Brad burst through the door. And he began yelling. Loudly. At her.

Chapter Sixteen

"Stop screaming!" Darlene yelled back at him after he'd unloaded on her. "I just got home and got Ansley's note."

"Well, I stopped when I saw her and Chad on my way home, and I told them to get their butts home." He chucked his briefcase on the couch. "They've never ridden horses before, and Chad was running his horse like he was some sort of cowboy or something."

"Was Layla with them?"

"Yeah, she was out there, but those kids shouldn't be on horses. They have no idea what they're doing."

"Brad . . ." She spoke calmly as she followed him into the kitchen. "I'm sure Layla wouldn't put them on a horse unless she felt it was safe." Darlene had counted on that, and in her effort not to be so overprotective, she hadn't felt the need to rush over to Layla's and drag them home.

Brad picked up the note. "They didn't even ask. They just went. Where were you?"

She flinched at his accusatory tone. "I went shopping. I haven't even unloaded the car." She touched his arm. "You heard Layla tell them at dinner the other night that they could ride the horses sometime."

Brad loosened his tie, her hand slipping from his arm. "And did you not hear me tell them that they needed some training before they just jumped on the back of a horse?"

"Well, what better person to train them than Layla?" She made the mistake of smiling.

Brad glared at her. "I'm serious, Darlene. I can't take it if one more thing happens to our children. After all Chad's stuff in Houston, now Grace . . ." He shook his head. "I don't want anything else happening to our kids."

Despite the harsh words they'd exchanged, it was clear to Darlene that Brad was just overwhelmed with worry. Determined to get past the way he was talking to her, she put her arms around his waist and squeezed. "Grace is going to be fine, and nothing is going to happen."

Brad eased her away, took a deep breath. "Where's my package?"

"Oops." Darlene frowned. "Sorry. I'm not sure if I got home in time. But I didn't see a note from UPS or anything. What is it anyway?"

"Nothing important, apparently."

She took a deep breath as her heart thudded a little too hard in her chest, a reminder about why she was late, fueled by the knowledge that the package was possibly a gift for her. "I'm sorry."

When he didn't say anything, Darlene pulled a package of chicken from the refrigerator, then turned when she heard the front door slam. "Someone's home."

Chad and Ansley scurried into the kitchen, and Ansley went straight to the refrigerator and pulled out the tea pitcher. "Want some, Chad?" Without waiting for an answer, Ansley pulled two glasses from the cabinet.

"Man, what a ride!" Chad walked to Ansley's side and

picked up one of the glasses she'd filled. "Thanks." Then he turned to his father. "It's cool, Dad. Really. The horses are super gentle."

Brad's face reddened. "I told you the other night not to get on the horses without me or your mom around, or until you had some training."

Ansley stepped forward. "Layla told us exactly what to do, and it was a blast, Daddy!"

"Yeah, that's the most fun I've had in a long time. The minute she opened the gate to the main pasture, the horses knew to run, and they just took off with us." Chad gulped down the rest of his tea as Brad's face turned a darker shade of red. He pointed a finger at Chad.

"No more riding the horses."

Chad sighed. "Yes, sir."

Then Brad turned to Darlene. "Can you please talk to Layla and tell her not to put my children on those horses again without our permission? I'm sure she heard me say that I didn't want them on the horses yet."

Darlene nodded before Brad walked out of the kitchen, and a few moments later, Grace walked in with Skylar.

"Hi, girls." Darlene smiled. "How was your day?"

"Good," Grace said. "We just hung out at Skylar's and played cards with her dad."

Darlene turned to Skylar. "How's your dad been feeling, Skylar?"

"He's better. And he loves to beat Grace at spades." Skylar smiled, as did Darlene.

"Can you stay for dinner, Skylar?" Darlene rolled the chicken in seasoned bread crumbs and Parmesan cheese.

"No. But thank you. I followed Grace home in my truck. She's—she's loaning me some stuff."

"Let's go upstairs." Grace motioned for Skylar to follow her out of the kitchen. Darlene wondered what Grace was loaning her, but Ansley caught her attention at the refrigerator. She stood with the door open, counting her eggs.

"Fourteen dozen," she said proudly.

Darlene walked to her daughter's side. "Ansley Marie, we are going to eat those eggs. Do you hear me?" Darlene had already been using them secretly to cook with. With four laying hens, they were getting four eggs per day, and Ansley's refusal to eat them was causing a huge backup in the refrigerator.

"That's so stupid, Ansley," Chad said, shaking his head. "Why are you saving those eggs?" Then he walked closer to her. "I boiled a dozen of them just last week, and Mom uses them all the time for cooking."

Ansley narrowed her eyes at him. "You know what, Chad? You're just mean." She walked out of the kitchen.

"Why do you do that to her?" Darlene asked after Ansley was out of the room.

Chad shrugged. "Because it's retarded the way she saves them."

Darlene spun around. "Don't use that word, Chad." Then she frowned. "You need a haircut before school starts."

"Yeah, I know." He grabbed a banana from the counter, peeled it, and took a big bite.

Darlene put the chicken in the oven. "I wonder what Grace is loaning to Skylar." From the little Darlene had gathered from Grace, Skylar and her father lived modestly. Darlene suspected they struggled due to his health problems and not being able to work much.

"I hope it's some clothes," Chad said, chuckling as he left the kitchen.

⧜

Brad fluffed his pillow, then flipped channels on the TV, finally settling on a documentary about space, one of his favorite subjects. Something to keep his mind off of life and the way he'd been acting lately. He'd been so irritable around Darlene, his kids, and his coworkers.

But even as he tried to listen to the show, his mind kept drifting. He wanted to be a better man, and all this worry was just causing him to act like a jerk. Plus, he'd never kept a secret from Darlene the way he was now. Guilt filled his days, and it definitely carried over into his interactions with his family.

All he wanted to do was to take his wife in his arms and love her the way she deserved to be loved, but he doubted she even wanted to be around him after the way he'd been behaving. He repositioned himself and tuned back in to the show. The narrator was discussing a new black hole found in a far-off galaxy. That's how he felt. Like he was in a black hole in a far-off galaxy, and there was no light, no escape.

He looked up when Darlene walked out of the bathroom and toward the bed in a short white nightgown. As she edged toward the bed, her blond hair flowing to her shoulders and still damp from her shower, he could smell her long before she reached him. He breathed in the scent of lavender as she sat down on the bed beside him, and he just stared at her for a moment. How was it possible that she was even more beautiful than the day he married her? He knew he was a lucky man. She climbed into bed, pressed her body next to his, then leaned up and kissed him tenderly on the mouth.

She smiled. "Who do you love?"

Brad swallowed hard, a knot the size of a golf ball in his throat. "You, baby," he managed to croak out in a raspy voice.

She kissed him again, and Brad pulled her closer. He could feel her heart beating against his chest, and he wondered if she could feel his accelerated pulse. As much as he could, he shifted his attention to his wife, but in the back of his mind, he couldn't stop thinking about the secret he was keeping from her.

⨒

Friday morning, the kids were still sleeping at nine o'clock in the morning, but Darlene could see Layla from her front porch, riding her horse in a far pasture. She slipped on her tennis shoes, then grabbed her keys. A few minutes later, she was turning into Layla's driveway.

"You look like you just crawled out of bed," Layla said as she dismounted from her horse.

"Leave it to you to always make me feel my best, Layla." Darlene sipped from a cup of coffee she'd brought with her. "Got a minute?"

"Uh-oh. What's wrong?" Layla frowned, one hand on her hip. "You have that look."

"What look?"

"That serious look you get sometimes." Layla sighed. "Let's go in. It's hot out here already."

Darlene followed Layla in, all the way to the kitchen. She waited while Layla drank some water, then they both sat down at the kitchen table.

"Brad was upset that the kids were riding horses here yesterday when he'd told them not to."

Layla pointed a finger at Darlene. "I asked those kids if they had permission to ride the horses. Ansley didn't say anything, but Chad said it was fine with you." She rolled her eyes. "I should have known better after the way Brad reacted the other night. But you know, these horses are gentle. There couldn't be finer animals for them to learn on, and I was right there with them."

"I know, but my kids wouldn't know what to do if one of them got spooked or something." She sipped her coffee. "But Brad's just been in a bad mood anyway. I guess he's been worried about Grace, and we hadn't been getting along very well."

"Things better now?"

Darlene recalled their time together the night before. "Yes. Things are much better." She decided to change the subject. "I haven't seen Tom's car here."

"He's out of town on business, but he's called." A soft smile lit Layla's face.

"I hope things work out for the two of you. I really do."

Layla shrugged. "They might. They might not."

Darlene waited a few moments to see if Layla would elaborate. When she didn't, she asked, "And that's okay with you?"

Layla tapped her finger to her mouth a few times. "Yes, it is. Either way. We've talked a lot. About everything. And that's something we didn't do after Marissa died. I guess it was too raw back then." She paused. "Oh, there were tears, for both of us. But there were things that needed to be said, and I think that whatever happens, we'll stay close." She smiled, shook her head. "You know, I prayed for God to bring Tom back. And He did. But I never expected things to turn out this way. I know that I'll be fine if we don't get back together. And Tom will be okay too."

Darlene touched the dove pendant around her neck. "You sound different . . . I mean, about everything."

Layla smiled. "It's been a long time since I felt the peacefulness that a relationship with God can bring. I've missed it."

They were quiet for a minute.

"Can I . . . ask you something?" Darlene ran her finger around the rim of her coffee cup. "It's about Dave."

Layla frowned. "Is he hitting on you?"

Darlene sat taller. "Why would you ask that?"

Layla raised her chin, lifting one eyebrow. "Because I saw the way he was looking at you at the gala."

Darlene shrugged. "I don't know. I mean, I think maybe. I went to his house to see some paintings that Cara had done recently, after I'd run into him at Walmart." Darlene scratched her head. "I don't know, Layla. Sometimes, the way he looks at me . . . I just get this feeling. Maybe I'm wrong."

"Stay away from him. You and Brad have a great thing going. Don't mess it up."

Darlene was insulted. "I would never do anything to mess it up."

"Never say never," Layla said as she stood up, walked to the sink, and filled her glass up with water.

"No, cheating is just not something Brad or I would do. It just wouldn't happen."

"Then why are you even telling me this? Are you attracted to Dave?"

"No!"

Layla sat back down. "It's okay if you are. He's a handsome man. Doesn't mean you have to act on it."

Memories of dancing with Dave at the gala flooded her mind, along with the tender way he treated her in Walmart, the way he looked at her in his bedroom. Yes, he was handsome, but she was never tempted for one second. Uncomfortable a few times, but never tempted.

"Of course he's nice looking. But I don't see him like that." She stood up. "Never mind. I shouldn't have said anything. He wants to bring Cara over to see the chickens from time to time."

Layla grunted, grinning. "I bet he does. Probably while Brad's at work and the kids are in school. They start school next week, right?"

"Yes. And, Layla, quit saying things like that. I'm going home."

She should have known that Layla would react exactly as she had. Problem was, Darlene was having a hard time arguing with her. Layla followed her to the door. Darlene turned around before she left. "See you at church Sunday?"

"You betcha. I told you, me and God are on good terms these days." Layla gave a thumbs-up. "Plus, I don't want to miss pancakes." She frowned for a few moments. "Is Brad going to still be mad at me?"

"No. He won't be mad. Just don't let the kids ride the horses for a while. I think Grace is doing better, and he and I are doing better, so hopefully he won't be as cranky."

"I just don't think my babies would ever throw your babies. Those horses have never thrown anyone."

"I know. And I'm sure he'll come around. The whole thing with Grace scared us both."

"But you think she's stopped cutting?"

"I don't think she's done it any more, and her counselor says they are making progress."

"Good." Layla waved. "See you Sunday."

❧

It started off just like any other Sunday. Church at eleven, followed by pancakes. Layla had sat with them at church, stayed for brunch, then hurried off to pick up Tom at the airport in Houston that afternoon.

Darlene agreed to kitchen cleanup by herself so all the kids could go shopping for last-minute school supplies in the afternoon. After a lengthy argument about whether or not Chad or Grace would drive, Ansley flipped a coin. Grace won, but Darlene wondered if Ansley rigged the toss since she disliked Chad's loud music as much as Grace.

She wiped the counters, dried her hands, and went to find Brad. He'd been quiet, but not nearly as cranky as he'd been the past couple of weeks. This seemed like a good opportunity to sneak in some time to themselves, maybe even drive to Brenham to go see a movie.

After checking around the house and calling his name, she figured he must be piddling in the barn, or the "Man Cave" as he called it. She was almost to the barn door when she heard him talking. No one else was home, so she knew he was on his phone. She was just about to turn the corner and go through the barn door when she heard Brad's strained voice.

"I'm telling you, Barbara . . . if my wife finds out about this, my marriage is over."

Chapter Seventeen

Darlene's white tennis shoes were rooted to the ground as her thoughts swirled in a thunderous tornado.

It was a beautiful, sunny day, birds chirping, cows mooing in the distance, and enough breeze to gently ring the wind chimes on the front porch. A beautiful day for anyone whose world hadn't just slipped off its axis.

She stood perfectly still. Listening.

"Fine. That's fine. I'll talk to you tomorrow."

She heard Brad click his cell phone off, but she still couldn't move. Taking a deep breath, she tried to assemble her thoughts. Should she confront him? Would he just lie to her? How long had it been going on? Who was she? Was Brad going to leave her?

Seeing a movie or spending quality time together no longer held the appeal it had a few minutes ago. She took a deep breath and edged forward. Until now, trust had never been an issue between them. That was one thing they'd always held sacred, and despite Brad's long hours at work, she'd never once suspected him of cheating.

But if he was, she wasn't going to play all her cards right here and now. She had children to think about, her life, their future. A future without him? She swallowed hard. There had to be some other explanation. She replayed his words over and over in her mind. *"I'm telling you, Barbara . . . if my wife finds out about this, my marriage is over."*

Hatred raged inside of her toward a woman she'd never met. And toward Brad.

She shook her head, despite the tears building in her eyes. There had to be an explanation. *Not Brad.*

She jumped when he walked out of the barn.

"Hey. Whatcha doing?" He walked up to her, his cell phone in hand.

"Just lookin' for you." She put a hand to her forehead and blocked the sun, her heart racing. "Everything okay?" She glanced at his cell phone.

"Oh." He lifted the phone, glanced at it. "Yeah, just work stuff." He dropped his arm to his side again. "All the kids leave in Grace's car?"

"Yeah. It's just us." She forced a smile, wishing her heart would stop pounding against her chest. It was everything she could do not to cry. Or punch him in the gut.

"I need to go run some errands. We need more chicken feed, and one of the Longhorns busted the fence again. I need to fix it before Layla sees it." He started walking toward the house, so Darlene got in step with him, looking at her first and only love. *This can't be happening.*

She recalled her conversation with Layla. *"Never say never,"* Layla had said when Darlene said she and Brad would never cheat on each other. She finally turned toward him. "Okay. I've got things to take care of around here."

Gritting her teeth, she followed him up the porch steps and into the house. The Brad who didn't cheat on her would have jumped at this opportunity for them to spend some time alone. Cheating Brad couldn't wait to get out of the house.

Ten minutes later, her husband pulled out of the driveway, and Darlene got to work. She went to her computer, logged into their cell phone account, then quickly pulled up the most recent activity for Brad's number, her hands shaking the entire time. She'd never looked at his phone bill, and despite her suspicions, she felt like a spy. She put her head in her hands and cried.

Please, God. Don't let this be happening. Please don't let me find anything bad.

After a few minutes, she lifted her head, sniffled, and decided she had to know. She scanned the numbers, starting with the most recent call, which ended with 2481, and according to the time, it would have been the call to Barbara. She ran her finger down the screen.

Covering her mouth with her other hand, her eyes teared up again as 2481 stuck out all down the page. They'd talked one . . . two . . . three . . . four . . . seven times yesterday. All were short conversations except for the last one. Thirty-two minutes.

Darlene searched her brain to recall what she and Brad did yesterday.

It was Saturday. She'd taken Grace and Ansley shopping for school clothes.

She tapped her finger to her chin. Brad had stayed home with Chad.

Scanning the rest of the page, the woman's number was scattered in between other calls, but there were several per day.

After an hour, Darlene had traced the calls back for about two months, most of them made by Brad during the workday. She closed the computer, cried again, and wondered if maybe Brad was trying to end it with this woman. His voice on the phone with Barbara had been harsh. The same tone he'd been using with Darlene—until recently.

Lord, I can't get past this.

She closed her eyes and brought both hands to her chest. Something Layla once said rang in her ears.

"When God decides your life is going too good, He will find a way to humble you, bring you back down to earth, even if it means destroying you. It's what He does when you sin. He takes, takes, takes . . . everything that means anything to you. Then He looks down on you with no mercy, even though you beg on bended knee for Him to stop the pain."

Darlene knew that wasn't true. That wasn't how God worked. And Darlene was pretty sure Layla would take back everything she'd said, comments that were the result of bitterness and too much wine that evening.

Even though Darlene knew it wasn't true, she couldn't help but think of it anyway, and she wondered what she'd done to possibly deserve this. Wasn't she a good enough wife to Brad?

What about Grace? How could she have missed the signs that her daughter was in trouble? Maybe she was too self-absorbed, always looking for ways to fulfill her own needs and not noticing her family's.

Please, Lord. I'm begging You. Please don't let this be true about Brad. I'm praying there is another explanation. I couldn't bear it without him in my life. And please, dear God, heal Grace of any pain she might not know how to express. Heal my family, Lord.

∽

Monday morning, Chad was glad to be back at school. That's where the girls were, although the first girl he ran into wouldn't have been his first choice. He was just closing his locker when Cindy walked up. She was still just as pretty as she'd always been with her big blue eyes and long blond hair. Her tan looked good too. But other than that, Cindy Weaver didn't interest him one bit.

"How was the rest of your summer?" She swung her hair over her shoulder and smiled. It was one of those no-teeth smiles that girls used sometimes when they were mad.

"Pretty good. What about you?"

"Great. I partied until I could party no more." She lifted her shoulders, dropped them slowly. "And you missed it."

"Uh, you know . . ." Then, just in time, he saw Grace. He'd know those pink jeans of hers anywhere, and she always wore them with the same pink and white blouse. "Hey, I gotta go. There's my sister. I need to tell her something." He didn't wait for a response as he hurried down the hallway, edging his way in between all the other kids hurrying to class. "Grace! Wait up!"

His sister didn't turn around. Typical. He picked up his speed, careful not to run, since Mr. Radcliffe was up ahead. "Grace! Are you deaf?" He grabbed her by the arm and swung her around, and—he thought he might fall over from shock. *Skylar?*

Chad couldn't believe the transformation. She was wearing Grace's clothes. Her hair was blond like Grace's, and her face didn't have all that black stuff on it. And no nose ring. She looked . . . normal. She looked . . . beautiful. He forced his jaw up, but all he could do was stare at her.

"Cat got your tongue?" Skylar adjusted a stack of books up on her hip.

"You—you look . . . Wow." Chad blinked his eyes a few times. This new look took her from friend of Grace's and friend of the family to something Chad couldn't quite wrap his mind around.

"I needed a change," she said as she raised an eyebrow. "Don't make a big deal about it."

Don't make a big deal. Every dude that walked by was checking her out, and Chad had a sudden urge to punch them all. "Okay . . ." He scratched his cheek, unable to take his eyes from her. Grace had told him that Skylar would be graduating early, which made Chad wonder if they might be in some of the same classes. "Where you headed, what class?"

"Ms. Johnson. English."

Thank You, God. "Me too. I'll walk with you."

Skylar started walking, so Chad got in step with her. He wondered if he should ask to carry her books, but that seemed dumb. He wasn't even sure if guys did that except in the movies.

"Can you please quit staring at me?" Skylar said through gritted teeth without looking at him.

Chad chuckled. "Skylar . . ." He shook his head. "I just really don't think I can."

She turned toward him and smiled.

The school year was starting off with a bang.

Oh yeah!

❧

Grace endured all the first-day-of-school questions her mother fired at her, and Ansley and Chad also received an ample amount of questioning. That was cool. Mom was just being Mom, wanting details about how her kids were doing. Ansley did most of the talking throughout the meal, half the time with her mouth full. Twice Grace told her to swallow before she talked, but that was just Ansley. She was excited, and it was hard not to be excited along with her. Turns out, her little sister had all the teachers she was hoping for, early lunch, and Tim Zimmermann in her first-period class. They'd all been hearing about Tim Zimmermann since they'd moved here.

"Uh, Grace . . ." Chad, also with a full mouth, looked at Grace and grinned. "You've been keeping a secret."

Grace finished chewing, and unlike her siblings, she swallowed before she spoke. "What?" Then she grinned. She knew what Chad was talking about. Although, after seeing Skylar and Chad huddled together after school, she wasn't sure how she felt about it. It seemed weird.

Chad glanced back and forth between their parents. "You should see Skylar. You wouldn't believe it. I mean, she's wearing normal clothes, her hair is blond, none of that dark makeup on her face." He focused on their father. "Dad, she's a knockout."

"Skylar's a sweet girl. She was just finding her way with all that goth stuff. Don't you think, Grace? What made her change?" Mom paused. "I guess being around you, maybe."

Grace shrugged, but she was pretty sure she knew what ultimately led Skylar to an overhaul. She'd asked about Chad a few times over the summer, and about Cindy, his ex. Grace could tell Skylar liked Chad, though she had no idea why. He was a slob, played his music way too loud, and his car was always filled with empty soda cans and trash. He usually needed a haircut, and he fell for girls like Cindy Weaver.

Grace had just been so glad to see Skylar ditch that outdated goth look that Skylar's motivation hadn't been important at the time. But if Skylar and Chad started dating or something . . . that would be too weird.

Something else was going on too. Grace could feel it, but she couldn't put her finger on it. Mom had served one of her best first-day-of-school dinners, something she knew everyone liked—tacos, beans, and rice. She was asking all the right questions, but something was wrong. Her eyes were swollen like maybe she'd been crying, and although she was trying to make sure everyone else was happy, which was Mom's way, she wasn't smiling much. She just seemed . . . down.

Dad wasn't much better. A for-sure sign that their father was worried about something was when he didn't eat much. He'd barely finished one taco and hadn't touched his beans and rice.

She hoped they weren't still worried about her. Tomorrow was another counseling session with Dr. Brooks after school. Grace liked the doctor okay, and she'd been trying to do what the doctor wanted. They'd been working on other ways Grace could handle her frustrations, and Grace had told her that she no longer had the urge to cut.

That's what everyone wanted to hear anyway.

⤝⤞

That night, Darlene waited until Brad was in the shower before she began searching his drawers, his briefcase, anywhere she could think of to find out more information about Barbara. She felt like a criminal, even though she wasn't the one who'd possibly broken their marriage vows. Every time she thought about what Brad had said to that woman, she felt a pain in her heart.

What had he turned her into? A pathetic sneak looking for clues to his infidelity? She hadn't been able to look at him all evening. Partly because she wanted to poke his eyes out, but also because she loved him with all her heart. She knew she would forgive him for anything, if he would just be honest with her, but she didn't know how to bring up the subject. And she didn't really want to without knowing more. Tomorrow she'd talk to Layla, if Tom's car was gone.

She closed her eyes. *Why is this happening, Lord? Why?*

It was all she could do to pray tonight. She'd always heard that God wouldn't give you more than you could handle. When she'd walked into Grace's room, with the blood, the cuts on her baby girl—at that moment, she was sure she couldn't handle anything else. Never in a million years would she have thought Brad would do something like this. And every time she tried to reconcile her thoughts, she wondered if maybe she was wrong. But what other reason could there be for his sharp tone with that woman, and his saying that if Darlene found out, their marriage would be over? And what about the many phone calls every day? Tears welled in her eyes, and she turned away as Brad walked from the bathroom, his hair wet, a white towel around his waist.

"You okay, baby?" Brad opened his drawer for some under-wear, and Darlene was glad he wasn't looking directly at her. She was already ready for bed. Dabbing at her eyes, she rolled onto her side, facing away from him.

"Yeah. Just tired."

"Me too. Long day."

She heard him slip into his boxers and a T-shirt, and he crawled into bed. While he flipped the channels on the television, Darlene fought the sobs in her throat. How could he just lie there beside her, like everything was normal?

Darlene had never felt more abnormal in her life, like she was in someone else's bad dream.

❦

The next morning, Brad dressed for work, ate a quick bowl of cereal, and kissed Darlene before he walked out the door. Just like he'd always done. She wanted to ask him about Barbara so badly that her stomach hurt. Maybe having it all out on the table would be better than the wondering, speculating— the horrible visions in her head. Or . . . would the truth be so terrible she'd never get over it? What if she confronted him and he wanted a divorce? What if he was in love with this woman?

The kids left for school shortly after Brad, and Darlene forced herself to do the household tasks that morning. But nothing could distract her from what she'd overheard. She looked out the window and across the pasture at Layla's house—again. Tom's car was still there, and she didn't want to intrude. She was happy for Layla and hoped things worked out for her and Tom, but right now she sure needed Layla's blunt honesty. Layla would tell her what to do.

Finally, around noon, Tom's car was gone. Layla might have gone with him somewhere, but Darlene grabbed her cell phone to find out. When Layla answered, Darlene hesitantly asked if she was home. When Layla said yes, Darlene invited herself over. Fifteen minutes later, she was on Layla's couch telling her everything.

"It's terrible that I went through his phone records and his briefcase and everything, isn't it?" Darlene laid her head back against Layla's couch and closed her eyes, waiting for Layla to tell her that she was perfectly justified.

"I don't understand why you don't just ask him about it." Layla crossed one leg over the other in the chair across from her. Once again, she looked like the movie star she once was, dressed in a bright-red halter sundress with lipstick that matched the dress perfectly. Her hair was long and loose below her shoulders, and she kicked one of her bare feet back and forth, the color of her toenails the same color red as her fingernails. Darlene didn't think she could ever look that glamorous, and it seemed to come so naturally to Layla. Even when Layla was in her blue jeans, work shirt, and boots, she was beautiful. And today, there was an aura of calm surrounding her. Her voice was softer, she spoke slower, and her movements weren't as sharp and quick as they usually were. Darlene felt terrible for dumping all this on her friend, but Layla was all she had. Now, more than ever.

"I'm afraid of what he'll tell me," she finally said, then swallowed hard.

Layla looked at her long and hard. "Tom cheated on me once, a few years after Marissa was born."

"So what happened?"

Layla shook her head. "Biggest fight we ever had. I threw things, punched him in the chest, and cried until I didn't have any more tears." She paused. "Then I forgave him."

Darlene raised an eyebrow. "Just like that? You forgave him?"

"We lived a crazy life back then." She gazed off for a few moments before she looked back at Darlene. "Opportunities to be bad were abundant. But I knew deep down that Tom loved me, and I wanted us to stay a family, to raise Marissa together. And no . . . I didn't forgive him just like that. It was hard to trust him for a long time." She paused again. "I punished him for probably longer than I should have, but . . . eventually we grew back into the couple we'd been before. Then . . ." Layla got up and walked to the hutch against the wall. She picked up a picture of Marissa. "Then I just couldn't look at him after Marissa died. I blamed him. I blamed me. I blamed God. And he did the same thing."

"But things are good now?" Darlene wondered if she and Brad would fall apart and eventually make things right. She wasn't sure she'd survive all that.

Layla brought the picture to her heart, pressed it there for a while, then put it back on the hutch. She turned to Darlene and slowly walked back to the chair and sat down. "Yes. Things are good. It doesn't mean we will get back together, but we are in a good place."

Darlene nodded. "So what do I do about me and Brad?"

"Talk to him."

"I can't. I'm afraid." She blinked back tears.

"What are you most afraid of?"

She thought about the question. "That . . . that he loves someone else."

"I doubt that. I thought you guys had a good marriage."

"Everything's been great, not perfect. I mean, we've had our moments when we're tired, stressed about money, kids, or something. But overall, yeah . . . we've had a very good marriage. I've always thought of Brad as my best friend, and I can't stand to have this between us, and . . ." She stopped when she started to cry. "I'm sorry, Layla. I just don't know who else to talk to."

"Yes, you do." Layla smiled. "You know exactly who to talk to."

"I guess I have to confront Brad about this." She blinked her eyes a few times, covering her mouth with her hand.

"That's not who I meant. If you hadn't given me a little push to pray again, I don't think I would have ever gotten the strength to press forward, to believe that it was okay to be happy again. Pray about it, Darlene."

"I have been." It was the truth, but Darlene felt like she was detached somehow from God, and she couldn't figure out why. "You said one time that when God thinks our life is too good, He humbles us by taking something away from us, and—"

"Oh, good grief. Forget all that, Darlene. Really. I was so angry at God, and a bottle of wine usually fueled my rage enough to blame everything on Him. I shouldn't have said all that, and you shouldn't take it to heart."

"I need you to tell me what to do." Darlene threw her head against the back of the couch again. "Should I just talk to him, get it over with?"

"I just told you what I think you should do. I think you should pray about it."

Frustrated, she got off the couch. She wanted Layla to lay it out for her, a plan, something besides the obvious. Darlene had been praying, about her and Brad, about Grace. Something wasn't clicking, and she needed some direction. "I better go."

"Oh, don't be mad." Layla stood up. "I know you came here for me to tell you what to do, and a few weeks ago, I'd have probably told you to string that boy up by his . . ." She took a deep breath. "But life is too short."

Then Layla did the unexpected. She walked over to Darlene and hugged her, and she let Darlene cry in her arms.

Despite the chaos in her life, Darlene knew one thing for sure: Layla was her friend, and she was thankful for that.

Now she needed to go home and get ready for the inevitable.

She had to confront Brad.

Chapter Eighteen

Brad pulled into the driveway, hoping the package from UPS had been delivered today. And he was glad that Barbara seemed to be listening to him, to his way of thinking. The woman was going to destroy him if he wasn't careful. He hurried up the porch steps. Darlene was in the kitchen.

"UPS show up today?" He kissed her on the cheek. "Mmm . . . smells good in here."

"No. I was at Layla's for a while around noon, but I've been home the rest of the day, and no deliveries." She pulled plates out of the cabinet as Brad helped himself to a glass of tea.

"Well, maybe tomorrow. I know it was back-ordered, so I'm not sure exactly when to expect it."

As she laid the plates on the table, Brad noticed her red and swollen eyes for the first time. He edged closer to her. "What's wrong? Did everything go okay at Grace's counseling session?" Brad had been praying a lot for Grace, and his heart raced as he waited for Darlene to answer.

"I spoke with Dr. Brooks after Grace's session, and she thinks Grace is making progress."

Brad breathed a sigh of relief. "Thank goodness." After he took another sip of his tea, he leaned down, touched Darlene on the arm. "Then why do you look like you've been crying? You okay?"

She eased away from him, opened the oven, and pulled out a casserole. "I'm okay. Just tired."

After she put the dish on the table, Brad walked up behind her and put his arms around her waist. He kissed her on the neck. "Maybe we can go to bed early."

"Maybe."

There was no mistaking the way she tensed up.

Darlene had been distant the past few days, but he knew better than to push his wife. She'd talk to him when she was ready.

Three days later, Darlene still hadn't confronted Brad. Talking to him might end everything she'd cherished and known to be true throughout her entire marriage. She wasn't ready to face a reality that might shatter her whole life. Her stomach was a wreck, but she thought that not knowing was better than what Brad's reaction might be. Would he adamantly deny being involved with Barbara? Would he say it was over? Would he lie to her?

If Brad lied to her, she would know. He was a terrible liar. When she'd guessed her Christmas present last year, Brad had looked her in the eye and denied getting her the pearl necklace she'd pointed out a few weeks earlier at a jewelry store in the mall. She'd just smiled and let him think that it would be a surprise. Brad loved to buy her gifts, but he never could keep a secret.

She sat down on the couch, stared at the ham sandwich she'd made herself, and forced a bite down.

Apparently Brad had been successful about keeping his secret about Barbara, so maybe he was a better liar than she'd thought. She put the sandwich on the plate beside her as she eased her feet up on the coffee table. Her house was the cleanest it had been in years. Staying busy had kept her mind occupied, but she'd run out of things to clean. And with the kids in school, it was quiet enough for her mind to wander to bad places. *Is Brad having lunch with Barbara right now? Are they in a sleazy hotel somewhere? Or maybe Brad ended it?*

She took a few more bites of her sandwich before she went to the kitchen and tossed it in the trash, knowing she needed to do something. As she looked around for ways to occupy her time, she heard a car coming up the driveway.

Peeking out the window, she watched Dave and Cara step out of Dave's car. Darlene pulled off her small loop earrings, tucked her dove pendant inside her T-shirt, and wrestled with her wedding ring until it slipped off her finger. She put everything on the hutch by the front door and walked onto the porch. Blocking the sun with her hand, she called out as friendly a hello as she could muster up.

"I hope it's okay, but The Evans School closed early today when the air-conditioning stopped working, and Cara and I were wondering if we could visit the chickens." Dave waved, and as always, he was perfectly put together in navy shorts and a yellow, collared shirt. Darlene glanced down at her blue jean shorts, white flip-flops, and her pink T-shirt with the Nike emblem on it. She'd had the T-shirt for as long as she could remember. It was a favorite, but it was as raggedy a thing as she owned. Why did Dave always catch her looking like this? She twisted her hair up on her head and secured it with a band she always kept on her wrist during the hot summer months.

Her short ponytail wasn't necessarily going to improve her appearance, but it was over a hundred degrees outside.

"Of course you can visit the chickens." Darlene walked slowly toward Dave and Cara. "Nice to see you." She turned to Cara and smiled. "Hello, Cara."

Cara didn't move toward her but instead pointed toward the chicken coop. "Ansley's chickens."

"Yes. We can go see Ansley's chickens."

Dave pushed his dark sunglasses up on his head. "I hope you don't mind us just stopping by. It was a last-minute thought since we found ourselves with a free afternoon. I looked up your home phone number and tried to call, but my cell kept losing service, and I couldn't get the call to go through."

"Cell service is touch and go out here, and I don't mind at all." Darlene welcomed the distraction. "Now, you know I'm not a big fan of these birds." She smiled as she motioned for them to follow her to the chicken coop. "So I might not be venturing in there."

"Oh no. It's all right. We can just look at the chickens from outside. You don't have to open the cage door." Dave was holding Cara's hand as they approached the birds. Two chickens were running around, and the others were perched in their roosting boxes.

Cara let go of Dave's hand and ran to the cages. "Feed Ansley's chickens!" She bounced on her heels as she pointed to the chickens. Cara looked so pretty in her red shorts, white blouse, and flat white sandals. The Evans School was open year-round, so a day off was a nice treat for Cara.

"Cara, I don't think we need to go inside," Dave said as he and Darlene walked up beside her.

"Feed Ansley's chickens," Cara repeated, this time looking up at Darlene.

"It's fine with me, if you don't think the chickens will scare her. I don't like when they start flapping and running around. Ansley doesn't mind when they do that, but Cara might."

"Maybe just for a minute, Cara." Dave leaned down and untwisted the piece of wire that kept the small gate closed. Cara walked inside, and as Darlene had feared, the chickens began to get worked up, flapping their wings and scurrying around. Darlene stayed outside while Dave followed Cara in. Cara didn't seem bothered as she moved about the chickens, giggling every time one of them made a noise or raced in front of her.

As Cara moved to the back of the pen, the unthinkable happened. Four of the chickens darted in front of Dave, past Darlene, and out the door. Knowing how Ansley felt about her beloved chickens, Darlene jogged across the yard to round them up. "Back! Back!" she yelled as she tried to corral the birds back toward the cage. It was one thing for Ansley to let the birds run loose occasionally, but Ansley also had a system to get them back in their pens.

Out of the corner of her eye, Darlene saw Dave pull Cara out of the coop, even though she screamed and tried to resist. He locked the door so the other two birds were secure. "I've got to help Darlene get Ansley's chickens, Cara. Don't move." He pointed a finger at her, but Cara scurried about, laughing and sending the chickens racing even farther away. One large brown hen disappeared behind the farmhouse.

"Darlene, I am so sorry," Dave said as he dropped his sunglasses back on his face. Then he ran to the left, and Darlene ran to the right, both of them waving their arms and making *shoo* noises as they tried to coax the chickens toward the coop. But every time one got close, Cara jumped up and down and scared it back in the other direction.

Ten minutes later, Darlene and Dave were both soaking wet

from sweat, and only one chicken had ventured back toward the cage. Darlene stopped and tried to catch her breath. Dave took her cue and also took a break.

"Are we doing this right?"

Darlene laughed. "Probably not."

Dave walked closer to her and eyed all the loose chickens kicking at the grass a few yards away. "Should we lure them with some feed in a pan?"

"That might work." Darlene went into the pen and picked up an empty feed pan. She walked around the corner to the barn and dipped the pan into a large feed bag. She jumped when she felt Dave brush up beside her. He was dripping in sweat like she was, and with only a small amount of light shining in through the barn window, she watched him run a hand over his forehead. Then he took the pan from her.

"Here, let me do that." He reached down in front of her, so close his chest brushed against her leg as he scooped deep into the almost-empty bag. When he lifted up, his face was within inches of hers. Sweat rolled down her cheeks as she locked eyes with him. She could hear Cara laughing around the corner, and she studied Dave's face. So serious, gazing back at her. She thought about the tenderness he'd always showed her, and for reasons she would analyze to death in the near future, she leaned her face closer to his. He didn't move as she leaned up and kissed him lightly on the mouth. When she eased away, Dave's eyes clung to hers, searching her face. He cupped her face in his hands, and even though she pulled against him, his lips were persuasive, passionate, and as he explored her mouth in a way that she knew was forbidden, she kissed him back.

When she finally pulled away from him, he whispered her name. "I've wanted to do that for as long as I can remember." He reached for her again, but Darlene backed up, a full realization of what she'd done slamming into her like a truck that wouldn't stop crushing her. She backed up even farther.

"You have to go. Now." She swallowed hard, Brad's face everywhere.

"Darlene, it's okay," Dave said, holding a hand out to her as he eased forward. "This was bound to happen, and—"

"No . . . It was *not* bound to happen. And it shouldn't have happened. I'm sorry. I don't know . . ." Her eyes started to burn with tears. No matter what Brad had done, two wrongs didn't make a right, and Darlene couldn't stand the person inhabiting her body right now. "Please go."

"Sweetie . . ."

"Don't, Dave. Don't call me that." She stared at the ground, not wanting to look up at him. He put a hand on her arm.

"I'll go. But please, Darlene. Don't beat yourself up about this. It was just a kiss."

Darlene knew it was more than just a simple kiss, and she was lost in a river of guilt. "I know," she said, for lack of knowing what else to say and not wanting Dave to think it was anything more than a kiss. "It just shouldn't have happened. I shouldn't have . . ." *I shouldn't have initiated it.*

Dave moved closer, and Darlene could feel her heart pounding against her chest. She didn't move when he leaned down and kissed her on the forehead. Instead, she started to cry. He pulled her into his arms. "Sweet Darlene. It's okay. We didn't do anything." He eased her away, touched her wet cheek with his thumb. "But I'd be lying if I said I didn't think about you all the time." He kissed her on the cheek.

"I can't do this." *I don't want to do this.* She backed away. "Please tell Cara bye for me. I need you to go. I'll worry about the chickens later."

Dave didn't move for a few moments.

"Please, Dave."

He held up a hand. "Okay. I'm leaving. But, Darlene, I'm here if you need anything."

She nodded, knowing that what she needed was a swift kick in the butt. She waited until she heard Dave's car pull out of the driveway before she left the barn.

It took her two hours to round up the chickens and get them back in their cage, and the entire time, she pictured the look on Brad's face if he found out what she'd just done.

Intermingled with that image was the image of Brad kissing another woman, possibly more. *What is happening to us?*

Once all the birds were secure, she slid down the outside of the chicken cage, put her head in her hands, and cried. Good Darlene would be praying right now, but Bad Darlene had nothing to say to God. Shame engulfed her, and she wished God couldn't see her, couldn't hear her thoughts, couldn't be as disappointed with her as she was with herself.

But He knew.

And she'd never felt more alone in her life.

Dave waited until Cara was settled at home, coloring at the kitchen table, before he allowed himself to think about what had happened with Darlene. Something had possessed her to kiss him first, but she'd clearly regretted it. However, his thoughts didn't end there. She'd kissed him back, passionately, the way a wife kisses her husband. And that left him feeling both hopeful and ashamed. He'd never kissed another man's wife. Nor had he ever wanted another man's wife. He dialed her home phone number, but as he'd expected an answering machine picked up. He didn't leave a message.

As he paced the kitchen, he thought about Julie and wondered if she was looking down from heaven, shaking her head. Worse yet, God knew what he'd done. But for all his knowledge of those facts, he knew that he wouldn't have changed anything. The feel of Darlene's mouth on his, and the way she'd responded to him, left him craving more. Husband or no husband.

Grace sat down beside Skylar at lunch, like she had since the first day of school this year, despite the looks she got from Glenda and her other former lunch buddies. But those girls weren't her friends. Skylar was her best friend.

When Chad slid into a chair beside Skylar and set his plate down, Grace's muscles tensed.

"What are you doing here, Chad? Go sit with that dumb group of guys you hang out with." Grace glared at him, then glanced at Skylar, who just smiled.

"Shut up, Grace." He turned to Skylar. "I got tickets to Festival Hill for tomorrow. There's a percussion performance that's supposed to be really cool. Wanna go?"

Grace's heart beat faster when Skylar nodded and said, "Sure."

She loved her brother, no matter how stupid he was sometimes. And she loved Skylar. But the thought of them together freaked her out. Skylar was her friend, and she wanted to tell Chad to back off and go find someone else to date. But when Skylar batted her eyes at Chad, Grace knew that she was losing her. Skylar would start hanging out with Chad, not Grace.

She thought back to the way she'd treated Skylar at school last year, and she figured she had this coming. But she wasn't going to give Skylar up without a fight.

"I heard Cindy telling some girls in math today that you guys were going to get back together." Grace stuffed a fry in her mouth.

Chad grunted, then quickly looked at Skylar. "Not true. Cindy lies about everything. There is no chance we are getting back together."

Skylar smiled, and Grace wanted to smack them both and say, "No, no, no. The two of you can't date." But she wasn't sure it was a rational thought, and for sure, it was selfish. Just the same, Chad didn't always treat the girls he dated well. Grace would warn Skylar about him later.

She sighed, knowing that if she did that, though, she would be hurting her brother. She didn't want that either. But she couldn't stand the thought of Skylar and Chad hanging out, without her.

❧

Darlene answered the phone on the third ring when she saw it was Brad calling. She broke out in a cold sweat at the sound of his voice, and she wondered how she was ever going to face him after what she'd done. But when he told her that he would be home really late this evening, her indiscretion suddenly seemed almost justified.

"How late?" She heard her voice shake and wondered if he did.

"I probably won't be home until around nine tonight. The meeting doesn't start until six."

"Who's the meeting with?" She stiffened as she wondered what Barbara looked like. Was she tall and thin? Was she younger than Darlene?

"It's a partners' meeting."

Brad hesitated before he answered. Or did he? Was she just paranoid? "Okay."

"Love you. See you tonight."

She heard the phone line go dead. *Love you too.*

⸺✣⸺

Layla jumped off her horse, tethered him to the pole near the barn, and walked to meet Darlene at her car. Her friend's eyes were red and puffy.

"I kissed Dave Schroeder," Darlene blurted out, throwing her arms in the air.

"You did what?" Layla looked at her friend for a long moment. This was the last thing she would have expected to come out of Darlene's mouth. She brushed the dirt from her clothes before taking Darlene's arm. "Okay. Come on in. Let's talk about this." Once inside, she put her arm around Darlene and led her to the couch. "Sit." Layla took the chair across from her friend. "What happened?"

After Darlene filled her in on the details of her hanky-panky in the barn, Layla's first reaction was to tell Darlene that what she'd done wasn't all that bad, but she suspected Darlene thought it was the most horrible thing she'd ever done in her life. "Then you just forgive yourself, Darlene, and don't let it happen again. Pray about it."

"I don't *feel* like praying about it, Layla." Darlene ground the words out between her teeth.

Layla grimaced. This seemed incredibly ironic. Not very long ago, it was Layla who refused to commune with God. But when she'd finally reopened that door, her life had changed so much. For the better. She needed to make sure that Darlene didn't close the door—and that she didn't leave it closed for as long as Layla had.

"Pray anyway." Layla spoke the words forcefully.

Darlene glared at Layla. "I'll pray when I feel like it."

Hmm . . . Darlene was itching for an argument. Probably needed someone to blame. And Layla knew from experience that God was an easy mark. "Okay." She kicked off one of her boots, then the other. "So what are you going to do now?"

"Tell Brad, I guess."

"Whoa, wait a minute." Layla leaned her elbows on her knees. "Sure you want to do that?"

"Yes. And while I'm at it, I'll ask him about Barbara. And I'll ask him how his so-called late meeting at work went tonight. Then I'll pull out the phone bill and throw it in his face. Then I'll . . ." She started to cry. "Why is this happening?"

Layla just stared at her for a minute. Her life in Hollywood had dealt her some hard blows, many of them self-inflicted, but she figured Darlene had led a relatively sheltered life compared to hers. This was hard on her. She stood up and walked to the couch.

"Honey, listen to me. You can get through all of this, no matter what you or Brad has done. The key word here is forgiveness. You have to forgive each other." She paused, reached for Darlene's hand. "And . . . you have to forgive yourself. Do you hear me?"

Darlene squeezed her hand. "I just want everything back to the way it was."

"It might not ever be the way it was." Layla paused. "But it might be even better. There'll be an honesty to your relationship that you didn't have before."

"Don't try to tell me that this is all good, that our relationship will improve because of bad choices we've made."

"You don't know why everything is happening the way it is. God has a plan, that's all I'm saying."

Darlene tensed at the mention of God, a reaction that was

painfully familiar to Layla. She knew she was being called to help Darlene the same way Darlene had helped her. Just through Darlene's kindness and gentle mentions of God, Layla had begun to open her mind and heart again, and through prayer, she'd found her way home to Him. Nothing would ever be the same for Layla, and even though she would never stop hurting over losing Marissa, a part of her was at peace. And she knew that was all due to God.

"Maybe I should just sleep with Dave, then we'd be even." Darlene shot her an icy smile.

"If you think that would make you feel better." Layla figured she'd fuel the fire a bit and help Darlene release all those emotions that Layla knew she had bottled up.

"Of course it wouldn't make me feel better, Layla!" Darlene jumped up from the couch. "Two wrongs don't make a right, as the saying goes. I'm not lowering myself to that!"

Layla stared at her. "Fine. Then what are you going to do?"

Darlene stomped her foot. "This is Brad's fault. I would have never kissed Dave if . . ."

Layla waited, figuring that within the next five minutes, Darlene would blame everyone she could, including Layla. She knew Darlene needed to feel it, go with it. Then, afterward, Layla would straighten her out once and for all.

Darlene blamed Dave for coming on to her, Brad for his infidelity, God for abandoning her, and herself for being a bad mother to Grace and a bad wife to Brad. Then, as expected, she threw Layla into the mix.

"I should have taken the hint . . . the way he's always looking at you, like he wants to . . ."

"That's enough!" Layla stood up and pointed a finger at her. "You don't know what Brad has or hasn't done, and now you're just making things up to justify what you did. So just stop it."

She nodded toward the couch. "You sit your butt down, missy. I'm going to tell you something, and you listen up."

"Don't boss me around like I'm a child." Darlene sniffled as she folded her arms across her chest, and Layla tried to remember who she was dealing with. She took a deep breath, let it out slowly.

"Darlene, please sit down on the couch so I can talk to you for a minute."

"I'll stand."

"Sit." Layla sat down on the couch and pointed to the spot beside her. Darlene huffed a bit, then sat down.

"Sweetheart . . ." Layla sighed. "You are in a dangerous place right now. Some people flee to God when they have problems, and others run from Him. I think I ran from Him because I was ashamed and blamed myself for Marissa's death, the breakup of my marriage, and I couldn't seem to get over all the bad things I'd done in my life. I felt like God gave up on me. But I think He used you, Darlene, to help get me back on track. And in a strange turn of events here, I'm begging you . . . turn to Him for guidance. Don't let yourself get so detached that it's hard to find your way back. Don't let it happen with Brad. And don't let it happen with God."

Darlene didn't say anything.

"I want you to know that for the first time in many, many years, I have hope. And everything that you are going through right now will pass. But, honey, turn to Him. You need Him now more than ever."

Darlene started to cry, and Layla reached over and pulled her close. She rubbed her hair like she'd done for Marissa when she'd been sad, and she cried along with her friend.

"I love you, Layla."

Layla wept as she silently thanked God for His wonder.

She'd never had a best friend. And Darlene was a gift. *Thank You, Lord, for Darlene. Please help her through this difficult time, and . . . don't let her lose her way.*

"I love you too, sweetheart," she said, sniffling. "And we are both going to be just fine."

Chapter Nineteen

Grace paced back and forth in Dr. Brooks's office after the doctor excused herself to take an emergency phone call. Then she made her way to the doctor's bookshelves. Mostly medical books, and she noticed books Dr. Brooks had written. There were also pictures of Dr. Brooks's three children. Grace thought they were around nine, fourteen, and seventeen. They'd talked about her children a little, and the doctor seemed like a good mother.

She turned around when Dr. Brooks walked in. "Grace, I'm so sorry. I had to take that call." Dr. Brooks took a tissue and dabbed at tiny beads of sweat on her forehead, then sat down in one of the high-back chairs. Grace took her position on the couch.

"Is everything okay?" Grace wasn't sure, but it looked like maybe the doctor had tears in her eyes.

Dr. Brooks locked eyes with Grace. "I hope so. I have a patient . . ." Dr. Brooks paused. "Actually she's a cutter, but she went too far, and now she's in the hospital."

Grace swallowed hard but didn't say anything.

"Does it bother you that I told you that?" Dr. Brooks put on her black reading glasses and moved her pad and pen to her lap. She scribbled something on the paper, then looked up at Grace.

"A little." Grace didn't like to hear about anyone hurt or in the hospital, cutter or otherwise.

"This patient had been making lots of progress, but she had a setback." Dr. Brooks leaned back in her chair. "How are you feeling?" She crossed her legs and peered at Grace over the top of her glasses. "Any problems? Any more urges to cut?"

Grace shook her head. "I feel great. No problems."

Dr. Brooks nodded, wrote some notes. "Good, good. How's school so far this year?"

"Good."

Dr. Brooks put her pen on her lap, then took off her glasses. "Grace, I'd thought we'd been making some progress, but lately I feel as though you just tell me what I want to hear."

Maybe the doctor was having a bad day, but she'd never spoken to Grace in such an impatient tone. "I don't."

"Yes, you do. And we've talked about this." Dr. Brooks leaned forward slightly. "So. Everything in your life is perfect? School is great? Not one worry in the entire world? Because if that's the case, you are indeed a lucky girl."

What kind of quack doctor is this? Bring back Dr. Brooks. Grace shrugged. "I guess I'm lucky then."

"I guess so."

Did Dr. Brooks just roll her eyes? Is she allowed to do that? Grace glanced at the clock.

"Oh, we'll still have our entire session. Don't worry."

Grace opened her mouth, unsure how to respond to this new Dr. Brooks. "Okay."

Dr. Brooks stared long and hard at her. "Still no urge to cut?"

"Nope." Grace folded her hands in her lap, bored with this

same line of questioning, although feeling a bit unnerved by the doctor's attitude.

"Really? Because I don't believe you." Dr. Brooks put her pad and pen on the table and raised her chin.

"Whatever." Grace looked away from her and tucked her hair behind her ears. "I feel fine."

Silence. Long, eerie silence. After a full minute, Dr. Brooks spoke up.

"I think you're lying to me, Grace. I think you do have the urge to cut, but you come in here and lie to me every week. That's what I think."

Grace's hands started to shake as her bottom lip trembled. "How can you say that? I don't lie."

"Really? Because that's what my other patient said, and she's in the hospital right now fighting for her life. So I don't want anything but the truth from you."

Grace couldn't believe this. "Look. I don't know what happened with your other patient, but it's unethical for you to even be comparing us. I'm pretty sure that's not allowed!" Grace heard her voice rise as she folded her arms across her chest.

"Don't talk to me about unethical. Talk to me about the things in your life that bother you. Everyone has things that bother them."

Nice try. "Well, I don't."

Dr. Brooks stared at her again, and Grace was tempted to run out of the room. "How are things at home?"

"Things at home are just fine." Grace was as sarcastic as she could be.

"Sounds like it."

And this time, for sure, Dr. Brooks rolled her eyes.

Grace pointed her finger at her. "Can you do that? I mean, roll your eyes like that at a patient?"

"Does that make you mad?" Dr. Brooks raised an eyebrow.

"It's unprofessional."

"Well, I'm rolling my eyes because you are lying to me, and I'm tired of it. Do you think that you come in here and fool me every week, Grace? I've been letting you get away with it lately, but this is unproductive, and I want to help you. No one can have as perfect a life as you claim to have."

"Maybe I don't need your help!"

"Maybe you do." Dr. Brooks's voice was softer now, which only made Grace feel like she might cry, and she couldn't do that. "Talk to me, Gracie."

"Don't call me Gracie." Her parents called her Gracie when she was younger, and now only when they were upset. She recalled her mother calling her Gracie when she found her that day. She pressed her lips tight, blinked her eyes.

"Okay. Grace. Please talk to me."

"What do you want me to say?" Grace knew she was practically yelling as she threw her hands in the air.

"Talk to me about things that worry you."

Grace didn't like the mean Dr. Brooks, but she liked this Dr. Brooks even less, the one who really seemed to care about her. That in itself was a lie. She shook her head, clamped her mouth shut. "Why do you pretend like you care? This is just a paycheck for you. You'll go home to your happy little life at the end of the day, and . . . do whatever you do."

Dr. Brooks sighed. "I'm not going to talk about my life with you, Grace. That's not what your parents are paying me for. But I assure you, it's far from perfect. And sometimes I get really mad." She paused, sighed. "What upsets you, makes you mad?"

Grace was trembling. She'd done a fair job—so she'd thought—of keeping Dr. Brooks a safe distance away. But she was getting really mad at this woman. "What upsets me is this questioning."

Dr. Brooks grunted and almost looked like she was grinning. Then she rolled those eyes again.

"Stop doing that!" Grace slapped a hand to her knee.

"What?"

"Rolling your eyes. You're not allowed to do that!" Grace threw her hands up in the air. "I know what you're doing, and it won't work!"

"What won't work, Grace?"

"You're intentionally trying to make me mad because you think I'll just spill and tell you everything that is bothering me!"

"So there are things bothering you?"

Grace slammed her foot on the floor. "No! That's not what I said!" Then she clenched her hands together so tight they hurt, and she closed her eyes.

"Tell me, Grace. Tell me about your life."

"I'm upset about stuff! I'm really upset!" Her eyes filled with water, and she wasn't sure she could do this. Her hands were trembling, her heart racing. She was losing control.

Dr. Brooks sat calmly in her chair. "Can you tell me about it?"

Grace pulled her eyes away from Dr. Brooks as she started to cry, then she turned back to her and yelled, "My brother wants to date my best friend, and I don't want him to! Something is wrong with my parents, and I don't know what it is! I miss having a boyfriend! And I go to bed crying every single night with a razor blade in my hand because I want to cut so bad I can't stand it!" Grace bent at the waist and sobbed. "There, are you happy?"

She heard Dr. Brooks get up, and she felt a hand on her head. "Yes, Grace. I am." Dr. Brooks sat down on the floor in front of her and gently raised Grace's chin until their eyes met.

Warm tears rolled down Grace's cheeks. "That is what you are supposed to do, honey. It's okay to get mad. It's okay to feel things. It is how you react to things that we are trying to deal with. And you should not have to go to bed every night with these feelings. We are going to get through this. Together."

Grace couldn't believe it when Dr. Brooks put her arms around her and squeezed her tight. "I'm so proud of you."

Grace eased away. "Why? I lost my cool. I screamed. And now I'm crying like a big baby." She was thankful that no one else was here to see this.

"Exactly. And that is what most people do to release their anger and frustrations. You might not see it, but we've just had a big breakthrough." Dr. Brooks folded her legs underneath her on the floor in front of Grace. She didn't seem as intimidating sitting down there. "Let's start with your parents . . ."

Grace slid out of the chair and onto the floor. She crossed her legs beneath her too and faced Dr. Brooks. Part of her wanted to talk, and part didn't. It took a few moments before she finally took a chance. "My parents are acting weird. I don't know how to explain it, but something is wrong."

She spent the next hour telling Dr. Brooks about all her worries, her fears, and her strong desires to cut.

By the end of the session, she felt something she hadn't felt in a long time, unless she'd been cutting. Relief.

⸞⸞

Darlene sat in Dr. Brooks's office after Grace's session and was thrilled to hear that Dr. Brooks felt like they'd made a break-through. But it upset her to tears that Grace was worried about her and Brad's relationship and that it was one of the issues that caused her pain and anxiety.

"I asked Grace to wait outside so we could talk, and I can tell you're very upset about what I've told you. Are you sure you don't want to schedule an appointment for you and Brad?"

Darlene shook her head. "No. But I don't want Grace worrying about us."

"I'm not going to minimize Grace's worries, but right now we are dealing with ways to help Grace deal with these issues. I felt like today was a starting point. She's admitted that she is worried about things, and she talked openly for the first time instead of pretending that everything in her life is perfect. I told you we had been making progress, and we were. But I felt sure Grace still had the urge to cut, and I needed to hear her say it. She needed to say it, so we can move forward and make sure she doesn't."

"I feel . . . so . . ." Darlene was so tired of crying, and every time she thought there were no more tears to spill, another one found its way down her cheek.

"I know you feel responsible, Darlene, but don't blame yourself. It sounds like you and your husband may have some things to work on. As for Grace, just be honest with her. As honest as you can be, even if it's a simple phrase like, 'Yes, Dad and I are going through some things, but we love each other very much,' or . . ."

Darlene didn't hear the rest of what Dr. Brooks said. Her focus shifted to whether or not Brad *did* still love her. She loved him with her heart and soul, and if she could take back the kiss with Dave, she'd do it in a heartbeat, no matter what Brad had done. The guilt was gnawing at her.

She eventually thanked Dr. Brooks, then focused on being as cheerful as she could with Grace on the way home, trying to put her daughter's mind at ease, even if her own was not.

"Grace, please don't worry about me and your dad. We've

been married a long time, and sometimes married people just go through things. We'll get past it." She turned to Grace and smiled. "I'm just glad that you and Dr. Brooks had a good session. And, Grace . . . I love you very much."

"I love you too, Mom."

Darlene was entering Round Top when Grace asked Darlene to drop her off at Skylar's house.

"Tell Skylar to let me know if she or her father need anything." Darlene didn't know how much she had to give these days—she felt drained in every way—but she wanted to keep things in perspective. She knew Skylar and her father struggled.

"I will, Mom. I'll catch a ride home with Skylar later."

Darlene nodded as she pulled into Skylar's driveway. "Chad's here," she said, noticing his truck in the driveway.

"Yeah." Grace turned to Darlene before she opened the car door. "I think they're going to start dating."

"How do you feel about that?"

"I don't like it." Grace grimaced but then smiled nervously. "But you know what? I'm going to go tell them both why I don't like it, and maybe it won't turn out to be such a bad thing." She shrugged. "Who knows, maybe Skylar will be my sister-in-law someday."

Darlene smiled. "Maybe so. See you tonight."

As she headed toward home, she thought about the past few days. Every time she'd tried to talk to Brad, one of the kids was around, or it was just a bad time. At least that was what she was telling herself most of the time. Truth was, she was just scared to death. When she finally confronted Brad, her entire life could change, and that thought terrified her. She'd heard what Layla had said, and she was praying. Not the kind of heartfelt prayers she'd said in the past, but it seemed God was listening because Dr. Brooks had said Grace was doing better.

If only Darlene—or Dr. Brooks—could magically fix everything between her and Brad. But Brad wasn't open to counseling, and Darlene didn't think she could mend things on her own. She tried to talk to God, ask Him for help, but shame rushed over her and choked her prayers. She knew what she'd done was wrong. How could she ask God to forgive her when she couldn't forgive herself?

She turned onto her street, exhausted and wanting to just crawl into bed, maybe stay there for days. But she had dinner to fix—and the anxiety of trying to find a good time to talk to Brad when the kids weren't around. She suspected there would be yelling, and she didn't want her children to overhear. She slowed down and pulled to the side of the gravel road to make room for two police cars whizzing by, something you rarely saw in Round Top, and never on her road. As she eased ahead, she had to move the car over again as an ambulance sped by, then a fire truck. Her heart started pounding. *Is something wrong at my house?*

She punched the gas so hard her tires spun. Her car sped down the road, a cloud of gravel dust in her wake, but she didn't stop at her house. All the activity was up ahead on the right. Including television crews.

All in front of Layla's house.

Chapter Twenty

Darlene pulled into Layla's driveway as far as she could, but too many vehicles blocked her way. She had to park behind two television vans near the gate. Outside her car, she hurried down the cobblestones and pushed her way through a media frenzy until she saw paramedics down in the pasture. Her heart pounded as she tried to move in that direction. A sheriff grabbed her arm.

"Ma'am, you can't go out there."

Darlene shook loose of his hold. "What's wrong? Is that Layla? Is she hurt?"

The tall man about her age pushed back his sheriff's hat. "Are you family?"

"No, but . . . I'm her . . . I'm her best friend. Please tell me what's going on. Please." Darlene was trembling as she glanced toward the pasture again.

"Evidently she fell off of her horse, but I need you to stay back. Got too many people out there as it is. We'll let you know something soon."

"Has someone notified her husband? Well, I mean, he's her ex-husband, but he needs to know." Darlene wiped the sweat dripping from her forehead.

"I'm not sure. I'll try to find out."

As the sheriff walked away, Darlene heard a rumbling in the distance. The helicopter wasn't in view yet, but she guessed it was for transporting Layla to the hospital. It wouldn't be long before it landed. Darlene's heart was racing. She nonchalantly weaved her way through the crowd, some of whom were Fayette County police officers trying to keep the media back. *Layla won't like all this.*

As soon as she found an opening, she darted past everyone and ran as fast as her short legs would carry her, weeds whipping against her bare calves as she tried to stay in her flip-flops on the uneven pasture. Six people surrounded Layla, and as Darlene came within a few feet of her friend, she could tell that Layla's eyes were closed. *No, no, no. Please, God . . . please.*

"Please step back. You shouldn't be out here," someone behind her said. A big, round woman carrying some sort of machine scurried past Darlene. Once she'd delivered the device to the two paramedics squatting beside Layla, she came back to Darlene. "Are you family?"

This time Darlene said, "Yes. I am her family." It was true, and the woman put a hand on her arm before easing her back a bit.

"She appears to be bleeding internally, and she has a large wound on the back of her head." The woman looked up when the helicopter neared. "They're taking her to Brackenridge Hospital in Austin."

Darlene tried not to panic. She knew they took the most serious injuries to Brackenridge as a precaution. It didn't mean it was life-threatening. She also knew that she wouldn't be able to ride with Layla in the helicopter.

"How—how bad is it? I mean . . ." Darlene took a deep breath as she glanced at Layla again. Layla's eyes were still closed, and there were no visible signs of injury.

"I don't know. It's hard to tell. But if you want to go ahead and drive to Brackenridge, you won't be there too long after the helicopter lands." Layla nodded, and the paramedic hurried back to her side.

Darlene knew the woman was right, even though she didn't want to leave Layla. "Okay," she said softly.

She watched them hooking Layla up to tubes and wrapping her head in a large bandage. The lady paramedic returned as the blare of helicopter blades grew louder.

"The helicopter is about to land, and the media is going to be all over that. I'd go ahead and get on the road. If you go now, you might beat the reporters that will be en route."

Darlene knew she should take the woman's advice, so she clambered across the pasture toward Layla's house. She wondered what Layla might need from home, and she was concerned about who would tend to her animals. *Will Layla be all right?*

Since everyone was farther down the cobblestone drive near the pasture, she made it to the front door without interruption. Once inside the house, she quickly went through Layla's bathroom, grabbing a toothbrush and a few other items, then putting them in a travel bag she found in a drawer. On her way out, she picked up a picture of Layla, Tom, and Marissa that sat on the hutch and stuffed it in the bag. After locating Layla's purse and keys, she locked the door on her way out.

She waited until she was on the main highway before she called Brad. He said he would leave right away for home so that both of them weren't so far from the kids.

"Baby, everything is going to be okay." Brad's voice was assuring, and even though there were issues hanging between them, the sound of his words, the soft-spoken way he talked to her when she was upset, gave her comfort. Right now, she just wanted to be with Layla.

Two hours later, she was at Brackenridge, but she hadn't beaten the media there. Television crews were parked outside, and Darlene was sure they were there about Layla. When she finally found the ICU unit, they told her she couldn't go in unless she was an immediate family member. In desperation, she lied, "I'm her sister."

A nurse escorted her back, but once they reached ICU Room 3, she asked Darlene to wait outside while she checked to see if Darlene could go in. A minute later, the woman returned and told Darlene that she couldn't go in just yet. She pointed to a nearby chair and asked Darlene to wait. Darlene did as she was instructed, and she could hear muffled voices behind the door a few yards away.

Almost an hour later, the doctors finally came out, pulling masks off and peeling gloves from their hands. Darlene walked quickly toward them.

"Is she okay?"

An older doctor with gray hair and gold-rimmed glasses locked eyes with her, and Darlene's heart flipped in her chest.

"I'm her sister," Darlene lied for the second time.

The doctor sighed. "Your sister has a broken leg, several cracked ribs, and some internal bleeding."

Darlene relaxed. That didn't sound too bad. But then the doctor's expression shifted, his eyes narrowing.

"She's suffered a bad head injury, and we'll be taking her to surgery within the hour." He paused. "She's in a coma right now."

Darlene blinked back tears. "Will she come out of the coma after the surgery?"

"We don't know." He stepped closer, and the wrinkles between his eyes and on his forehead deepened. His expression reminded her of the vet's on the day he'd told her that Buddy wasn't going to live. Darlene's heart raced faster. "Her injuries are severe. I would let the rest of your family know, and—and if there is a member of the hospital clergy you would like to call before surgery, there should be someone on staff from several denominations."

Darlene went weak in the knees, but she nodded. "A chapel? Where is the chapel?"

The doctor offered a faint smile. "Right off the lobby near the entrance." He touched Darlene's arm. "That's really all you can do right now. Pray."

Darlene cried the entire way to the lobby, and she was glad to see that the chapel was empty. She had lots to say to God.

Brad got home as soon as he could, but the kids were already there. When he walked in the front door, all three of his children met him.

Ansley wrapped her arms around Brad's waist, sniffling. "Is Layla okay?"

"I don't know anything, sweetheart." Brad kissed the top of her head before easing her away. He tossed his briefcase on the couch, then glanced at the TV, which was on extra loud.

"It was on the evening news earlier." Chad pointed the remote at the television and turned it up even more. "Maybe they'll give an update soon." He turned to Brad. "Dad, they said Layla wasn't expected to live." Chad's eyes watered up. "Is that true?"

"I don't know, son." Brad sat down on the couch. "Turn that down some, Chad." His head was splitting, and his heart hurt. For Layla, and for his wife. He knew how close the two women had become, and if anything happened to Layla, they'd all be devastated, but especially Darlene.

They were all quiet for a few minutes as the weatherman predicted some much-needed rain. When it appeared that they weren't going to say anything else about Layla, Brad asked Chad to turn the TV off for now. Then he asked his son to go to Layla's to check on the animals.

"I'll go help too," Ansley said.

After Chad and Ansley left, Grace sat down beside Brad. "Dad, should we say a prayer for Layla?"

Brad swallowed back a lump in his throat. "I think that's a great idea."

They lowered their heads, and Grace reached for Brad's hand. He fought the tremble in his bottom lip. Things hadn't gone well when he'd talked to Barbara today. And now this. "Why don't you lead us in prayer?" Brad said in an unsteady voice.

Grace squeezed his hand.

⤶

Darlene was still in her raggedy shorts, T-shirt, and flip-flops. There hadn't been time to change clothes, nor had she grabbed a bag for herself. She'd just wanted to get to the hospital as soon as she could. Earlier she'd worried that Tom wouldn't get the news of Layla's accident, but in the waiting room, she'd seen it on two different TV channels already.

Both broadcasts said that Layla was not expected to live, then they gave a brief history about her, showing clips of the films she'd made in her twenties. Darlene knew enough about the media to know that they were just building hype. They didn't know anything more than Darlene knew. There were six men and one woman in the waiting room with her. Two of the men appeared to be waiting for news about someone else's surgery, someone named Sam. The others appeared to be waiting for news about Layla.

In the chapel, she'd prayed for Layla, questioning God, crying, begging for forgiveness, and begging Him not to take Layla when her friend was so close to happiness again. She'd also covered just about everything in her life, including Grace's continued recovery, healing in her marriage, no matter what the causes of their discord were. But mostly she'd asked for the Lord to lay His healing hands on Layla.

She laid her head back and closed her eyes, said a few more prayers. But the conversation between two of the men caught her attention.

"She was a beauty back in the day, huh?"

Darlene glanced to her left. The man doing the talking didn't look much older than Chad, though he likely was, maybe a recent college graduate.

"She still is," the other, slightly older man said. "I have a cousin who lives in Round Top. We bumped into her one day at a store. She's still a beautiful woman."

"Kind of a has-been, huh?"

"Yeah. She dropped out of the limelight after her daughter overdosed on pills." He paused. "That's what I heard anyway."

"I heard that she hates the media, and that one time she kicked a cameraman in the shin, then pushed him down."

Darlene grinned.

The older man chuckled. "Yeah, I've heard that story too. And a few others."

Darlene jumped when the door to the waiting room opened. A herd of reporters piled into the room, some toting television cameras. Darlene frowned, knowing Layla wouldn't like all this. She'd worked hard to stay away from the media.

A scowling African-American woman entered the room

behind the crowd. She spoke loudly. "Which one of you is trying to pass yourself off as Layla's sister?"

Darlene froze for a moment, then stood and walked over to the woman. She leaned close and whispered, "Can we talk somewhere else?" Darlene hurried out of the room, hoping the woman would follow.

Not only did the woman follow, but so did the reporters. Darlene opened a door that said Private and hurried inside, followed by the woman. She glanced around, glad that no one was in the business office, then closed the door and locked it.

"I'm her best friend. I knew they wouldn't let me be with her unless I said I was her sister. Please don't say anything. She'd want me to be here."

The slender woman looked to be in her midforties, and she was well dressed in a tan pantsuit. Darlene thought briefly about her own appearance.

"You her neighbor?" The woman folded her arms across her chest.

"Yes. My family lives down the road from her in Round Top. Have you heard anything from the doctors?"

"No. But I've heard plenty about you." She extended her hand. "I'm Sheila, Layla's agent."

Darlene shook her hand, again glancing around the private office and wondering how long they could stay in there before they got thrown back out to the media outside the door.

Sheila's left eyebrow rose a fraction. "Layla's told me about you. She obviously cares about you a lot, so I won't blow your cover, but be careful what you say around those vultures. They're gonna latch onto you as Layla's sister and quickly report that you're a fraud." She paused, shaking her head. "I might as well go out there and give them some sort of statement so they don't complicate your life. I'll tell them you are her best friend, and as such . . . you call each other sisters. They'll probably still hound you for a while, but it won't make you look like a groupie fan trying to get in to see Layla."

Darlene nodded. "I'm guessing Tom found out from the news reports. Do you know if he's on his way?"

"He's in Thailand on a movie shoot, but he was booking a flight to leave when I talked to him."

"Oh. I didn't even know he was a movie star."

"I don't know if the term 'movie star' is accurate, certainly nothing like Layla, but he steps into a few small roles here and there." She dug into her purse. "I live in New York, but I happened to be in Houston and saw the report on the news." She handed Darlene a card. "I'm going to go out and speak to the media, then I'm going to have the hospital kick them all out, which should have already been done. Wait here until I'm through."

Darlene did as Sheila asked, worried that the doctor would go into the waiting room to report on Layla and Darlene wouldn't be there.

About ten minutes later, Sheila returned. "All clear." She motioned for Darlene to follow her. They walked back to the waiting room where Sheila walked up to the TV in the corner and turned it off.

"I checked with the doctor, and they are still operating on Layla." Sheila blinked several times, pressed her lips together. "They don't know if she's going to wake up, and if she does, if she'll ever . . . be the same."

Darlene sat in a chair, bent at the waist, and laid her face in her palms. *Please, Lord . . . heal Layla. Please.*

Sheila sniffled as she sat in a chair next to Darlene and put a hand on Darlene's leg. "I tell you what. They don't get any better than that woman in there." She paused, pulled her hand away. "She comes across as one tough broad sometimes, but she'd give you her right arm if you needed one. I guess you already know all that."

Darlene still had her head in her hands, but she nodded. Then she sat up straight.

They were quiet for a few moments, then Sheila stood. "I have to go. Unfortunately, I'm having a crisis of my own. I was in Houston at St. Luke's Heart Institute at the Medical Center because my husband is scheduled for a triple bypass this afternoon." She dabbed at her eyes. "I have to be there. But I wanted to come check on Layla for myself. It gives me comfort that you're here, and I know Layla appreciates it. I've got a three-hour drive back to Houston." She handed Darlene a card. "Please call me at that number the minute you hear something, and I'll be back to visit Layla as soon as my husband is stable."

Darlene nodded. "I will."

A minute later, Darlene was alone.

She called Brad to check on the kids, and once again, the sound of his voice was a comfort to her. Everything had to be all right. It just had to be.

Then she prayed. And she prayed some more. Surely God would answer her prayers.

Forty-five minutes later, a doctor emerged from behind a door that was marked Surgery. He pulled off his surgical mask, wiped his forehead with a handkerchief, and approached Darlene. She stood up, a pulsing knot in her stomach. She could tell by his tense, drawn face that her prayers had gone unanswered.

Chapter Twenty-One

Darlene cried in the waiting room until she felt like there was nothing left in her. The doctor's words rang in her ears. "I'm very sorry. The surgery on her brain went well, but her internal injuries were too bad. Her kidneys and other major organs are failing. You can go see her, but she doesn't have long."

The doctor had said that Layla was in and out of a coma. When she'd fallen off her horse, her foot had gotten caught in the stirrup. They thought something must have spooked the horse, maybe a snake, and that she'd been dragged across the pasture for a long time before the mailman came by and saw what was going on.

Darlene finally lifted herself out of the chair in the waiting room and made her way to Layla's room. She opened the door hesitantly. Layla looked surprisingly calm, even with the many wires and tubes. A large bandage was wound around her head and across her forehead, but no ventilator or anything else obstructed her face. She had two long cuts on the left side of her face, both with stitches, and several smaller cuts on the other side of her face. Her upper lip was swollen, her eyes closed. Darlene pulled the chair closer to Layla's bed and reached for her hand.

How was it possible that she could still cry? She gulped hard and blinked as fast as she could, but hot tears slipped down her cheeks just the same. A few minutes later, the door opened and a nurse walked in. She checked Layla's breathing, her pulse and heart rate, then put a hand on Darlene's shoulder. "It won't be long, honey. Can I get you anything?"

Darlene just shook her head.

For the next six hours, she sat with Layla. Twice she'd called Brad with updates. Nurses came in and out, each time seeming surprised that Layla was still hanging on. Twice Layla had opened her eyes and stared at Darlene. Darlene had squeezed her hand and tried to talk to her, but Layla closed her eyes again. One time, Darlene thought she was gone. Her heart monitor still showed a heartbeat, though, and her breaths were shallow but there.

Darlene hadn't realized she'd dozed off until she felt a gentle squeeze on her hand. She opened her eyes and met Layla's glassy gaze. "Hey," Darlene said as she leaned forward.

To her surprise, Layla whispered, "Hey."

Please, God, don't let me cry. Give me strength. And when Layla goes, take her to Your kingdom in paradise where there's no more pain.

"Do you need anything?" Darlene didn't know what else to say, and she didn't know how much Layla knew. She couldn't help but wonder if a person knew when life was slipping away. Or did Layla just think she was temporarily in the hospital, anxious to get back home?

"Tom?" Layla's face twisted in pain as she spoke.

"He's on his way, Layla. He took the first plane out of Thailand." Darlene squeezed her hand again. "Is there anyone else you want me to call? Sheila was here earlier. She had to leave for her husband's heart surgery."

"No. You stay." Layla's voice was low and raspy.

Darlene's entire body was trembling, and the knot in her throat made it difficult to swallow. She wasn't sure how much longer she could keep from crying. Her chest hurt from the effort, but she was determined to be strong for her friend.

Then Layla whispered something Darlene didn't understand. "I didn't hear you, Layla. What did you say?" She leaned her face closer to Layla.

"Tell—tell Tom . . ." Then she closed her eyes, and Darlene started to cry. She shook her head, forced herself to stop.

"I'm listening, Layla. What would you like for me to tell Tom?"

Layla slowly opened her eyes again. "Tell him that I'm sorry I won't be around."

Darlene's entire body shook, tears pouring down her face. "I'll tell him."

"Tell him he's always been the one . . ." A slight smile formed on one side of her mouth. "Tell him snow bunnies never freeze. He'll know what it means."

Darlene squeezed her hand. "I will, Layla. I will tell him."

Layla locked eyes with her. "Thank you."

"You're welcome."

Layla closed her eyes again, and Darlene yielded to the sobs that burst out of the heaviness in her chest. She couldn't take her eyes off of Layla's breathing, and relief washed over her when Layla opened her eyes again.

"Thank you, Darlene, for nudging me back onto the path. His path." She said something else, but Darlene didn't hear her. She leaned closer, but Layla's eyes shifted to her right. Layla smiled again, and a tear rolled down her cheek. "Marissa . . ."

Darlene looked to the far corner of the room, to where Layla's eyes were fixated and glowing now. She looked back at Layla and saw her smile broaden.

"Marissa . . . ," she said again.

Then Layla closed her eyes for the last time.

❧

Layla's funeral was three days later in Round Top, and Sheila made sure that the details were kept from the public. Tom and Sheila agreed that Layla would have wanted a small gathering, so after the funeral, Sheila had organized a meal at Layla's house, catered by a local company. Darlene couldn't have eaten anything if she'd tried. And seeing Dave among the guests only upset her more, especially when she saw him talking with Brad in a corner at one point.

She knew she had to tell Brad, but it might be awhile before she was mentally able to focus on anything. She was trying to be strong for her children. All three kids had liked Layla a lot, and Grace was taking it the hardest, crying uncontrollably on and off throughout the funeral and even now. Darlene stayed close to her, and she thought it was touching the way Ansley never left her side. Chad had cried during the funeral, and Darlene had hardly been able to breathe, but he was holding himself together here at Layla's.

Throughout it all, Brad did everything in his power to ease Darlene's pain—having food brought in the past few days so she didn't have to cook, running her hot baths, tucking her into bed, keeping the kids occupied. And always telling her how much he loved her, which made her cry harder.

One thing gave her comfort. Layla had formed a strong faith and renewed her relationship with God before she'd passed. But Darlene worried about her own relationship with God. What if she died tomorrow? Would she have the same kind of peace that Layla seemed to have in the hospital? She'd prayed and prayed the past few days, but not always with a clear conscience. Sometimes she knew she was talking to God because there was no one else. She couldn't confide in her best friend about how guilty she felt, the regret in her heart. And she couldn't talk to Brad about her guilt, her suspicions, and her need to have things right between them. So she'd talked to God. For hours.

And even though it seemed to her that she'd chosen God last, He made her feel like she was number one to Him, and love, comfort, and strength had come from those prayers the past few days. Her conversations with God were honest, tearful, and genuine. She'd talked to Him like she would a best friend, often aloud when no one was around.

Her thoughts were interrupted when Tom walked up to her. She'd met him before the funeral that day, but they hadn't been able to talk. Everyone had been so upset, including Tom, who had cried hard. His eyes were still red and swollen.

"I'm glad you were with Layla when she went," he said, then swallowed hard. "She said you were the first best friend she'd ever had that she trusted."

Darlene forced a smile. She wanted to go home, to bed, to cry in private. "I'm going to miss her a lot," she finally said. Then she remembered Layla's last words, which she should have told Tom earlier. "Tom, Layla wanted me to tell you that you were always the one." She took a deep breath. "And that she's sorry she won't be around."

He covered his eyes with one hand for a moment, then looked at Darlene. "Layla and I were in a good place." He blinked back tears.

"She also said to tell you that snow bunnies never freeze."

Through tears welling in the corner of his eyes, he chuckled. "That's my girl. Thank you for telling me that." He kissed

Darlene on the cheek. "I hope to see you again soon, to stay in touch."

Darlene nodded. Sheila was Layla's executor and would be putting Layla's house on the market, so Darlene doubted that she'd ever see him again.

She walked out of the crowded living room and down the long hallway to the bathroom. She ran right into Dave on the way. She'd done her best to keep her distance from him and avoided eye contact whenever she caught him looking at her.

"Can I talk to you?" His tone was urgent, and even though now wasn't the time to talk about anything to do with them, she briefly wondered if maybe something was wrong with Cara.

She followed him into a large library off one end of the hall. "What?"

"I'm just worried about you." He touched her arm, and she quickly jerked away.

"I'm heartbroken. My best friend just died." She knew her tone was laced with resentment, but being around Dave only served as a reminder of what she'd done.

"I know. We're all going to miss Layla." He paused, and Darlene could see the sincerity in the depth of his blue eyes. She looked away.

"I don't regret it, Darlene. The kiss." Even though his words said otherwise, Darlene detected a hint of apology in his voice.

Darlene glanced behind her, then back at him. "I do, Dave. I regret it very much, and I'm going to tell Brad about it."

"What? Don't do that, Darlene. Why would you do that?" He shook his head, frowning. "That's a mistake."

"It's a mountain between me and my husband, and I want it moved." Although she wondered if her confession might just dirty up the already polluted air. Either way, she couldn't live with it anymore.

"It was just a kiss. I don't think you should tell him."

"Dave . . ." She took a deep breath. "It shouldn't have ever happened. I regret it. Please stay away from me. And Brad."

She left the room, even though she could hear him calling after her. She found Brad as fast as she could. "Can we go?"

"Sure, baby." He put his arm around her, and they found the kids. She nestled herself into the safety of his arms as they went home, knowing that whatever Brad had to say to her about Barbara, she would love him until the day she died.

❧

The next day, Darlene assured her family that she was fine, although the void in her life and in her heart was colossal. She insisted the kids go to school. They needed to keep busy, and Darlene wanted to hole up and cry, stop having to be strong in front of everyone. Brad had offered to stay home with her, but she'd insisted he go to work. They would have to talk soon, but she didn't have the strength for it today.

"Are you sure you don't want me to stay home today?" Brad kissed her on the forehead.

She shook her head. "No. I'm fine."

He finally left, said he'd call her later that morning to check on her. He wasn't even to the end of the driveway when Darlene lay down on the couch and cried, loud thunderous sobs she wouldn't want anyone to hear. She'd been bottling it up since the funeral, and she pulled her legs to her chest, wrapped her arms around them, and allowed herself to feel the pain of losing Layla. Even on her drive back from the hospital the day Layla died, she'd forced herself to suppress everything, knowing she had to drive back to Round Top, arrive safely, and be there for her children.

She knew that her continued conversations with God had gotten her through all this so far, but she was going to need His help to get her through one more thing. Tomorrow, she'd talk to Brad.

For the next twenty minutes, she cried, prayed, and cried some more. She was crying so hard that she didn't see or hear Brad walk into the room. He ran to her side. "Baby, honey . . ." He threw his arms around her. "I was afraid of this. I got about ten minutes down the road, and I decided to turn around. I knew you were having a hard time with this." He sat down on the couch, pulled her into his lap, and stroked her hair. "I'm here, baby. I'm here. What do you need?"

She didn't answer, but buried her face in his chest and cried. For a long time. When she was done, she eased out of his lap, squeezed her eyes closed for a moment, then took a deep breath. She stared at him for several moments. "I need you to tell me about Barbara."

Brad tensed as he reached up and scratched his chin. "Who?"

She wasn't sure she had the strength for this, but she knew she didn't have the emotional energy to carry the burden for one more day. "I know about Barbara." Brad's expression clouded, and fear squeezed Darlene's heart. "How long has it been going on?"

Brad stood up and paced the floor in front of her in the living room. "A couple of months."

Confirmation. She felt light-headed as she put her feet on the floor, elbows on her knees, and face in her hands. *God, I need You now. More than ever. I can't do this. I can't.*

She sat taller, but through her tears, she didn't look in his direction. All of her loneliness and anxiety melded into one upsurge of determination, and she asked him the one question that was fueling the worst of her fears. "Do you love her?" Just thinking about it shattered her, and she squeezed her eyes closed.

"Who?"

She opened her eyes and turned to face him, a war of emotions raging within her, as she wondered how he could innocently ask her that. "Barbara." Her stomach clenched tight, and the seconds ticked by in slow motion as she waited for her world to change forever.

Brad's jaw dropped. "Why would you ask me that?"

She sniffled. "Because I just need to know if you love her."

"Of course not!" He sat down on the couch beside her. "Baby . . ." He reached up to put his hand on her cheek, but she slid over on the couch.

"Don't touch me, Brad. You tell me everything! I can't take one more day, one more second of this! I've known for weeks, but I've been too scared to ask. Then with Layla . . ." She cried so hard she could barely breathe. "I need to know how long you've been having an affair with this Barbara woman."

"What?" Brad dropped his jaw again. "You think I've been having an affair with Barbara Rollins?" He gave his head a shake. "What? Why?"

"I heard you on the phone, Brad. I heard you say that if your wife found out about the two of you, then your marriage was over."

"You never heard me say that, Dar. I'd never say that because there was nothing going on with—" He stopped, stared at her, then sighed. "Oh . . . you must have overheard my conversation with Barbara when I was out in the barn, didn't you?"

"Yes."

"Dar . . . Barbara is a stockbroker. The insurance wasn't covering Grace's visits to the psychiatrist, and I wanted you to be able to redo this house the way you want to." He paused, then spoke slower than before. "I invested a large chunk of our savings in a plan that Barbara suggested. And it lost a lot of money almost overnight. I told Barbara that she better figure out a way to reinvest it or get the money back, because"—he took a breath—"if you found out about it, our marriage was over." He shook his head. "I was just trying to make her understand how important it was." He sat down on the couch, reached for her hand, then squeezed. "The market shifted, and the money is finally back in a much safer investment program." He narrowed his eyes. "Did you really think that I would *cheat* on you? I'm so sorry that I didn't tell you about what I'd done, but it all turned out okay, and I was just trying to make some extra money. I'll never do anything like that again without discussing it with you, but, Dar . . . I would never, ever even so much as touch another woman."

Darlene pulled her hand from his, stood up, paced, and chewed on her fingernail. She could barely breathe. She wanted to run away, to run back to a time when Grace wasn't cutting herself, to a time when she and Layla were sitting on her couch talking, to a time when she and Brad were laughing and loving each other, to a time before she'd ever met Dave Schroeder. "Oh, Brad," she whispered as she bent at the waist.

He ran to her, wrapped his arms around her. "I'd never, ever betray our love. Never. I'd never cheat on you."

She shoved him back, then glared at him. Despite the warning voice whispering in her head, the one saying, *Don't tell*, she tossed the words into the air, knowing she would be the one to fall. "Well, I thought you did. And I kissed Dave Schroeder! I kissed him twice. Here, out by the barn."

The color drained from Brad's face as he stared at her.

"I don't feel anything for him. It was a mistake, and I'm so, so sorry. I thought you were having an affair with someone named Barbara." Darlene dropped to her knees. "I'm sorry. You are the love of my life, my everything. I'm so sorry."

The silence thickened between them like a heavy mist, and Brad's nostrils flared. He looked like a volcano on the verge of erupting. "You and Dave? Making out in the barn? Our barn?" Brad was yelling now, and Darlene knew she deserved it. She just wondered if he could get past this. And if she could forgive herself.

Darlene stood up and faced him. She reached for him, but he backed away. "Brad, who do you . . ."

But before she could even finish the question, he turned and walked out of the house, slamming the door behind him.

Chapter Twenty-Two

For the next two days, Brad spoke to her as little as he could. He stayed up late and fell asleep on the couch. She knew he was sending her a message, one that she deserved. It was all out now. Ultimately, she'd been the one to betray Brad, to keep a secret worse than the one he'd been keeping. And she was sure, beyond any doubt, that she'd never seen Brad as angry as when she'd confessed to him—his eyes blazing, his words filled with utter contempt. She felt empty. Lost. And she missed Layla.

She'd been relying on God for strength. In her heart, she knew He was listening, hearing her cries for help, but guilt and regret were suffocating her. The only thing she knew to do was to keep busy.

Despite Brad's promise that they would replace the old wooden floors in the den, Darlene had rented a floor sander yesterday. It was hard work and torturous on her back. She'd hardly been able to crawl out of bed this morning to resume the task, but idle time was her enemy. She started running the sander right after the kids left for school and Brad left for work.

Every time she moved, her body ached. And she deserved it. But with each push forward, she could see the reward for her efforts. As the top layer of weathered wood turned to sandy residue throughout the den, there was a fresh surface underneath, worthy of restoration. She coughed, groaned from the exertion, and stopped to cry when she needed to.

❧

Brad left the office early that afternoon. He missed his wife, but bitterness wrapped around him so tightly that he couldn't breathe. As he pulled into Dave Schroeder's driveway, he had every intention of punching the guy in the gut. But when Dave opened his front door, Brad held his breath. Cara was standing beside him, a gentle smile across her beautiful face.

"Can I talk to you?" Brad stuffed his hands in the pockets of his slacks as Dave's eyes met his.

"Sure." He hung his head, swung the door wide, then he and Cara stepped aside so Brad could go in. His heart was beating hard in his chest as he fought the images of Dave kissing his wife.

Dave wrapped an arm around Cara, the color draining from his face. "Let me go get Cara settled in her painting room, and I'll be right back."

Brad picked up a picture of Dave standing next to a beautiful woman outside of this house. He realized the woman must've been Dave's wife. A chill ran down Brad's spine at the thought of ever losing Darlene, but before he had time to discern whether or not he was feeling sympathy for Dave, the man returned. And so did the bitterness Brad felt.

"I know what happened with you and Darlene. You stay away from my wife." Brad's voice trembled as he spoke, and he still hadn't ruled out a swift punch.

Dave rubbed his forehead and looked at the floor for a few moments. When he looked back up, he swallowed hard. "I've never kissed another man's wife, and I can't tell you how sorry I am that it happened with yours." He paused, nervously rubbing his forehead again. "It goes against everything I believe in."

Brad was glad Dave was nervous, but he was upset with himself for feeling a wave of sympathy for Dave. The man appeared sincerely sorry. Brad glanced at all the pictures of Dave and his wife on a hutch near the door. Again he thought about how hard it would be to live without Darlene, and he suddenly wanted to get home to her.

"I don't want you in our life." Brad's voice was stronger, his eyes fixed on Dave's. "It's a small town, and we'll run into each other, but I don't want you around my family."

Dave nodded, looking down again. "I understand."

Brad knew Dave wasn't fully to blame, but right now that logic was buried beneath Brad's own need to fix things with Darlene. Blaming her wouldn't achieve that result. He needed Dave to take the blame, which he seemed to be doing.

Brad turned and headed toward the door. He was almost there when he heard a whisper that made him pause.

For if ye forgive men their trespasses, your heavenly Father will also forgive you.

He didn't move for a moment as his own indiscretions rose to the front of his thoughts. Was what Darlene and Dave did worse than what Brad had done by lying to his wife, or at best, avoiding the truth? Who was he to decipher the importance of one sin over another? Sadness, bitterness, and shame fell over him. He needed to blame Dave and Darlene, but had he not looked in the mirror lately? He turned around and faced Dave.

"I forgive you." He wasn't ready to forgive Dave, nor did he want the man around his wife, but something in his heart cried for him to mean it. He said it again, "I forgive you," and hurried out the door.

❧

When Darlene's back couldn't take any more, she stowed the sander in the corner and admired her work. More than anything, she wanted Brad to be pleased, to be proud of her work on the floors.

She sat down on the couch, sweat dripping down her face. The front of her T-shirt was soaked as she laid her head back. Here it was—idle time, when her thoughts turned sour. But she was sure she couldn't do one more thing around the house. In addition to sanding the floors, she'd scrubbed the bathrooms, washed all the linens, and even polished the dove pendant. She reached up and grasped the bird in her hand, praying that the Holy Spirit would fill her, give her strength.

Ten minutes later, Brad walked in, almost two hours early. He was carrying a slender box about three feet tall, but only four or five inches wide. He put it down in front of the couch. "This was on the front porch."

Darlene wiped her face on her shirtsleeve. "I guess I didn't hear UPS come." She glanced at the sander, wondering if Brad would comment on the floors. When he didn't, she asked, "What is it?"

"Something I bought for you months ago."

She covered her face and started to cry. "Back when you still loved me."

Brad sat down beside her on the couch and pulled her hands away. "I never stopped loving you, Darlene. But I need to know . . . Do you feel anything for Dave?" He gave her hands a slight jerk. "Do you, Dar? Because I don't think I could take that."

She shook her head. "No!" Tears poured down her face. "I love you. I've always loved you. I could never love anyone else."

She put an arm across her stomach, her body trembling, her heart breaking. "I'm so sorry, Brad. I just—"

He put a finger to her lips. "Darlene . . ." He spoke softly, tenderly, as he locked eyes with her. After a few moments, he brushed back her hair on both sides and cupped her face. "Who do *you* love?"

As tears poured down her face, she said, "You, baby. Always and forever."

He wrapped his arms around her. "I'm sorry for not being truthful with you."

"I'm sorry—sorry for everything." She buried her face into his chest, his love as necessary to her survival as food and water. "I'm so sad, so incredibly sad, about everything. I can't breathe."

He lifted her chin until she was facing him. He kissed her softly. "I know you are. And I'm going to stay with you today, tomorrow, and as long as it takes until you feel better." He paused, gazed into her eyes. "I know you, Darlene. So listen to me." He kissed her on the nose. "I know you love me. That's why I don't ask you all the time. I know I'm the only one for you. So please . . . forgive yourself. Because I forgive you, and I need you to forgive me for keeping a secret too."

"I do."

He pulled her into his arms. "Losing Layla is a big loss, and it's going to take some time before you feel better."

She started to cry. "Brad . . . I need you. More than ever."

"I know, baby. I need you too."

❧

The following Saturday, Darlene, Brad, Chad, Grace, and Ansley found a nice spot in the far corner of the front yard. Darlene carried her gift from Brad, a fruit salad tree that didn't look like anything more than just a stick. About three feet long, it resembled any number of broken branches in the yard that had fallen from their trees.

The instructions said to soak it in water for a few days, then once it was planted, it had to be watered every day. Darlene planned to nurture that tree into the most luscious fruit salad tree anyone had ever seen.

Brad was hauling a shovel, and Ansley carried the small plaque they'd had made so they could plant the tree in memory of Layla.

"So that tree is actually going to bloom all different kinds of fruit on *one* tree?" Chad had already asked the question several times. Darlene had pointed the tree out to Brad in a catalog months ago and was thrilled he'd remembered.

She assured her son one more time. "Yes." Darlene smiled at Chad. "Ours is a stone fruit tree, and it'll have peaches, plums, nectarines, and apricots."

It didn't take long for Brad to dig the hole and get the small tree packed in. Grace reached for the water hose nearby, then soaked the ground under and around the tree. Ansley placed the marker at the tree's base. *In loving memory of our friend, Layla Jager.*

"Let's all bow our heads," Darlene said after a few moments. They formed a circle around the tree and held hands. "Lord, we miss Layla, and . . ." Darlene swallowed back the sob in her throat and took a deep breath to go on, but Brad squeezed her hand and spoke up.

"Why don't we all say something about Layla, and something we're thankful for. I'll go first." Brad paused. "Lord, we know Layla is in a wonderful place, Your kingdom. And she's enjoying all the love that You have to offer all of us, whether in heaven or on earth." He squeezed Darlene's hand again.

"Blessings for her and for us as we all heal. I'm thankful for my wonderful family." Brad nodded to his left where Grace stood.

Grace cleared her throat. "I'm going to miss Layla, Lord, but I know that she is with You and Marissa."

Darlene felt a tear roll down her cheek, but she smiled as she recalled the last word Layla had spoken on this earth.

"I'm—I'm . . ." Grace took a deep breath. "I'm thankful for my family. And also for Dr. Brooks."

Darlene knew that after their breakthrough, Grace was truly on the mend, and much of the credit went to Dr. Brooks. They all looked at Ansley.

"I'm going to miss Layla too, Lord. And I'm thankful for my family, my chickens, and my friends at school."

They all looked at Chad.

"Hi, God. I'm really gonna miss Layla too." He bowed his head for a moment, and Darlene hoped he wouldn't cry. But he raised his head, and a smile spread from ear to ear. "And I'm thankful that Skylar finally let me kiss her."

"Chad!" Ansley sounded disgusted, and Grace picked up the water hose and shot Chad in the chest. Darlene was glad that Grace had accepted—even encouraged—the budding relationship between Chad and Skylar.

Next thing Darlene knew, they were all running around, laughing, spraying each other with the water hose, and darting around a tiny tree—a sprig of life no bigger than a twig. But with proper nourishment, the tree and its various fruits would be forever grounded, rooted together for life, for generations to come.

Just like a family.

Reading Group Guide

*Guide contains spoilers, so don't read before completing the novel.

1. Throughout the story, there are several instances of symbolism. Can you name three?

2. When Darlene takes a job outside of the home for the first time in her marriage, she admits to herself and others several reasons for her choice. What are these reasons, and why do you think she chose a job working with children?

3. Every member of the family keeps a secret at some point—except for Ansley. Whose secret is never revealed?

4. Overcoming guilt plays a large role in several of the characters' lives—Darlene, Brad, Chad, Grace, and Layla. How do they each get past it? Have you ever let guilt bog you down, and if so . . . how did you handle it?

5. Teenage "cutting" is a growing problem. Have you ever heard of it before or known a family that has been affected by it? If so, did the problem resolve itself, or did the teen seek counseling?

6. When Layla dies, she says her daughter's name. Do you think she really saw Marissa? Have you ever had a friend or loved one who experienced something similar as they passed on?

7. There are several times when characters unrightfully judge one another. The most obvious would be when Darlene and Brad judge Skylar by the way she dresses. What are some other examples of passing judgment?

8. When Brad lies to Darlene about the investments he made, we know that he was doing it to provide for his family, and in the end it all worked out. But if Darlene hadn't caught him on the phone in the barn, do you think he ever would have told her about it?

9. Layla shows up in church to thank God for answering her prayers about Tom. At this point, is she still somewhat nonchalant about the Lord's role in her life? And if so, when does she truly begin to have a relationship with Him?

10. God has a plan for everything. Why did He bring Darlene and Layla together? What roles did they play in each other's lives that neither of them could have foreseen?

11. Do you feel like Darlene and Brad have a good marriage? Could they have benefited from counseling, as Darlene suggested?

12. What are your thoughts about Dave? Did he pursue Darlene? Did you have compassion for him and his situation? How much do you blame him for his indiscretions in the barn with Darlene—or do you? Do you hope that he finds someone to spend his life with and to be a good mother to Cara, or does he not deserve such happiness after almost wrecking Darlene and Brad's marriage?

13. Do you think Darlene would have ever kissed Dave in the barn if she hadn't suspected Brad of infidelity? What were her motives? Did she feel justified? Lonely? And how did her betrayal ultimately affect her?

14. When Darlene and Brad are arguing a lot, their discord is fueled by their worry for Grace. But what inner feelings are each of them harboring that cause resentment of the other?

15. If you live in the city, have you ever dreamed of escaping to a quieter life in the country? Does geography really have anything to do with the peace we have in our hearts?

16. Do you think Darlene and Brad's betrayal and lies will make their marriage stronger now? Or would they have been better off without any of it? Has there ever been a time within your own marriage when poor judgment ended up strengthening your bond?

Cutting is a dangerous coping method that can be addicting. If you or someone you know is engaging in self-injury, talk to a health professional—such as a counselor, social worker, doctor, or nurse— and ask about resources in your area. The Substance Abuse and Mental Health Administration (SAMHSA) offers a national directory of mental health facilities on its website, store.samhsa. gov/mhlocator, and The American Psychological Association's website has a Psychologist Locator, locator.apa.org. SAMHSA's public education website "What a Difference a Friend Makes" contains information—including a community forum—for anyone trying to help a friend through a mental health difficulty: www. whatadifference.samhsa.gov. A large Internet forum specifically devoted to self-harm is www.recoveryourlife.net.

Don't leave God out of your pain. Pray for His guidance and healing so that this behavior releases its hold on you. "Come to me, all who are weary, and I will give you rest."

MATTHEW 11:27-29 NASB